Taste of Lust

Taste of Lust

LeBlanc

www.urbanbooks.net

Urban Books
1199 Straight Path
West Babylon, NY 11704

ISBN- 13: 978-1-933967-82-0
ISBN- 10: 1-933967-82-X

First Printing May 2009
Printed in the United States of America

10   9   8   7   6   5   4   3   2   1

Distributed by Kensington Publishing Corp.
Submit Wholesale Orders to:
Kensington Publishing Corp.
C/O Penguin Group (USA) Inc.
Attention: Order Processing
405 Murray Hill Parkway
East Rutherford, NJ 07073-2316
Phone: 1-800-526-0275
Fax: 1-800-227-9604

Dear Love,

I dedicate this book to you. The world's best husband, father, and friend. Thank you for taking your time with me, showing compassion and empathy when I needed it. I thank you for having faith and supporting my dreams, adventures, and crazy ideas. I thank God for you daily, because he truly showed favor on me when I met you. I love you and appreciate everything you do. Keep on being our hero and pursuing your dreams because the best has yet to come.

Love Always,
LeBlanc

Acknowledgements

I would like to give thanks to God, my husband (greatest man alive), my children, mother, father, brother, nieces, nephews, cousins, pastors, friends, book clubs, bookstores, reviewers, fellow authors, my editor, and readers for your support during the writing of this book. Your encouragement and faith in me was greatly appreciated, and will be cherished forever. May the blessings of our Savior Jesus Christ rain upon all of you.

MEET SHELBY

The rain was pouring down uncontrollably. Wind was blowing water through the porch screen as Shelby sat in her long, hot pink nightshirt daydreaming about her life. Who was she? She knew she was a wife, mother, and professional. But what happened to her? Six years of marriage and two babies had stolen her identity. She gained twenty pounds, isolated herself from her friends, and wrapped herself into her family. And in the six years of her marriage she had never been away from her husband or kids. She was a psychiatrist who suffered from separation anxiety and displayed dependent personality characteristics.

"Happy birthday," shouted Shelby's husband and two kids, waking her from her self-analysis of her life, stealing her privacy. "We've been looking all over for you. How old are you, Mommy?"

"Twenty-five," Shelby replied before the kids finished their question. She hadn't seen that age in years, but it seemed like life raced by after twenty-one. Reality was, she was finally in her dirty thirties and hating every minute of them. Dexter Junior looked at his mom with his big pretty eyes and long eyelashes, not knowing she was lying about her age. Then he tapped her arm and pointed to his sister. "She said the B word. She said the B word, with her bad self."

Savannah's little hands tapped her mother again. "No, I said Ima a bad bithz. Ima bad bithz."

"Don't say that," Shelby scolded her daughter, feeling guilty because she had learned the vulgar word from her. Ever since her identity crisis she walked around the house singing "Check" by Stef 'G.'

"I farted," the little girl added with her small thumb in her mouth.

"It's *I passed gas* and say excuse me," her father said, shaking his head.

"It stinks, Daddy. Me farted." Savannah giggled, crumpling up her nose. Dexter turned to his wife and smirked. Their kids were always making them laugh. "Why you out here anyway?" he asked, handing her a medium-sized gift bag and two cards.

"Hiding from you and yo kids. I need some privacy sometimes," Shelby taunted, rolling her teary eyes at her family. "Go in the house with your granny and your cousin. And you, watch your mouth, Savannah. No more B words."

"Mommy, open our card first," her son yelled, exposing his missing front tooth.

"No, let me give it, she's my mommy, D.J."

"Give it back, stupid," her son taunted, snatching the card from his sister.

"D.J., you a big-head monkey."

"No, you are."

Shelby ignored the kids as they argued back and forth. "I told you guys not to get me anything." She sighed as she opened their cards, feeling guilty for hiding from them. Happiness invaded her soul as she read the sweet pink, card from her kids with Snoopy on the front. But nothing was more heartwarming than the card her husband gave.

"Thank you," she cried out as tears darted across her flushed cheeks.

"Dook in Daddy's bag, Mommy," her two-year-old daughter ordered, not pronouncing her L correctly in *look*, before following her big brother back into the house.

The bag opened and Shelby's eyes protruded out. There was a twenty-five-dollar pear berry candle before her and a gray extra-large fleece warm-up suit. She wiped her tears, rolled her eyes, and tightened her mouth.

Didn't he pay attention to what I liked? she wondered.

"Honey, I only buy vanilla sugar-cookie candles from that company. I don't know what were you thinking?" She picked up the Nike warm-up suit and placed it close to her body. "This looks like Chuck E. Cheese's rat suit. Why didn't you ask Megan to help you?"

"I forgot. I can't remember everything," he retorted with a little attitude in his voice.

"You could be more observant and pay attention to what I like and what size I wear. I've been telling you for months to call one of my girls if you needed help."

"Aight. I can keep that suit for myself," Dexter replied, grabbing the candle and warm-up suit back. "I can't do anything right for you if I let you tell it."

"No, it's me. I've centered my entire life around you and the kids and I don't know who I am. I know I'm a wife, mother, housekeeper, bill payer, cook, and a hooker in the bedroom. And I also have to work to help pay half of the bills. A man would be a fool not to get married. Hell, you bastards have your own personal servants called wives," she ranted. "And I need a break!"

"Whatever." Dexter stood up over Shelby, peering down at her with slits in his light brown eyes then walked away without looking back.

Was I being hard on him? The thoughts kept pouring in. *Hell, it is my birthday. Six long years, Dexter should know what I like by now. But no, he never paid attention when we went to the mall or the boutiques. Nor did he ever listen when I'd say "I like this or that." All I want is for him to be a little more observant and romantic* she thought as she watched the glass on the patio door vibrate after being slammed shut by her husband.

Shelby's emotions changed from anger to empathy in seconds. Guilt overwhelmed her as she wondered how she could want a break from such a wonderful family. After all, she realized she was blessed. Dexter was the best husband and father in the world. He was rich, intelligent, thoughtful, attentive, caring, and compassionate and although he didn't always express himself verbally or buy the perfect gift, he always found the right card to communicate his feelings.

Smiles dominated her being when she decided to go back and read back over Dexter's card. He had written a special note to her on the blank page of the card.

My Dearest Wife,
   You've had two beautiful babies for me. And for that I love you. Your body has gone through so much to give life and I wanted to do something too. Consider this vasectomy as a token of love and gratitude for all the sacrifices that you've made for our family.
   Loving you always and forever,
   Dexter

Dexter returned to the patio where his wife was sitting in a chair, crying. He serenaded her neck with kisses. "Shelby, I love you. I'm sorry. I'll do better. You do need a break. Go take a trip by yourself. I'll be fine with the kids."

"No, bay, I'm sorry. It's the thought that counts. I would've been happy with the card . . . and as far as leaving you guys . . . you know I can't leave without you and my babies." She wept aloud, allowing his hands to explore her curvaceous body.

He lifted her nightshirt and delicately licked her stomach. "Am I being spontaneous now?"

"Yeah, but I look disgusting. These C-sections have destroyed my teenaged figure," Shelby said with a smile, pushing his mouth away from her stomach. "Look at this pouch," she growled, pulling on her skin. "I never had a stomach. If anyone sees me from high school they are going to get a kick out of my fat butt."

"Shelby, you look fine. I always tell you how sexy you are," he replied, sitting up to face his wife. "Don't worry about what other people think. You just had a baby. Look!" He pointed down to his pants. "You still turn me on. I get horny every time you walk by." His face became serious. "That's why I'm getting that vasectomy. You don't have to worry about birth control pills or patches making you gain weight. The recovery is two days, I only need a local anesthetic, it's cheap, and most importantly I won't be putting your body in jeopardy."

She perked up, just thinking about how wonderful sex would be without condoms and worry about getting pregnant again. The thought alone made her pussy wet. "You act like you want some of this *bad bitch's* big juicy ass at seven in the morning."

"I always want some. No matter the time," he answered,

attacking her neck and ear with more wet, affectionate kisses. "Come on, let's do it right now."

Shelby moved her husband's hand. "No, the kids are inside. What if D.J. walks out here or your mom or nephew?"

Dexter's groin area connected with his wife's firm, shapely butt and he rotated in a circular grinding motion. Shelby's mouth flew open, her head swung back, and soft moans escaped her lips. His spontaneity excited her. The thrill of making love with company awake in the house made her juicy morsel swell up. Miss Clit began pulsating, beating like a heart. She wanted him bad, but there was no way she was doing anything with everyone up and moving about.

"Let's go to the bedroom. We can lock the door," Shelby whined, wanting to have sex but not wanting to be adventurous.

"No, let's do it out here in the rain."

"We can't."

"Come on, baby. I thought you wanted to be free," Dexter said, dismissing his wife's paranoia and pulling her by the hand to the side of the house.

They escaped like two mischievous teenagers in love. The humidity swept over them like heavy clouds as Dexter flipped up the long nightshirt. "Put your hands on the side of the house and bend over." Like an obedient child she obeyed, placing her hands on the stucco siding, scaring the green lizard away. The rain beat down on her body, setting her free as Dexter slipped her panties to the side and squatted down on the grass with his head against the house.

His long, thick tongue plunged inside of her sopping wet vagina like a plumber hard at work. She screamed each time his tongue attacked, grabbing his head with her thighs.

"Come on. Hurry up. I want some before anyone catches

us," Shelby pleaded with her husband. "Oh, I'm so wet and gushy. Just stick it in. C'mon, give it to me now."

Dexter continued to indulge in his wife's sweetness. Taunting and teasing her with his tongue, letting the rain drench her aching body.

"Fu—fuc—Daddy, give it me! I need you so bad! Please fuck me!" she said, emphasizing the letter F in the word *fuck*.

Dexter removed his mouth from between his wife's legs, rain dripping from his body as he stood up. He smacked her butt and watched it jiggle.

"Naw, you a bad bitch. You're going to appreciate whatever I give you next time," he said as he smacked her butt again. "I want you to beg me."

"Baby, you know I'm sorry. I respect you and I'm going to be that Proverbs: Thirty-one lady. Now chill out and come on and give me some. Hurry up, I don't want anyone to catch us," Shelby begged, allowing the rain to plaster her mouth.

Dark clouds, heavy rain, lightning, and thunder planted itself among them, but that wasn't a concern for Shelby. All she wanted was her husband, longing to feel the warmth of his big, long dick growing inside of her.

"I'm going to fuck the shit out of you." Dexter sighed, pulling off his T-shirt and leaning his six-feet-four-inch body over her back. Raindrops plastered on his tattooed-engraved back.

"Yeah, baby, talk dirty to me." She massaged between her legs. "Look at how wet and fat this is. Feel this juicy pussy," Shelby demanded, pointing to her hard, erect clit.

He licked her finger then sucked it. "Umm . . . you taste so good."

"Hurry up."

Dexter shut his wife up with one swift motion. His long

thickness glided in, replacing her begging with moans of pleasure as the two became one. He reached his mouth over her arm, seized her hanging juicy, ripe mango breasts, and caressed them with his hungry mouth, taking a taste or two between licks, squeezing and massaging them as he prodded in and out of her creamy pussy.

He took his mouth off her breast. "You like the way I'm giving it to you. Say it's good. Tell me it's good. You want me to make that pussy cum."

"Oh yeah! Make me cum! Make me cum! I have to cum . . ." Shelby groaned as she held her hands on the side of the house.

"Work that pussy. Come on girl, work that pussy. Bounce that juicy ass on Daddy's dick."

"You like how this big ass feels," Shelby yelled back to her husband, enjoying their wild rendezvous, her bottom banging against his pelvic area, making a loud smacking sound like a ping-pong match.

"Oh, yeah, Daddy loves it. Your pussy is so wet. Grrr— Grrr—" Dexter shouted as he grinded deeper in her.

"Fuck me harder! Fuck me harder!" Shelby groaned and inhaled deeply, enjoying her husband's powerful thrusts.

"Yeah, ummm . . . This is the best pussy in the world."

Shelby continued to whimper with sighs of pleasure, taking in ten of her husband's inches, her vaginal walls gripping tight on his girth with each rhythmic movement. "Baby, this is how I want you to make love to me all the time. You hitting this pussy right. I can feel that shit in my navel." She moaned enjoying the sexual pain.

"Like that, you like that, huh . . . kiss me, give me that tongue so we both can cum." Dexter reached over and tongued his wife. The two entangled in lust. Their mouths filled with each other's liquids.

Minutes later, Dexter broke away from his wife's quick

tongue. He quivered and gasped for air. "Oh that's that spot, you about to cum, huh? Cum on that dick."

"Yes . . . I'm a . . . bout to cum. I know you came already and you bet not pull it out. Fuck me harder. Fuck me until I cum. Take this pussy. Oh yeah . . . yeah . . . that's it." Shelby screamed and exhaled while releasing her orgasms as Dexter removed his flaccid penis. Giggles exited her mouth and a look of satisfaction covered his face until the two adults locked eyes with their eighteen year old nephew, Chad who was recording them on his brand new digital camcorder.

TWO

Shelby sat on the plush caramel colored leather passenger seat of their Mercedes with her eyes blindfolded. She was dressed in a sultry spaghetti-strapped short satin dress with silky textures and a bubble bottom. Her feet were adorned in black patent leather stilettos and her toes were painted in neon pink. Dexter looked over at his wife and smirked. He was finally surprising her and she had no idea. Shelby always had to have her hand in everything and wanted to be the boss of any event, but this time he was in full control and Miss Bossy was totally clueless.

"You think the kids okay? Your mom is in her sixties. She may not be able to handle Savannah and D.J., maybe they should've came with us."

"Shelby, the kids are fine. You said you needed a break, this is our time. And Chad is there if she needs extra help."

Shelby wiggled in her seat. "Don't mention that pervert. He was filming us having sex. If he wanted to see me naked all he had to do was ask."

"Chill out, Chad didn't see anything. You are so paranoid. The boy was filming the clouds. He had no idea I was tearing that ass up. I told you I checked his camera."

"Okay, but if I end up on the Internet with my ass in the air, I'm going to beat them braces out of his mouth." Shelby giggled, trying to peek from the blindfold.

Dexter smacked his wife's hand as they drove pass LaPlace, Louisiana and onto the long bridge over the swampland. "Don't peek. You want me to surprise you and that's what I'm doing."

Dexter turned on Tchoupitoulas Street and valeted his black beauty. The two pranced inside the restaurant, which was one of the top five picks in New Orleans. But that wasn't why Dexter choose the fine dining establishment. He, Shelby, and the kids watched the Food Network faithfully and they adored the *Iron Chef*. Dexter watched his wife for weeks, observing the comments made as the New Orleans cook prepared meals. She had mentioned driving to New Orleans on several occasions to visit the restaurant, so Dexter thought her birthday would be the perfect time to wow her with a meal at the famous restaurant, *August*.

Refinement filled the air as Dexter led his blindfolded wife into the elaborate restaurant. The dark wood walls and subtle lighting of the bar and gilt-edged décor in the central dining room showed distinct signs of wealth. Over one thousand crystal prisms, dangling from four huge chandeliers, illuminated the damask-covered walls and French-style chairs.

The hostess opened the doors to the private room and Dexter untied the black blindfold, revealing over seventy-five of their closest friends and associates dressed in sexy costumes and masks. "Surprise!" the crowd yelled, standing at their round cocktail tables, covered in white linen with pink calla lillies peering from the tall, twenty-inch crystal vases. Shelby was stunned. Tears dribbled down her light brown eyes. Dexter had never been able to pull off a surprise in their six years of marriage. And this event took the cake. There was a masked cartoonist in the corner dressed in a black tuxedo with a hot pink bow drawing pictures of guests. The all-male waiters were also dressed in the same attire, passing out pink hurricane drinks and appetizers. The place was so elegant and decorated just right, everything planned to perfection as if she had done it herself. In addition, a 13-by-15-inch canvas photo of Shelby stood on a silver easel right on the ebony grand piano. Minature bottles of champagne labeled *Happy 30th Birthday Shelby* and small gift boxes of Godiva candy wrapped in silver and pink personalized ribbons with Shelby's name and birth date on them traced the base of the easel.

"Thank you," she managed to say between weeps as she placed kisses on her husband's lips and all around his mouth several times. "Oh, you have poetry reading, singing, and door prizes," Shelby stated in a stunned, excited voice as her eyes scanned the place.

"Your girls helped too. They said you wanted all of this," Dexter replied, looking over at Shelby's friends. "Brooklyn got that author, Naiomi Pitre to read some of her erotic poems and Megan flew Lissa in from Atlanta to sing a few songs until we arrived."

"Oh my God, I can't believe none of you whores told me about this," Shelby yelled aloud to her best friends, Megan, Kelly, Blair, and Brooklyn, nearly forgetting she had business associates in the room. Seeing her childhood friends made her feel like that eighteen-year-old girl from the south side of Chicago again.

Kelly's eyes opened wide like a deer about to be shot.

"Watch your mouth, young lady. Don't let Satan enter your vocabulary. Just because we're in the city of sin doesn't mean you have to act like it. You need to be careful about what you let in your spirit. Now give me a hug," Kelly told Shelby with a huge smile and open arms. The two hadn't seen each other in years and Kelly was still the same. But Shelby preferred the radical preacher than the old jezebel who lived in Kelly's body six years ago.

"Crab cake? Oysters Rockefeller? Crawfish pie? Seafood pasta?" the waiter carrying the silver platter asked Kelly.

"No, thank you. I'm cleansing myself for the Lord, but God bless you for asking."

"Look at you, Kelly, you are so skinny. My hand can wrap around you," Shelby stated with a haphazard smile dashed with a little anxiety. "And your dress is beautiful," she lied with a shaky voice, not knowing what else to say because her facial expression had said it all. The dress Kelly was wearing was hideous. It was the kind of outfit that only a resale shop would own. It was a long, pale pink, loose, lace dress that reached her ankles with ruffles around the collar. She thought it was a costume but realized it wasn't when she saw how modest freckled-faced Kelly looked.

"I'm glad you like it. I couldn't get down with that mask and costume theme. I have to keep things real. And I'm a Christian at all times. I wish I could say the same about you and that provocative dress you're wearing," she said with a cute smirk. "You are turning thirty, not twenty. A married woman, especially one that is supposed to be of the Lord, should think twice before decorating her body with the devil's wear," Kelly said as nice as she could with a pinch of Shelby's cheek. Shelby hummed to herself and inched toward Megan, who was sitting at the round table with Kelly, Blair, and Brooklyn. She greeted Megan with kisses and hugs, before anything ungodly came out of her mouth.

"Hey, diva! You look so, so, good. Like, oh, my, goodness a nun costume," she said in her best Valley Girl voice, looking around. "Like, where is your husband?"

"Nuns are single, and this is a girls-only trip. We came to party in the best city in the world to celebrate our girl's birthday. And my husband is at work, working one of his many jobs because I want that new Porsche truck."

Shelby giggled a few seconds, then her smile disappeared. She inched closer to Megan's chair, moving the satin headpiece to the side to whisper in her ear.

Megan responded in a light whisper. "You know she's been fasting and praying for a husband. I told her to be more specific and tell God she wants a rich one. She's losing a lot of weight, but you can't tell Reverend Kelly anything. She only listens to God, which is a good thing." Megan pointed to Blair, who was sitting across from her wearing a huge black Afro wig and a tight short black dress on with go-go boots. "Now, that's the one you need to worry about. Something is going on, I just haven't made my way to Eighty-seventh Street to find out. I can't stand to go over there. You know how hood Blair can be."

"Would you ladies like a pink hurricane? Pink champagne?" the tall, dark waiter asked in a chipper voice, ending the two ladies' gossip session.

Blair stood up, took two drinks off the silver tray, and inched over to Shelby. "Look, do I have to wait all day for you to make your rounds? Do the snob and nun get all your attention?" Blair gave Shelby the tightest hug ever. "Happy birthday, baby girl. You are beautiful. Who did your makeup and toes?" Blair asked loudly as she popped her gum.

"Germs! Blair, can you please step back. You're squirting spit everywhere," Megan said as she took out a mini can of Lysol and began to spray. "Shelby, please tell her who did your face before I drown in saliva."

"Flawless Creations. Girl, Flawless is a fool. She'll make you look like you're twenty again, as you can see. And Nikki did my toes at Escape to Paradise Nail Spa."

Blair's eyes traveled down Shelby's body. "Okay, I'll have to check them out when I'm in town. 'Cause you look great." She sucked her teeth. "You have really filled out a lot, you and Megan both. The bigger the better. I need some ass from the whispering ass sisters." Blair added in. "If I had an ass like Megan and Shelby, I'd show you all how to make it do what it do. Shit, I may go get me one in the Quarter tonight and show you bitches how to drop it like it's hot and make that booty clap." Blair turned around and pointed across the room. "You see Max checking out that phat ass." She pointed to a dark, short gentleman wearing a black suit and a mask.

Shelby turned around and met the eyes of her ex-boyfriend and childhood friend, Maxtin Brooks, who was also her husband's best friend. Dexter and Max were closer than thieves before Shelby met Dexter. You didn't see one without the other, it was like their names were intertwined.

In Shelby's early twenties she was saved, a lot like Kelly, but not as radical. She didn't go to the club, curse, drink, dress seductively, or have any intimate interactions with men. Her routine was school, church, and Bible study, until she ventured out to the club with Blair, Megan, and Kelly on a cold March night. And that's when she bumped into Max, they reconnected, and her Christian life vanished.

Max manipulated Shelby; he said he was a changed

man, no longer a controlling, arrogant, womanizer. He
told her he knew how Sebastian, her first love, had taken
her for granted and he would never do that. Max said he
was a man, not the cruel boy she dated in middle school,
a grown man who was ready for a serious, monogamous
relationship with the woman he loved. But he lied, he was
the same old Max. He cheated on Shelby with more than
one woman, and was living with the mother of his baby. It
bothered her slightly, but when she fell in love with his
best friend, Dexter Jean Pierre, nothing Max did mattered.

Shelby and Max never had sex; however, that wasn't
the case with Dexter. The two were drawn to each other.
He listened to her every word, showed respect, and wanted
to spend every free moment with her. They crept around
for months behind Max's back, having wild sexual escapades. Dexter wanted to tell Max how much he loved
Shelby, but she wouldn't let him. She wanted to avoid con-
frontation so she broke up with Max without any explanation. A year later, Shelby rededicated herself to the Lord
and married Dexter, her soul mate. The two men remained
friends, but after Shelby married Dexter, Max never said
another word to her again. He spoke with Dexter on his
cell phone and their paths had not crossed until now.

Shelby brushed her hair out of her face with her fingers.
"I don't know why Dexter invited Max to my thirtieth
birthday."

"What did he do? Remind you that you are human. Get
over it. You slept with and married your boyfriend's best
friend. Love has no boundaries," Brooklyn said as she
stood up wearing a black, red, and white poker-girl cocktail dress costume with a hat to match and a black mask
on, placing a kiss on Shelby's forehead.

"Yeah, that nigga can't keep his eyes off of you. Why

don't you put an extra twist in those hips since he's watching," Blair said, turning Shelby around so that Max could get a good look. Then she popped her girl on the butt and mimicked to Max. "You want some, don't ya? Yeah, that ass den got fatter since you last seen it."

"See, this is why I didn't want to come with you women of the world. You guys promised to be good. I can't block my blessings by filling my spirit with foolishness." Kelly preached.

They all ignored her and kept on talking and taunting like she didn't exist. "Come on, girl, fuck with that nigga's head. Here he comes," Blair chimed in, pushing Shelby toward Max.

THREE

At two in the morning, hours after her surprise birthday party, Megan, Blair, Brooklyn, and Shelby left their suites that Dexter had booked them at the Ritz-Carlton Hotel, and journeyed down to Bourbon Street, one of New Orleans's most famous streets, which was closed down to traffic at night and filled with walking tourists. The girls were mesmerized by the fact that they could drink liquor in the streets, so their first stop was at the Tropical Isle. The spot was known for housing the most powerful drink on Bourbon, and the hand grenade was it. The melon-flavored, neon-green–colored drink was sold in an exclusive one-half yard souvenir cup shaped like a hand grenade.

"Megan, you sure you don't want one? This drink is the bomb!" Brooklyn stuttered between slurps.

"I don't drink, especially in the street and my husband is a minister."

"Pish-posh! Since when don't you drink?" Brooklyn asked.

"Stay out of my business. I just prefer not to drink in

the filth of this place. That stale beer smell is making me nauseated. Oh, God I need to wash my hair again. . . . And if one more drunk person bumps into me I'm going to scream." Megan spat the words out quickly to a drunk lady who had just bumped into her. Then she sprayed her shoulder with a miniature bottle of Lysol that she pulled from her purse. "I can't even look in my mirror and check my makeup good."

"Put that damn Lysol and mirror up. You should have stayed your beautiful ass in the room with Kelly," Shelby replied. "I'm kid- and husband-free and it's my birthday. We about to party. I'm thirty and I'm a bad bitch. I thought you knew. It's time to live and enjoy life."

"Pay no attention to me. I'm just having mood swings. I'm gaining too much weight," Megan said without giving any eye contact. "Didn't I buy you bitches these cute pink sweaters and designer jeans," she said, rubbing on the diamonds on her XL sweater.

"Yes, you did. Because every girl needs a good pair of designer jeans that cost over two hundred dollars," Shelby answered back, mocking Megan's favorite statement about designer jeans. She ridiculed Megan, but she had to admit there was a major difference in the way expensive designer jeans looked versus the others.

The girls continued traveling back toward the front of Bourbon Street, passing many strip clubs, bars, restaurants, and souvenir shops. *Now kick* . . . Shelby shoved her drink into Megan's hand and ran to the middle of the street and started dancing to the lyrics of the "Cupid Shuffle." "Come on. Let's dance. Walk that shit out," she shouted as she turned her body around and swung her hands in the air, dancing without a care in the world. Brooklyn joined her, but didn't let go of her drink, which had two extra shots more than everyone else's.

"I represent for the dirty south," Shelby sang as she kicked her legs out. "Come on kick. One, two, three, four, now turn and shake that big butt."

"Can you shake all of that on me. You ran from me earlier at the party," Max whispered into Shelby's ear. His groin area connected with her backside. "You know I've been mad at your low-down ass for the last six years. You were supposed to be my wife and you marry my best friend. I still say that was some ho-ass shit. But what goes around comes back around. Karma is a bitch," Max said with a cute chuckle, walking away before Shelby could reply.

Just the feel of the small notch between his legs made her want to puke. *I should've been his wife, yeah, right,* Shelby thought to herself after the dance was over, glad none of her friends heard Max's ignorant comment. "There is nothing little dick Max can do for me with his lying, histrionic self. He'll say anything for attention," Shelby recited in an non-audible voice as they walked down Bourbon.

The girls giggled down the street, their bodies tightly huddled together. "We doin' it big in the Big Easy, a hurricane can't destroy the spirit of New Orleans," Blair stated before she pulled her huge breasts out of her triple-D bra. "Throw me something, mister," she yelled up to the guys on the balcony of a hotel.

"This place comes alive at night," Brooklyn chimed in and pulled out her 34 C's as beads fell from the balcony.

Megan spoke into her small, pocket-sized sterling mirror with her named engraved in it. "Can you picture me, Megan Cole Myru, dancing in the street? I don't think so. I am just too sexy for words. I am the most beautiful one of them all. Yes I am."

"Are you sure you didn't have anything to drink? Cause I'm the only bad bitch out here."

"What's up with you? You are so ghetto. I would never believe you were a psychiatrist. And wasn't no one checking you out except Max's tired ass," Megan said, rolling her eyes at Shelby, wanting to snatch the furry pink crown tiara off of her drunken head.

Before Megan could finish checking her face out in the mirror, Shelby dismissed her and popped into a club named Razzoo and by the time they all made it in she was on the stage jumping up and down criss-crossing her legs to another song.

"Super soak that ho. What kind of song and dance is that?" Megan asked, patting her chest as her friends ran onstage for Shelby to teach them how to do the somewhat complicated dance for young people.

"Come on, Megan, it's easy. This dance is old," Shelby yelled out from the stage. "My nephew and nieces taught me this dance in ten minutes."

"No, I'll watch. That dance is too interactive for me. I may sweat too much. And speaking of sweat, I need to wash my hair as soon as we get back to the room." Megan stood back and watched as her friends swayed left to right like they were sixteen years old. She made sure no one touched her or bumped into her because she knew the purse snatchers were on duty just watching to catch someone slipping.

"Crank that soulja boy. Crank that soulja boy," two guys yelled from behind Megan in an intoxicated tone.

She grabbed her gold designer purse tight, her eyes refusing to venture. Her neck locked. "I know what crank that souja boy means. They are trying to rob me. Well, he won't get this four-thousand-dollar Oscar de la Renta python bag," Megan whispered to herself, then typed something into her cell phone, which was in her hand.

"Crank that soulja boy," One of the guys yelled louder. Megan refused to turn around. Her shoulders stiffened up and her grasp around the purse tightened. She looked down at her feet. "Thank God, I have on these flat shoes. Okay, Emporio Armanis, I paid almost four hundred dollars for you. I hope you run fast," she mumbled to herself as her feet tapped the floor at a fast offbeat rhythm and her hands rubbed her stomach in a circular motion.

Without notice a dark brown masculine hand adorned with platinum jewelry reached over Megan's shoulder, landing on the side her purse strap rested. She nearly jumped out of her skin as his arm extended around her.

"Give me your purse! Go ahead. Crank that soulja boy."

"You know you almost got Mace sprayed in your face," she managed to say between her heavy breathing and punches as she put her Lysol bottle back in her purse.

"Oh, you were gonna Mace me with Lysol? What the fuck did I do?" Max asked, wondering why she had a bottle of Lysol.

"You tried to scare me. I thought you would have grown up in the last twenty years, but I see you haven't. You still two feet tall and very immature." She stressed to Max as she looked down at him and rolled her eyes. "You are still the same stupid, mean, arrogant little boy who tormented me in grammar school."

Max tried to embrace his childhood friend to stop her verbal attacks, but she was on a mission and there was no stopping Megan, so he backed up off of her.

Megan and Shelby grew up with Max and he would tease, throw rocks and dirt at them like many boys his age did, yet Megan never forgave him. She held on to the childhood hate.

"And give me back my damn Michael Jackson button you stole. It's probably worth millions now. And my official Chicago Bulls hat with my name embroidered on the back. Those were valuable items yo black ass took from me," she shouted with rage and a few more punches.

Max didn't reply. He just sipped on his large cup of beer, staring out onto the dance floor at the woman he should have married.

Shelby dropped it low to the ground and brought it back up. She was attracting a lot of attention; it appeared the whole club was looking at her on the dance floor. Max could see why as he fought with the man in his pants who bulged out to see what was going on. Shelby was untamed and rowdy with her tight pocket-less skinny jeans and pointed toe gold heels on.

Max wanted her bad. He watched with an eager eye as two guys grabbed Shelby's waist from the back and followed her movement. "Them niggas dancing a little too close to my boy's wife," he mumbled, still ignoring Megan, who was now putting sanitizer on her hands.

"What's up with that? Back the fuck up," Blair cursed, pushing the two men in their chest, shoving them off the dance floor.

Brooklyn and Shelby kept on dancing. And a few seconds later a new set of vultures were back on the ladies' side. Max couldn't stand still. He marched to the dance floor in an attempt to put an end to the dirty dancing.

"Man, come on, let's go," Max said, pulling Shelby's arm. "And get your girl too."

"What? I'm just dancing. Are you stalking me? You need to go back to Chicago and watch who your wife is dancing with," Shelby sang to Max, yanking her arm back and dancing. "This my song, I-N-D-E-P-E-N-D-E-N-T. She got her own house. She got her own car."

"Look, you my girl no matter what. We been friends over twenty years and I'll always care about you. And ain't no country-ass nigga gon' be pushing up on you. Now let's go," Max voiced in a more assertive manner. "You never could hold your liquor," he said, hugging Shelby and Brooklyn off the dance floor.

"Yo boo, I thought we were dancing?" the man from the dance floor asked, trying to stop Shelby.

"I got this," Max said, stepping in front of Shelby.

"You didn't look like you had it. You heard me?" the guy mumbled as he walked up closer to Max.

"Do it look like I got it now? Or do I have to stick my foot off up in yo country ass," Max answered back, pointing to his gun, which was tucked in his pants.

"Naw, I'm straight. You heard me," the guy stated as he backed away from Max and Shelby with swift movements toward the exit door.

"Now, I ought to tell your husband how yo ass was in here letting another nigga feel you up. Good thing I was here to check that weak, lame-ass brother. Y'all better be glad I followed—"

Shelby rolled her eyes at Max and dismissed him before he could finish his long sermon.

There was no way she was letting him chastise her on her birthday. She had one father and didn't need another one. She left Max standing, conversing with himself.

At four, the girls and Dexter's crew, including Max, met up and made their way toward the end of Bourbon Street near Canal Street. Everyone was drunk except Megan, who was dry as a fresh diaper. She was tired and exhausted, but that didn't stop her from text messaging on her high-priced cell phone.

"Last stop is the Bourbon Cowboy," Shelby yelled out to everyone in a tipsy voice. Her friends looked at her like she was crazy when they examined the outside of the western-looking saloon. The name fooled them cause when they entered, it was another story. Sounds of hip-hop gyrated from the loudspeakers. And a mixed crowd greeted them.

After Blair, Brooklyn, and Shelby took a few shots of top-shelf tequila from the bar, they jumped up on the bar, counter and danced to the old song "Walk it Out." The whole setup looked like a scene from the movie *Coyote Ugly*. Dexter stood back and admired his wife. For the first time she was forgetting she was a mother, wife, and professional. She was letting loose, being free and enjoying life. And he was elated that he was able to make her thirtieth birthday a happy occasion.

"Let's ride the bull," Blair roared, searching for her cigarettes as they jumped down from the bar.

Megan looked at the Caucasian girl who was topless on the bull. Her tattooed breasts were flopping everywhere and her back was being yanked around in every direction.

"Have you lost your mind? I'm not doing that, not Megan Myru. I am just too sexy and mature to ride a bull. That is so beneath me."

"Can somebody shut this bourgeois bitch up? She's fuckin' up my high," Blair shouted with a long cigarette in her mouth.

Megan pointed to the topless girl, whose breasts were splattered to the mat after riding the bull only a few seconds. "I'm going to sit right here at this bar and text-message my man. You three hood rats have fun."

"Pish! Posh! That bull ride ain't nothing. I'm getting on first," Brooklyn said as she grabbed Shelby by the hand, heading toward the bull.

While the birthday bash were riding mechanical bulls and dancing to New Orleans favorites, Megan sat at the bar sipping on ginger ale. She laughed aloud as she watched Shelby bend over and back it up on Dexter. Blair had taught her how to do the stripper bounce and the two were gyrating, bouncing, and jiggling like video vixens. Dexter spanked Shelby's bottom as she danced. They looked good together, fresh like newlyweds and she wished her and Victor could be the same, but he knew that wasn't possible. Her husband was a minister. A proper speaking, rigid, boring man who did everything by the book.

"Hey beautiful? What's so funny?" A tall, Caucasian man asked.

Megan turned around and all the unhappiness she was feeling disappeared with the blink of an eye.

"You got my text message?" she murmured to the familiar, handsome man.

"I sure did," he replied with a soft kiss to her lips, thinking about the text picture she sent of him hitting it from the back.

Megan blushed, loving the feel of his thin, soft lips. "I've been acting like a complete ass tonight. You know how I get when I miss you. Megan wasn't happy. She was uptight and horny. And you kept her waiting."

He kissed her neck, stuck his tongue in her ear, then whispered, "Princess, I got here as fast as I could. I told you we could book another night. Come on, let's go."

Megan looked around. Her friends were loaded and hadn't noticed anything she was doing.

"Come on, no one is looking. Your husband is in Chicago and your friends are having a good time, like we should be. Let Doc make it up to you."

Megan perked up when she heard those words from Jackson, her young, rich, handsome Caucasian lover who she met on the Internet dating site Date a Millionaire Doctor.

"Oh, yeah. I love makeup sex, especially when it's good," Megan purred as she caressed her lover's hand and exited the club. She pulled out her phone and texted her friends a group message: *Don't worry about me. I'm back at the Ritz in my presidential suite enjoying the good life.*

MEET KELLY

Kelly tossed and turned her beautiful, flawless body against the pink satin sheets. She was elated to be home away from her wild friends. Not that she was judging anyone. Kelly was a demon, back in the day. She considered herself one hundred times worse than any of her girls. She slept with any and every man she could. Even had a journal that kept track of her weekly rendezvous and measured each man's size. Morals, she had none. Self-esteem, what was that? And talking about selfish, Kelly was loyal to herself and no one else mattered.

Years, maturity, and a lot of praying had changed Kelly-anna Swanson into a different person. A born-again Christian, living for the Lord and loving all of his people. She promised in the name of Jesus that she would never sleep with a man that was not her husband. "Fasted and prayed and it's been five years today. Pure and clean, a born-again virgin for my husband to be. I'm speaking things into existence. Thank you Jesus, for sending me a husband," she repeated several times before drifting off into a deep sleep.

The blue, leather-covered NIV bible with gold writing crashed to the floor. Kelly ran to the door after the second knock. "I'm coming," she announced loud enough for the person to hear on the other side of the door. Standing on the tip of her toes she raised her four-eleven frame and looked out the peephole. "Am I in hell? What is a giant chocolate chip cookie doing at my doorstep? Devil, you're a liar! Get behind me, Satan! I'm seeing things," she bellowed in a daze when she saw a delivery person dressed in a huge cookie costume. "May I help you? Do you have identification?" she yelled through the door with shaky hands.

"I have a delivery for you. Are you Kelly Swanson?" the Caucasian girl said in a loud, friendly tone as she pulled out her Illinois identification.

She opened the door without hesitation, with a huge Price is Right smile on her face. "I'm Kelly in the flesh, saved and baptized in the blood of Jesus."

The lady stepped, but didn't move. Her eyes peered at the baby roaches crawling over the plate of old food. "Do you have a clean table I can put these things on?"

"Bless you, sister. Follow me." Kelly looked back at the cookie costume and wondered if her feet where glued to the wood floor in the foyer. "Come on, it's okay. I should be afraid of you," Kelly said in a chipper voice as she led the woman to the cocktail table. "Just move those daily devotions out the way." The cookie lady placed her laptop on the table and

*keyed in something. Then she opened the huge box.
There was a heart-shaped cookie decorated with red
and white icing inside. Kelly's face became flushed
she almost fell out when she read the cookie. "Will
you marry me, Kelly?"*

*"Lord, I know I told all my girls I was praying for
a husband, but that was quick. I had no idea my
prayers would be answered today," Kelly testified
as she glanced up at the white swirling ceiling.*

*Before she could collect her thoughts, the blond-
haired lady dressed up as a cookie began to sing
and dance. "I'm a chocolate chip and so are you.
Please tell me you'll say I do."*

*Kelly looked down at the cookie box and that's
when her eyes were blinded by the huge emerald-cut
diamond engagement ring. The girl dressed like a
cookie smiled and picked up the ring and placed it
on Kelly's small, skinny finger. Kelly's hands trembled like a person with Parkinson's disease. Karl,
her classmate from theology school, appeared on the
thirteen-inch laptop computer screen. "So Kelly, my
love, will you marry me? Move to Los Angeles and
be my first lady and wife?" Her breathing became
erratic. She covered her eyes as tears rolled down
her freckled, blushed cheeks, but uncovered them
quick as she looked into the computer screen. Kelly
stood up. "Yes! Of course I will! I receive it, Lord!
Thank you, Jesus! Jesus, yes!" She jumped up and
down and twirled around in circles, then made the
Father, Son, and Holy Ghost sign with her hands.
"I'll meet you next Monday night in Chicago at
twelve midnight, at the chapel on Seventy-third street."*

Kelly's mouth gasped open. She leaped up out of her bed from her deep sleep and dropped to her knees. She thanked the Lord for the revelation, sent out her wedding invitations, ordered a cake, and reserved the church hall for her wedding to take place next week. She was already in preparation and glad that the Lord had come to her months ago in a similar dream and said that she would be married soon. She just didn't know to who and when. But she was obedient. Kelly bought her dress at the local thrift shop on a big bargain Wednesday, awaiting her word from the Lord. "Well, the time has come and God isn't a liar. I's gonna be married next week. Thank you, Jesus"

Kelly busied herself around the house, excited about her up-and-coming wedding. She was leaving everything to God, even telling her husband-to-be about their wedding. She picked up the phone off of her wicker nightstand to call Blair, Megan, and Shelby on three-way.

"My darlings, guess what?"

"What, Kellyanna?" Megan asked, upset because someone was disturbing her from searching the Web for her father.

"I claimed it. I received it. I spoke it into existence. God sent me a husband. Remember the older man I went to theology school with?" Kelly asked her friends, almost jumping through the phone.

"Now what is a retired ho going to do with an old man?" Blair asked.

"You need a young, twenty-year-old white boy with some stamina and money. I'm telling you if I was single I'd have a young, rich white man. . . . Peep the game, the white boys are loving some black women these days. Pay attention the next time you go out," Megan stated in an eager, blunt way as she gazed at a message from Jackson.

"White boy? Jesus knows, I've never dated anyone outside of my race," Kelly said in a defensive manner, even
though her mother was white.

"Yeah, white boy? Megan, ain't nobody down with the
interracial thang except Shelby," Blair exclaimed.

"So what. I only dated one Asian. He wasn't white,"
Shelby replied, thinking about Sebastian, the boy she gave
her virginity to in high school. "Just be happy for Kelly,
our praying paid off. A husband is a husband at this
point." Shelby exhaled, motioning for her kids to get out
of her room.

"But Mommy, D.J. looked at me," her two-year-old
daughter whined.

"I didn't look at big-head Savannah," her son replied.
Shelby covered the phone receiver, squinted her left eye
and pointed her finger toward the door.

"Shit, I remember that bowlegged minister. He looked
like he had a horse dick that dropped down to his knees."

"Blair! Don't talk like that. Lord forgive her. But, yes,
that's him. He's the one. It came to me in a dream last
night," Kelly said, full of joy.

"A dream? Have you consumed any controlled sub-
stances? Are you back drinking?" Shelby asked.

"The bitch is just crazy or smoking that shit with her
mama," Blair screamed through the phone.

"Don't say that, Blair, something may be really wrong
with Kelly. Have you been under a lot of stress? Any depression?" Shelby asked in her doctor voice.

"No, I am not crazy or depressed. Minister Karl will be
my husband and that's that. God isn't indecisive nor does
he lie. My visions always come true."

"But, when is the last time you've spoken to this minister? And does he have any money," Megan interjected.

"It's been six or seven months, since graduation," Kelly

said, bothered by their series of questions and inappropriate language. "He moved to Los Angeles and is head minister over a huge congregation of about five thousand members."

"Wait . . . Kelly, are you telling us you are getting married off of a revelation from God?" Megan asked slowly, with a calm voice.

"Yes, how many times do I have to tell you guys? God told me that I was getting married."

"Just like I thought. Your God forgot to tell him to ask you to marry him. Shit, no dick for you," Blair answered in a sluggish tone, twirling her long blond weave around her finger.

"Girls, chill out. You know Kelly is joking. If she's planning a wedding then I'm sure the guy asked her," Shelby replied in a weak voice, not wanting to believe Kelly was exhibiting schizoid characteristics. "What do y'all know about divine intervention anyway?"

"Thank you, Shelby. Your two friends are so negative. If they had faith, they'd understand the power of prayer and speaking things into existence. And he doesn't have to ask me, God has already spoken."

"Oh, Shelby is the one that asked if you were on psych medications. And I have faith. How do you think I've made it this far? It was God's grace that led me to a rich man," Megan replied with plenty of attitude as she glared down at her busy fingers, decorated with diamond rings, typing away on her laptop.

"Kelly, I can use a laugh. I wouldn't miss it for the world. We can wear the same dresses we bought for Brooklyn's wedding that never happened," Blair replied, then guzzled down a glass of wine.

"Ha-ha . . . My wedding is real. You ladies don't have to come if you don't believe."

"You know I'll be there to support you, girl. Dexter has recovered from his vasectomy too. I'm there. He can handle the kids. This will be my first trip away from him and the kids since we've been married."

"Kelly, yo ass is crazy, but I guess we can meet up. This is some soap opera drama or are you sure we didn't get picked for a reality show? You need to let me know so I can be looking my best on television."

"Do you guys actually think I'd have you come to something that wasn't ordained by God?" Kelly shouted.

"Hell yeah, you ain't wrapped too tight," Blair giggled. "Like I said, I'll be there, I can use a good laugh."

After Kelly hung up the phone she thought about her girls. They were a trip, but she loved them, especially Shelby. Kelly had cleansed herself and had been a faithful servant to the Lord since her battle with cancer five years ago. And Shelby was there through it all, she even turned her life back around. Kelly and Shelby met in junior high and had a love-hate relationship. Kelly thought of her as "Miss Goodie" because she was always doing things morally right. Shelby was almost like a parent figure to Kelly when she lost her father. And when Kelly was out in the world living the whorish life, Shelby was at home praying. She had become a born-again Christian and was quick to keep Kelly in line, who was wild and didn't have respect for her body.

Kelly jotted a note to pray for Shelby then she shook her head, and added Blair and Megan down too. They just didn't understand that there was no need for Miss Kelly to intervene in what God had for her. She placed her hand together like a church steeple, dropped to her knees and thanked Jesus for blessing her with a wedding date and a husband.

MEET BLAIR

It was after five and the Dan Ryan Expressway was fierce. Cars were bumper to bumper inching south. The road was covered with dirty sleet and gigantic flakes of snow mixed with rain were invading the windshield, making Blair's commute home a bitch. "This rush-hour traffic ain't no joke. It's still taking me almost two hours to get to Seventy-ninth street from the north side. They need to expand the Dan Ryan," Blair complained aloud as she swung her long, blond curly weave from side to side, puffing on her cigarette.

Without warning, a black, ghetto, fake Bentley with twenty-four-inch rims leaped in front of Blair's vehicle, forcing her to slam down on her brakes and horn abruptly. "You reject wannabe gangsta!" she shouted as she reached under her seat, grabbing her piece then lunging out of her car toward the overpriced vehicle, which was at a halt. Evil, hazel-colored contacts met with the young punk who was wearing knockoff diamond studded Chanel sunglasses and dressed in an artificial black mink coat. His little body was sitting low in the driver seat, which was swallowing him. He was so short you could barely see his head peering over the steering wheel.

"You almost killed me! You sorry, imitation pimp!" Blair yelled as she banged her gun on his window and kicked at the door of the gaudy car before the driver sped off onto the curb.

Things like this happened weekly in Chicago. If Blair wasn't blowing her horn she was giving drivers the finger and banging her fist on windows. And if someone cut her off she was kicking at the back of their car and cursing them out every chance she got. Blair had always been a little violent, but every since she took herself off of her antidepressants her aggression level was out of control; and her mood swings were fierce.

The black iron gated security door of the south side home swung opened before Blair could turn the lock. "Come on in. How was work?" Bryan asked with a big kiss on his wife's chocolate painted lips.

"It was fucked and that damn traffic is a bitch. I almost had to bust a cap in a little midget." She looked around, noticing their home was silent. Her son, Blairson, whom she had before they were married and their new addition, Bryanna, were nowhere to be found.

"Where are the kids?"

"At Madear's. Don't worry about them. Give me yo' shoes and sit down, relax. Let Daddy make you feel better." He pulled her size eleven heels off and placed them under the cocktail table, then he handed over his paycheck. "Take those panty hose off. I want to taste my brown suga's toes." Her stockings came down quick. Bryan grabbed his wife's feet the minute they hit the ottoman. "These feet is beautiful. My baby is always decorating and color coordinating everythang. Emerald green toe polish with diamonds shaped into clovers. You are one creative lady," Bryan said in his frantic country accent as he kissed Blair's big toe. "But, bay, St. Patrick's day is over. Let me redo your toes."

"Naw, I got to get them done for Kelly's wedding," she said, pushing him away with her hand. "Just pass me my cigarettes."

Bryan handed his wife a lit cigarette. "But, um . . . What about Kelly getting married?" he asked with a surprised expression on his face.

"Bryan, she's been fasting and asking the Lord to send her a husband and he answered her prayer just like that," Blair said, snapping her fingers.

"Well, that there is wonderful. When you faithful to the Lord he'll answer your prayers. And Kelly has been a devoted servant. I see her every week in Bible study and Sunday school."

"Whatever? I knew you'd believe in your girl," Blair giggled with a little sarcasm in her voice, remembering Kelly and Bryan had snuck out to a Keith Sweat concert together before they were married.

"No, I believe in you," Bryan sighed as he kissed her feet again.

"And I in you," Blair responded in a light, phony tone, enjoying the kissing and massaging of her feet at the same time. "Ooh baby, it feels so good. I just love for a nigga to suck my toes."

"I'm glad, cause I'm that nigga there," Bryan said as he took the palm of each foot and kneaded it in all the right places, sending chills up his wife's back. "Ohh! I really need this. I don't know how much longer I can take living in this big city. Traffic is too crazy, not to mention the high cost of gas, cost of living, and these crazy-ass wannabe gangstas killing everybody."

Bryan ignored her ranting, placing each toe in his mouth, making hasty, loud, sucking noises. He loved Chicago like he'd given birth to it and there was no way he was leaving. He was born in Mississippi in a small country town and had no plans to return.

"You're making me hungry. You're eating on my toes like they're pickled pig feet. What's for dinner?"

"Gurl, I've already prepared a special meal just for you, baby boo. I had to do a taste test first to make sure it would meet your standards."

"You are so sweet. What are you serving?" Blair replied with a grin the size of Australia, loving every minute of the pampering her husband was giving.

Moments later, Bryan seized the tip of Blair's hand and escorted her to the table. He pulled her chair out, placed a linen napkin in her lap, and rushed to the kitchen for her meal. Blair lit another cigarette and waited for her husband to return.

"Madam, we have broiled *chilapia*, fresh from Lake Michigan, steamed *asparagust*, wild rice and praline and cream-cheese cake for dessert."

"Aren't we being the perfect husband? But honey, the fish is called *tilapia* and it is *asparagus*." Blair chuckled, laughing at the way her husband pronounced words.

"You know what I was talking about," Bryan replied, a little embarrassed that after all the years of living in Chicago, his old Crosby, Mississippi accent still dominated his speech. "Anyway, this is for you," Bryan stated as he placed the plate down in front of his wife and pried the cigarette out of her hand.

Blair's eyes flowered open. Saliva formed in the side of her mouth. "Thank you, sir."

"Can I get anything else for you?"

"No, thank you. Everything looks wonderful." Blair picked her fork up and started to eat that very second. "Honey, this is delicious. You have really outdone yourself this time. It tastes better than yesterday's dinner."

"Why, thank you. There is more if you like, but let me bless the food first," Bryan lectured, smacking his wife's hand as he quoted a holy prayer.

"Amen!" Blair yelled before he could say "in Jesus' name." She dug back into the plate and continued to eat. "I definitely want seconds. This food is the bomb!"

Ten minutes later, Bryan looked into his wife's eyes and smiled back with his hazel, now green eyes as he hurried to the kitchen to fix her another plate. When he returned the food was piled up high on the plate this time. "More of Bryan's special of the day."

Blair couldn't stop grinning as she gazed at the huge plate of food; her mouth watering for more. "This is so good," she said, exaggerating her words.

"Good, there is mo', you can have as many helpings as you like. You know how I love me a big, fine, healthy woman."

She picked up the fish with one hand and began to eat. Her fingers and mouth were moving quick as if this was her last meal on earth.

"Bring me some more fish and a glass of white zinfandel!" Blair ordered, sucking on her long fingernails.

"Sure! I love to see my little lady enjoying my cooking." Bryan rushed back to the dining room, but stopped midstream, admiring Blair from afar and winking. A good cook always took pleasure in watching people overindulge in their cooking. Blair looked up at her wonderful husband and beamed with joy. Cooking was one of the many reasons she married him. "Honey, join me."

"No baby girl, I just want to watch you. I'm here to serve you. Daddy is yo servant for the night," Bryan said with a seductive smile as he placed more fish on the plate and sat down the glass full of wine. Blair didn't argue as she tore back into her plate, shoving asparagus into her mouth four at a time.

Bryan sat down next to his wife at the table and stared into her eyes. He licked his lips and blushed. She smiled back, adoring her husband.

Guilt has turned my husband into an amazing man. He brings home the check, cleans the house, takes care of the kids, and cooks like a chef, she thought to herself, at the same time her mouth embracing the rim of the wineglass.

"You want some mo' wine?"

"Yes," Blair replied then paused and smacked her lips. Bryan stood up, grasped her glass and poured more wine in it. "Thank you, baby. I could really appreciate this if I were a cheap-broke ho!" Blair yelled as she threw the entire glass of wine in his face. "I do not drink from cheap, thick-ass wineglasses. Why didn't you serve my wine in a crystal glass? Hell, all I tasted was cheap lead. Bring me a crystal wineglass. Megan brought us those Waterford crystal glasses. Use them!"

Bryan wiped the dripping wine from his forehead and backed away from the table. "Baby girl, I'm sorry. You need to stop that there playing so much. I'll get you a crystal glass. Just calm your little self down."

Bryan returned with a plate of cheesecake and a crystal glass filled with wine. Blair sipped from the crystal glass. "Yes, much better. My wine tastes more crisp and I don't have a mouthful of thick-ass bulletproof glass." Then she turned to the dessert like nothing ever happened. Since her miscarriage she had experienced drastic mood swings and unexplainable manic episodes. She was like a time bomb, any little thing set her off. But Bryan was patient and tried hard to keep her calm and comfortable at all times.

"Honey, that looks so good. I need about five more pieces. You know how much I love cheesecake with praline sauce. Put extra praline sauce on my pieces."

"Sweetheart, I am here to serve you. I made that there entire cake for you. Let me get my little lamb some more," Bryan said, trying very hard to say the right words, not wanting to ruin their special date.

"Thank you, suga pie," Blair stated as she rubbed her hands together, anticipating his return with the dessert.

Bryan returned with the entire platter of cheesecake with praline sauce dripping to the floor. "When you finish eating, I'm gonna eat you with a little praline sauce," he chuckled trying to soften the mood.

"And you can eat all you want of me because I'm fat-free," Blair announced with her chest poked out, rubbing her hands all over her body.

"Baby, let me feed you," Bryan cooed as he put the fork in her mouth.

She rolled her tongue around the fork. "Give me more, Big Daddy." Bryan placed more in her mouth. She glowed, loving every taste on her palate as she swallowed the delicious cake. "Baby, you ain't to be played with. You should be on the Food Network."

Bryan seized his wife's hand. "Sorry about the cheap wine glass. I forgot all about our good crystal and I wanted to make this night special. It's the anniversary of our first date." Her husband kneeled down before her and started to sing. *"Could you be the one for me? Could we dance the night away?"*

Minutes later, Bryan stopped singing the Brian McKnight oldie. "Do you think you can love me the rest of our lives? Blair, I've loveded you since the first day we met. Thank you for being my wife."

"Yeah, Bryan, I can love you until this world ends. I forgot how sweet your voice is. My heart is crying and my panties are too." Blair looked down, feeling a little embarrassed about throwing wine in his face. "You even remembered our wedding song. I forgot about the anniversary of our first date."

"That's all right," Bryan stated as he kissed cheesecake off of her lips. He picked his fork up with the cheesecake on it and inched it toward her hungry mouth. Blair's tongue seized the fork before it reached her face, like a lizard seizing its prey.

"More, more, more," she cheered, like the lady on *Nutty Professor*, closing her eyes and wiggling her tongue.

"Baby girl, I live to make you happy. Open your mouth wide, this here is the last piece."

Blair sat there waiting for her husband to place some of that delicious homemade cheesecake dripping with praline sauce in her mouth.

"Ummm. This is like heaven. I love it," she screamed, waiting and wiggling in her seat for another forkful, but instead of giving her the last taste he treated himself. An expression of bewilderment masked her face. She opened her eyes, stood up over her husband and started pointing in his face. "How can you claim to love me and take food out of my mouth? You selfish motherfucker!"

"What I do now?" Bryan asked, not aware that he did anything wrong.

"Look at you with your big fat ass! You are disgusting. Lose some weight, why don't ya. I should stab your big greasy lips together with this fork." Blair chuckled aloud.

"Sitting up there like a giant moose munching on a dick full of cum."

Bryan continued to eat the cake. "What you talking 'bout?"

Blair's voice was stern. "I'm talking about you, Jabba the Hutt, and I'm not joking. You need to do something with yourself. Look at your jacked-up feet. They feel like cactus plants." She stared at the bottle of white zinfandel. "You fat country hog. Your hands look and feel like alligator paws. Look at your dried up, cracked ashy hands and your burnt fingertips. Don't get me started. With yo bumpy-dick ass," she hollered with rage as she grabbed the bottle of wine. "That last piece of cake was for me. You said you made everything especially for me. I didn't expect your hillbilly ass to down the last taste of cake."

"Baby boo, I'm so sorry. I can make another cake, you know. I didn't mean to upset you."

Blair became angrier when she saw how calm he was. "Yeah right, you sorry-ass nigga! You fat punk. When I met you all that fat wasn't hanging down to your knees. Look at your big sloppy gut! You have five stomachs. We have all this weight equipment collecting dust. There is no excuse for your gigantic butt to be as big as you are. Fuck around and catch a heart attack. With yo nasty ass."

"News alert, *Rasputia*, you aren't small," Bryan mumbled under his breath. "You look like you're twelve months pregnant. All you do is eat."

Blair hovered over Bryan. "What the hell did you say?" Without thinking, she grabbed the bottle of wine and smashed it into Bryan's head. Glass flew everywhere and wine mixed with blood poured down his face. "How dare you say I look pregnant? I just lost your baby two years ago."

"Yeah, you lost my baby! My mama told you pregnant women not supposed to smoke, especially weed. You didn't want to listen to her. But you always listen to that there Morgan," Bryan said with his hands grasping his head.

"Her name is Megan."

"Well my mama is a nurse just like that Morgan girl, but you didn't want to listen."

"Your mama ain't shit. She wishes she was a nurse. She's nothing more than a nursing assistant, who has worked in a nursing home half her life. That black bitch has never stepped into anyone's school. Looking like a bald-headed jack-o'-lantern with that missing tooth in the front."

"I see yo girl was smart enough not to smoke. She still pregnant."

He had to go there. When Shelby told me Megan was pregnant, something came over me. I couldn't pick up the phone to congratulate her. How could I? She was carrying a baby, a precious life in her stomach and my belly was filled with emptiness. Bryan, you are going to pay for that comment. Do you know how it feels to lose a child that is growing in your stomach? To prepare for a life that doesn't make it?

"Bring me some more food," Blair ordered, determined to fill the empty void in her belly, not concerned or apologetic for knocking her husband in the head.

Bryan paced back and forth, shaking glass and wine out of his dreads. A huge cut was plastered across his forehead and right eyebrow. Thick, dark blood oozed from the cuts. He was furious, but he didn't want to lash out at Blair. Bryan had hurt her in the past and he was trying to make it up to her. He did the unthinkable and he felt he deserved to be punished. "I'll bring you something to eat, but don't talk about my mama again. Watch who you call a b—"

"Okay, okay, I'm sorry. And don't get any of that blood in my food. Get you a Band-Aid," she voiced in a low, hurried, fake, empathetic manner.

He bit his lip, rolled his eyes, and headed toward the kitchen holding the cuts on his head.

"Here's your food," Bryan said calmly, placing the plate in front of her. He raised his hand up toward Blair, wanting to slap her head off. His eyes flickered shut as he thought about the huge cut on his face. He lowered his hand and walked toward the front door. "I'm outta here. I can't take this shit no more."

Blair took the plate of food and threw it as hard as she could. It was like she was trying to cut his neck off. "You wanna duck? You fat yellow bastard" she bellowed, watching the food fall to the floor from the door.

"Oh! I'm leaving for good this time, you crazy."

"What?" She could barely get her words out between cries. "If you leave you better not come back."

Bryan placed his hand on the doorknob and looked back at his wife. "This whole argument is bull. Look at me, girl. I have blood running from my head. And for what?"

"No, you look like a bull. Take your wide load to Bally's and work some of that lard off!" Blair ranted like a wild woman as she raced upstairs to the bedroom closet, grabbing racks of Bryan's clothes that were still in plastic from the cleaner's. "You want to leave me?" she screamed, opening the bedroom window, tossing his clothes out.

Bryan raced after her, snatching his Rocawear jersey and some more throw backs out of her hand before she could toss it out the window. Blair slammed the window down with all her might, smashing his three middle fingers.

He let out a piercing cry. "Blair, please lift the window back up."

"No, you goin' respect me."

"Blair, you goin' to break my fingers. How can I work if my fingers are broke?"

She hesitated for five seconds, then lifted the window up.

Hell, I do need his paycheck. And if his hands are broke, who's going to do the cooking?

"You still leaving?" she asked, pacing back and forth.

"Yeah, I need stitches and some air and I don't want to hurt you, Blair."

"What?" she howled before taking the palm of her hand and slamming it against Bryan's cheek. "Hurt me? You've killed me inside already. I don't know why I stayed with yo sorry, dirty-dick ass."

He acted as if he was startled by her behavior, clutching his face with his fingers.

Blair showed no emotion as she spoke to her husband. "The next time you better think before disrespecting me. You did the unthinkable."

Tears mixed with dried blood rolled down her husband's cheeks. He blew air out of his nostrils and released a loud, roaring sound. "I'm trying to be a Christian man and not hit you back." He bit his lip and grunted, speaking very slow and composed. "I promised God and Madear I would never touch a woman, but you taking it too far. My father beat my mama, our family is cursed with that there kind of domesticated violence stuff and I refuse to continue this sin," Bryan cried while looking up toward the ceiling. "I'm turning the other cheek, yeah, but Lord, I don't know how long."

After noticing the crazed expression on Bryan's face, a stench of fear graced Blair's body. She loved Bryan more than life, and she didn't want to lose him. Her mood swings were out of control and she couldn't help herself.

"I'ma head out. I really need to pray about some things," he said, shaking his head, not believing what just happened.

Blair clutched her husband's hand tight and kissed it several times. "Bryan, don't leave. I'm sorry. I'll start taking my medicine again. I'll get counseling. I just want my baby back." Hysteria housed her body. She fell to the floor and wept like a woman having a nervous breakdown. "I forgave you. Please forgive me. Please, I love you," she moaned, kissing at Bryan's feet. "Don't leave me."

MEET MEGAN

Megan sat at the chaise with her feet under her bottom and her laptop computer on her mocha-cream–colored thighs. She glided her glossy red fingernails through her silky black hair as she stared out of the huge bedroom window, thinking about her life. How she had a master's degree in nursing, a large home in the suburbs, a baby on the way, and a devoted husband. But she still wasn't happy. More money was needed to take her to the next level of happiness. She had more than others, but not enough. Megan felt someone as beautiful as her deserved to be a millionaire.

"Megan Myru, you need to decrease your expenses. You need to stop using your cell phone. You are over on your minutes and that credit card bill is over ten thousand dollars this month. I am working at the university full-time, the hospital, and the church and we still have outstanding bills," her husband communicated to her in an aggravating manner. She rotated her neck from left to right and lifted her hair to the middle of her head. Then she glared down at her computer screen and logged onto Date a Millionaire Doctor.

Victor's short frame shadowed over Megan, only because she was sitting. The two were actually the same height. "Honey, did you hear me? Are you on there looking for your father again?" She never looked up from the screen. Megan wasn't looking for her estranged father this time, she was looking for a man. Finding her father could wait. She didn't know who he was all these years and a few more years wouldn't hurt.

Megan had no idea who her father was. She was a love child from a relationship her mother had in college. When her mom found out she was pregnant with Megan, she left school and never returned, never telling the father-to-be about her pregnancy.

"Sweetheart, did you hear me?"

Megan smiled, her eyes glued to the computer screen. Victor kissed Megan's forehead.

"Honey, why are you ignoring me?"

"Victor, I am not going to live like a poor woman. I should not have to count my minutes or limit how much money I spend. If I want something I'm going buy it. It sounds like you need to get another job or stop sending your family in Africa money. Or maybe it's your trips to Kenya three times a year. I know one thing, you better write that thousand-dollar-check for Kelly's wedding gift."

"Megan, you fully understand I go to Africa on grant money, none of those expenses come out of my pocket. You, on the other hand, have a shopping problem. That child has a million dollars worth of possessions and he or she is not born yet."

It's a she, Megan thought to herself as she stared into her mirror, admiring her gorgeous, unblemished skin. She too was in her early thirties and still looked twenty.

"And I am still paying for our fifty-thousand-dollar wedding you were dying to have. We could have replicated your girlfriend Blair's wedding, and traveled to Jamaica or Barbados."

"Victor, you are really getting on my nerves. You should feel privileged to be married to me. I would've never did the Jamaica thing. How dare you? You just can't please an ugly brotha. Why did I let Shelby introduce me to Victor? She could've fixed me up with any other professor. Hell, I didn't know psychiatrists were the bottom-paid doctors. This broke Negro is running out of funds," she mumbled to herself. Then she spoke aloud. "Whatever. Just make sure you write that check for Kelly's wedding gift." She rolled her eyes and looked down at the platinum ring. The diamond baguettes in her ring were sparkling as she pecked down on the keyboard, posting a comment on Jackson's page. When she completed her message she gazed back at her ring, counting the diamonds in silence. A mask of gloom covered her face.

Megan quickly changed her Web browser. "Honey, I'm sorry. I just get so frustrated. I want my child to know his or her family. My child could date or worse, grow up and marry a relative. Roots are important. Hell, if you weren't African you could be my brother. Heritage is so vital. You know your whole family tree," Megan moaned, upset because her husband forced her to think about her situation.

Megan was embarrassed about her family history. She was the only one on the block who didn't have a father. All her friends had some type of dad. Margaret's father was a drunk, Darlene's dad was a drug dealer, Shelby had a stepfather, Thomas's dad was a minister, and Max's dad lived out of town, but he visited. You see, no matter what kind of dad they had, they had a dad.

"It hurts to grow up and not know where you come from." Megan began to cry. "Why do you think I overcompensate with clothes and other material things. I want to be beautiful. I want to be important, I want to be someone special, but no matter how much money I have, I'm still a bastard. My life is not complete without knowing who my father is," Megan said pitifully.

Victor rubbed his head, which was thinning in the middle. Megan was his life and he loved every inch of her self-absorbed body. His mission on earth was to make her happy and he promised to take care of her and provide all of her needs and desires. "Megan, I'm sorry that you are hurting. I will hire a private detective and we will find your father before our child is born. I love you and I will do anything to gratify you. And if spending money and shopping cheers you up then, my goodness, go for it! Buy the baby anything your little heart desires. And I'm writing the check for Kelly's wedding gift now."

The frown disappeared from Megan's face and was replaced with a mischievous grin. Blissful thoughts of shopping struck her as she stood up and wiggled her fingers. Megan couldn't wait to see her friends' faces when Kelly opened her card with the thousand-dollar check inside. Most importantly, she couldn't wait until Monday morning to parade up and down the gold coast on Michigan Avenue, better know as the Magnificent Mile.

Victor stood behind Megan, admiring her bowed legs and plump round buttocks, shaped just like a Georgia peach. His hands couldn't resist; he rubbed her bottom in a circular motion and murmured in her ear, "I know how to put a smile on my wife's face."

She turned around and displayed her freshly whitened teeth. "You sure do, Big Daddy!"

"Big Daddy? Are you referring to me? I like that name.

Keep on talking dirty to me, Mother, and I will buy you that Porsche truck you want."

"You're a naughty pastor," she said, pushing her laptop to the side.

Megan gazed into his dark-colored eyes, then her eyes darted to his navy blue turtleneck, which matched the color of his skin. Victor was blushing like a nerdy cartoon character. She couldn't help but chuckle when she glanced across his huge pearly whites that resembled horse teeth.

She spoke softly into his ear like a Forty-seventh Street hooker. "You can release it all in me tonight. I want to feel the hot sizzling juices of your ancestors in me. Knock a hole in da bottom of this pussy."

"Megan, don't use that degrading word when you're referring to your vagina."

"Shut up and make love to me," she said, hushing her husband up with kisses.

Victor became enthused. He pushed her bottom up the three marble steps leading to their bed like she was a stalled vehicle on the road. In his deep African accent he stated, "I am going to rock your world. Our baby will get plenty of protein tonight." Megan twisted her lips to the side. She hated that nasty stuff inside of her. Not to mention his bare skin. They used condoms up until the time they planned for the baby, which only took two tries. She got away with the famous, "I can't take birth control pills," for years. Now that she was pregnant, there was no alibi. They continued the bareback thing after Megan became pregnant, but she insisted he pull out before ejaculating. Tonight was different. He could deposit all of his check inside of her bank for a brand-new Porsche truck.

"Hurry! Hurry, baby! Take a shower. I can't wait to feel that hot lava of yours stream down my thighs."

They made it to the middle of the bed and Megan spread out with her legs opened as wide as a Chinese split.

Victor gazed at her with his small brown eyes. "Megan, this is so out of character for you. I usually have to beg and pray for sex around here. Now to hear you carry on like this is really an enormous shocker and turn-on, I have to admit," he giggled and snorted. "I feel guilty. Condemn me now. This has to be immoral. It sounds so pleasing to my ears and my . . ." He looked down and pointed to his erection.

She rolled over and propped her bottom up in the air. "Just rip my clothes off and take this!"

His eyebrows rose up. "We cannot do it that way. I have to be on top."

"Baby! Give it to me from the back. I'm tired of the missionary position."

He motioned for her to lay flat on her back, the ordinary boring routine. She could have received an Oscar award as she flipped over. "My favorite."

"Yes, I know what you like. We don't need to try the ways of the jezebel. Lay back and let me loosen things up."

Megan bit her bottom lip and sucked her chest in just thinking about his habitual displeasing sex. "Anything to get my Porsche," she mumbled.

"Wait, brush your teeth first and please make sure you're clean," Megan urged Victor, pushing him away from her.

Megan's husband returned and she swirled her head back and massaged her lips with her tongue. Victor slid his long, strapping tongue inside of her like a frog ripping into a fly. Her eyes flickered as he explored hidden crevices in every bit of one minute. She squirmed like a caterpillar inching down a tree bark as his minty-fresh tongue connected with her wet vaginal lips.

"Ahhh! You make me feel so wonderful."

"I do?" Victor asked with raised eyebrows, pulling his head from between her legs.

"Yes," Megan said, trying to keep a straight face.

"I savor the flavor of your body."

What? This man can ruin a beautiful moment with his dry, corny conversation.

"Are you prepared for my bulk deposit?"

Bulk deposit? I wanted to say, "you wish." You were biting my clit and my boyfriends in high school ate better pussy.

She put on her best actress voice and pushed his head back down. "Yes, take control! Have no mercy on me! Tear it up!" Victor continued his pitiful act and Megan was just counting the minutes for the dreadful oral sex to be over.

"You've got mail from Jackson," echoed from Megan's laptop. Victor stopped mid-stream when he heard the loud announcement. He raised his head and stared into his wife's startled eyes.

SEVEN

"**P**raise the Lord! I'm so happy to see you," Kelly confessed, kissing her hands, welcoming Shelby into her mother's home. She looked around and behind her. "Where are the kids and hubby?"

Shelby stepped into the foyer, pulling off her pink helmet, her long, layered hair falling over her shoulder. "I did it. I flew here by myself and I didn't cry. I told you, I'm a new woman," she said with so much spunk. "I rode my brother's Harley over here from my parents' house too. You know I'm taking motorcycle lessons," Shelby said, patting on her curvaceous hips then reaching her hands in the air, turning them like she was riding a motorcycle.

Kelly looked at Shelby, wearing tight hot pink leather pants. "You look like a biker." She gazed at her pink leather jacket with silver studs. "You're getting like men when they turn forty. Having a female midlife crisis?"

"No." Shelby blushed. "I'm just doing me and being free."

And she was definitely doing her. A stench of jealousy graced Kelly's consciousness as she took in Shelby's loveliness. Her deep-tanned skin was the color of light, fluffy butterscotch which matched her oval eyes. Shelby was stunning in her thirties and happiness was written all over face.

"Lord forgive me, I confess my sin to you. You are faithful and just to forgive us of our sins and to cleanse us from all unrighteousness," Kelly recited to herself the minute she closed the front door to the house and looked back at Shelby. Embarrassment engulfed her for being so envious.

Shelby's face displayed enthusiasm but when her eyes ventured off shock and disgust overpowered her expression. She hadn't been inside the Swanson home since high school and a lot of things had changed. Now she knew why Kelly always met them outside and was always moving in with any old guy she met. Kelly knew what Shelby was thinking. Her jealous spirit was so apparent and that's why the Lord chastised her to repent. But to Kelly's dismay, Shelby's gaze was glued to the kitchen table where her mom and five male friends sat drinking vodka, playing poker, and snorting white powder.

"I'm getting ready to go," Shelby voiced, turning toward the front door and reaching for the doorknob. "Them niggas doing drugs and I'm not going to jail for you or nobody else."

"Calm down. I need your help. It's my wedding day," Kelly begged, grabbing on Shelby's arm. "I had no idea he was doing drugs. I stay downstairs in the basement." She looked toward the man and shouted, "Jeff, respect this house. I am a minister, a woman of God. Get those drugs out of here before I call the police." Kelly looked up at the men and shook her head. "Don't you know that you yourselves are God's temple and that God's spirit lives in you?"

"What? You can't preach to nobody. You use to give the best head in town," Jeff hollered.

"Lord, forgive him," Kelly whispered, looking up toward the ceiling, inching down each step. Insults didn't bother her anymore because she lived for the appreciation of Jesus. Negative remarks about her past just reminded her of how good God is. How he brought her from nothing and turned her into something special.

Shelby followed Kelly down the wooden stairs with her mouth wide open, bewildered by the activity that was going on right before her eyes. She never witnessed anyone doing cocaine nor had seen the hideous drug before. If she didn't trust Kelly and love her like a sister she would have fled the Swanson home the minute the front door opened.

As the girls made it down the last step, Estelle Swanson appeared at the top of the stairs. "Kellyanna Swanson, who in the hell do you think you are? Jeff is my guest," her mother yelled down. The loud mouth of Kelly's mother, Estelle Swanson, didn't scare Kelly. She ignored her as if it was the norm and continued trotting into her bedroom, singing gospel music.

"Where the fuck are you two tramps going? Shelby, you brought your supposed-to-be-educated ass up in my house and haven't said shit. Looking like the Pink Panther. No good morning, no hello bitch, nothing."

"I'm sorry, Miss Swanson. How are you?" Shelby replied, unbothered by her harsh words. She giggled to herself, remembering how they all hated Kelly's mom in high school. Shelby even thought about the time she and Blair prank-called Miss Estelle and played NWA's "Just Don't Bite It." What great fun they had before caller ID. "Oh, Miss Swanson, give me a hug," she recited in a fake voice as she walked toward the stairs with her arms extended to hug the petite lady.

Estelle Swanson was high. White powder covered her

nose and her glassy blue eyes bulged out. Wrinkles mapped her ghostly white face. A black scarf covered her head, pieces of silky black hair peeped out, showing her ethnicity. Black eyeliner smeared under her eye, pink lipstick was painted over her thin lips. Huge diamond rings and silver bracelets decorated her arms and hands. Tattoos etched in her loose skin. She looked just like a gypsy and Kelly was at a lost for words as she saw her mother through the eyes of someone else.

Estelle staggered down the stairs to hug Shelby and Kelly looked like she wanted to faint. "Come on, Shelby," Kelly pleaded, trying to rush her away from the lady who gave birth to her. "Flee from here, devil. Trust in the Lord with all your heart and lean not on your own understanding," she prayed aloud, but when the two embraced Kelly knew her secret was revealed; the second she spotted Estelle's potent drool dripping down Shelby's cheek. The minute she caught a glimpse of Shelby holding her breath, trying not to inhale the deadly fumes. Exposed by the reeking smell of old sex, alcohol, crack cocaine, cigarette smoke, and pot that absorbed her mother's body.

"Mama, have a seat. I don't want you to fall," Kelly said, wiping the slob off of Estelle's face, escorting her to the white wicker chair in her room near the base of the steps. She kept rubbing her red, pale nose. "Kelly, it's just so good to see you and Shelby back together again," she said in a slow, hesitant manner. "Darling, look how beautiful my Kelly is. She's a princess," Estelle said as she played in Kelly's long hair, staring at Shelby with great uncertainty. "Darling, Shelby. What happened? Did the fat bug bite you? Those babies have plumped you up all over. I don't remember you having ass, hips, and tits," Estelle stuttered in a French Cajun accent. "Kelly, take a good, long look at

Shelby. Are you sure you still want to get married? You only get married if you want to have kids."

Shelby was calm with Estelle's first few crazy comments, but feelings of anger were stepping in. Her nose was flaring and her eyes were cutting slits in Ms. Swanson's chest. She didn't know how much longer she could ignore the sick woman. "Just pretend like she's one of your clients. You deal with crazy people daily. Do it for Kelly," she repeated to herself in an inaudible voice.

"Jeff! Come down here now. Please get my momma," Kelly howled to avoid conflict.

"All I'm saying is look at Shelby. She used to be so thin and cute. Now look at her with those fat cheeks and them huge black-woman hips and ass. You don't need to ruin your thin figure. Remember, you have your dad's black genes and the minute you get pregnant, you'll start looking like your black friends."

"Miss Estelle, I've heard enough of your racist insults," Shelby said firmly, loud enough for everyone to hear upstairs.

"Racist? I had a black husband. I love black men. Hell, I voted for Mustafa." Miss Estelle laughed.

"It's *Obama!* And you love money and black di—" Shelby replied, but paused when she looked at Kelly's stunned, saddened face.

Jeff entered the bedroom with his pants hanging and his hat tilted to the left. The timing was grand, the superb moment to sweep Kelly's mother back upstairs before she embarrassed her any further. "What's going on, old girl?"

"Nothing, my dear, we are having girl talk. My precious lamb, my little princess is getting married tonight," Estelle stammered, tripping over her tongue.

"Let me hit it one more time then," Jeff said with his slick voice, looking at Kelly. "Shit, remember how my boys and I used to bang the hell out of your deep-ass pussy? Yeah, Estelle, your little princess was a freak in high school. She gave killer blow jobs too. She swallowed it," he sang, rolling his hands to a beat in his head. "It don't matter just don't bite it."

Shelby let out an embarrassed sigh, remembering her prank again and all the stories about the good head Kelly gave in high school.

"Boy, you need to go home and pray. We are not in high school anymore and the old Kelly don't live here. Lord, he know not what he say," Kelly replied with a happy smile, snapping her fingers.

"Just get out of her face. My daughter is a reformed whore; she doesn't want anybody like you. She's a damn minister. Why don't you hit on her fat friend, Shelby?" Estelle panted, almost out of breath.

Jeff turned around and stared. "Now, that's what's up. I thought I knew you. Shelby Tate? Girl, you finer than a muthafucka now. Sebastian missed out. I ain't gon' lie. I've always wanted a piece of yo tight ass back in the cut. And I wouldn't mind getting with ya now." Shelby looked at her high school classmate like he was a meager crackhead and clearly not worth responding to.

Shame enmeshed Kelly's body. She didn't want Shelby to leave, but how many insults could she take? How many could the both of them take, for that matter? The thoughts kept pouring in and Kelly's eyes started to fill up with water. Moments like this made her miss her father. He would never let anyone hurt his precious Kellyanna. Her mother, on the other hand, was another story. She disgusted Kelly. And at times she despised her, but the Holy Spirit reminded her daily to pray for her mother's salvation.

"Kelly, it's okay, I deal with worse. Look at your mom. She's in another world." The two looked over at Estelle slumped over in the chair. "Let's get your mother in bed so we can get you ready for your big day." Estelle rose and willingly followed as the two ladies led her by the hand to her bedroom.

Black and brown dog hair was all over the rose comforter. The bedroom was a disaster. The stench of urine lingered. Plates of old food, forks, spoons, and empty vodka bottles were on the floor along with insulin needles, which were scattered about. To make matters worse, the dog was sitting on the bed and a pile of crap was at the end of the footboard. Shelby held her nose. Her eyes focused in on the dirty roach-covered plate on the floor. Goose bumps attacked her body and she started scratching her head. A creepy feeling hit her. "Kelly, this is a damn shame. This room needs to be cleaned. Hell, this whole house needs to be fumigated. How can you let you and your mother live in this filth? Those no-good junkies need to be cleaning up around here. This is unsanitary. You better be glad your neighbors haven't reported you. How long have you been hiding all of this? "

Kelly knew Shelby was right, but no words would come forth. The selfish part of her knew why. To be honest, she had not stepped foot in her mother's room in years. She lived in a fantasy world. Praying and meditating daily in her clean, peaceful sanctuary in the basement. Hell was upstairs and she wanted no part of it.

"Do you hear me?" Shelby snapped, attempting to pick up the garbage in the pink-colored bedroom with stained walls and torn carpet.

"Yeah," Kelly whined, humiliated by the whole ordeal.

"You too damn holy for your own good, too busy praying and not doing anything. Snap out of denial. God gives you wisdom," Shelby preached.

Kelly looked down at her mother's pale skin. She was passed out in the bed and was so pitiful. It was true. Her little frail body had been abused so much, while she did nothing. Part of her secret was out. The horror she had been living for years; watching her mother abuse alcohol and drugs (pills, heroin, cocaine, marijuana, crack). Witnessing Estelle's sexual escapades and prostitution, doing nothing while young men her age had sex with her mother, countless times. Kelly ignored illegal gambling and all the immoralities that followed. She repressed it all, holding on to the life she had when her dad was alive. Wishing he'd come back from the dead and save her from the wretched life she lived as a teen.

"Kelly, you should have told us. I'm here for you. I'll never leave you. You don't have to face this alone. It's not your fault. There's help," Shelby cried, not able to hold in her tears any longer. She was always very compassionate and cried at the drop of a hat.

"It was pride and selfishness. The Lord has been dealing with me about this for some time now. I was praying for a husband to take me away from this mess. I didn't want to deal with it. Thank you for being here for me. I think you are the only one who believes in me. Blair doesn't think Karl will show up and Megan is just coming because she thinks it's a reality show." She grabbed Shelby's hand and knelt down on the dirt-stained carpet. "Will you pray with me?" Shelby nodded yes and Kelly prayed aloud. "Your word says, when two or more come in agreement count it as done. Lord, I kneel before you thanking you for my husband. And right now in the name of Jesus! I ask you to restore my mother. Free her from drugs, alcohol, and her jezebel lifestyle. By your stripes she is healed. . . ."

Shelby latched on to Kelly's quivering hand with a firm grip and said her own prayer too. This was a part of Kelly she didn't know, the missing puzzle piece, the reason Kelly was so promiscuous in high school. Her friend endured years of senseless pain. This time things were going to be different. She was going to refer Kelly to counseling and help admit Miss Swanson into a drug rehab program. "Lord, please let this man show up at the altar tonight because if he doesn't, Kelly is going to lose it," Shelby whispered silently to God.

EIGHT

Kellyanna Swanson's special moment had finally arrived. The night she had been waiting for all of her life. She couldn't wait to be with Mr. Karl Hughes, a man of God who lived his life according to the scriptures, a Christ-like being who was sent to her by the Lord himself was her belief.

"Lord, he's eighteen years older than me, rich, and well-built and I will love every inch of his body. I've fasted. I'm pure, clean, a born-again virgin, and I'm ready for my husband-to-be. It's been five years since the last time I've had sex and I'm ready to consummate this marriage." Kelly conversed with the Lord without opening her mouth. When she finished she turned to her friends. "Thank you, girls, for coming to support me," she said graciously, reaching over to kiss Megan, Shelby, and Blair. They had all showed up on time too, which was pretty amazing because Megan was usually late for everything. But not today. She winked at Shelby for not spilling the beans about her secret family life. The girls already had doubts and she didn't want anything to stop them from showing up.

"Here's your gift," Megan said, handing Kelly a small white gift bag with Gucci written on it, and a big coral bow. "Open it." Kelly opened the bag and box, pulled the long white leather wallet with Gucci written in gold out of the fabric dust bag. When she examined the inside of the wallet her eyes popped open in disbelief. She knew the wallet cost a minimum of five hundred dollars, but a generous check for one thousand dollars was also enclosed. Kelly fixed her teary eyes on Megan and shook her head. "Thank you so much. I can't believe this is for little ol' me. Blessed is his name."

"I figured you could utilize the cash. You know, maybe buy you some clothes for that rich husband of yours. A first lady of the church has to be on point at all times."

Megan turned to Blair and Shelby. "So what did you guys get Kelly?"

"We're saving it for the reception," Shelby answered nonchalantly and turned back, talking to Blair.

"Nada, I ain't buying Sister Theresa nothing until I see her get married," Blair interjected with gleeful gestures of the hand. "And when are the guests, going to show up?"

"I only invited a few people; my theology teacher and my Bible study group," Kelly answered in a low tone as she bit down on her fingernail.

"Did you invite your husband-to-be? 'Cause he ain't showed up yet," Blair said with a slight tilt to her head.

"No, God invited him so I know he'll be here. The Bible says in the book of Matthew eighteen: nineteen, that if two of you shall agree on earth about anything you pray for, it will be done for you by my father," Kelly testified, standing up to Blair this time.

The church bell rang twelve times at midnight. Kelly stood at the altar before her pastor, looking like a true princess. Her black silky hair was pulled back flat into a ponytail with long, soft curls around her face with a pearl-beaded tiara on top of her head. The dress that graced her body was elegant. It was white with swirling beaded pearls on the satin bodice with a triple-tiered chiffon skirt, empire waistline, and a chapel train. Hints of makeup traced her face, natural earth tones. She looked amazing, a beautiful bride-to-be.

Megan, Shelby, and Blair stood on the side of Kelly wearing their halter, coral, chiffon, tea-length dresses with side-draping flower cascades, lit candles in their hands. And Bryan, Victor, Brooklyn, and two people from Bible study sat in the pews with scroll wedding programs in their hands, awaiting the grand wedding ceremony.

At two Brooklyn and the associates from Bible study left and Victor and Bryan waited around with their wives, Kelly was still standing, waiting for Karl Hughes, her husband sent by God. A man who knew her by name but had no idea he was supposed to marry her. It was Kelly's vision from God and her strong faith that led her to believe in love. And no one, not even the minister, could tell her that her groom was not going to show up because she knew what God had planned for her. He was an awesome Lord and his word was gold. Shelby was asleep, Blair was reading a book that someone left on the pew, Megan was on her laptop, and the pastor was sitting in his chair, but Kelly refused to sit. When Karl arrived she was going to be standing, waiting with much respect.

"Look, Cinderella! It's three in the morning. I've been positive for three hours, but sorry, looks like you'll remain a desperate single female. Your prince didn't show up to turn you into a wife." Blair giggled with an "I told you so grin" and beckoned for her husband. Bryan rushed to the choir pew, picked up Blair's shoes, and reached to give Kelly a hug. He had a big gash on his head with about twenty stitches in it. Blair said he was in the wrong place at the wrong time when three dudes jumped him. But Blair knew the truth. She had assaulted her husband and he endured her abuse. She agreed to start taking her anti-depressants and he vowed to stay with her. He forgave just like that. Whatever Blair had on him was deep and Bryan was giving their marriage his all.

"God answers all prayers. Keep your faith. If your hand or your foot makes you lose your faith, cut it off and throw it away," Bryan whispered in Kelly's ear before exiting the church—a scripture he needed to abide by himself.

"Bryan, don't play. I'll fuck you up in this church," Blair snarled, banging her fist into his arm.

"I will," Kelly murmured in a soft reply to Bryan, watching them walk out of the church, wondering where her heaven-sent husband was. "Megan, you and Victor can go too. You're pregnant and shouldn't be out this late." Megan looked up from her laptop with her white veneers glowing. "If you insist, I'm fine, really . . . The Internet has been keeping me busy. I'm trying to find my dad. I can't have my baby not knowing who her granddaddy is. It pisses me off that my mother hasn't told me anything about him. I know she knows how to find him."

"Okay, Meg, don't get worked up. The baby and I need you. I think we should leave. No one is televising us and you really need your rest. You are carrying our little African princess," Victor replied in his strong West African accent.

"You are right. I really thought this was going to be a TV reality show. Oh well, it's been real, but a diva needs her rest," she said staring at herself in her silver engraved pocket mirror vanity, noticing her eyes were a little puffy. She put her mirror up after she applied makeup and turned toward Kelly. "Keep the money. You'll need it to pay for this event," Megan whispered into Kelly's ear. Kelly hugged Megan tight. "I believe I will see the goodness of the Lord in the land of the living. It's raining and I'm sure Karl's plane from L.A. was delayed," she chanted as she watched Megan wobble out of the sanctuary with Victor.

Four hours had passed and a faithful Kelly was awake, kneeling and praying. "Thank you Jesus! Thank you Jesus!" she said loud as she stood up and gazed down the aisle in amazement. Her face was covered with tears of joy as she thanked God for her husband-to-be. "Lord, you are worthy to be praised." She looked around, wanting someone to share in her excitement "Come on, let's get this wedding started. Thanks be to Jesus!" Grrr . . . Grrr . . . snored the pastor from his chair on the pulpit, sounding like a nine-hundred-pound grizzly bear. She looked at her friend, who was also asleep. "Well, God, it's just you and me. I know you will never leave me or forsake me." Kelly kneeled back down and turned to the cross on the altar draped with purple linen.

Music played from Shelby's cell phone. "Hello," she answered in a sleepy voice, after four rings.

"Bay, where you at? I called your mom's house and didn't get an answer."

"Dexter, I'm asleep at the church with Kelly. We are still waiting on her husband to show up."

"What? Shelby, it's after four, go home. Her husband isn't coming. The man doesn't even know Kelly exists. Let's be real."

"Honey, I know that. I'm not crazy, I feel sorry for her.

She isn't going to leave and I can't leave her here alone. This may send her into a nervous breakdown."

"Well, be careful and call me when you get home. I love you."

"I love you too. I miss you and the kids so much. I should've never left without you guys," Shelby cried out.

"Bay, stop crying. I keep on telling you, me and the kids are okay. You needed to get out by yourself. You've been up under us for six years. Enjoy your independence. Remember you're a bad bitch." He chuckled, making fun of Shelby's search to find herself.

"Just kiss my babies for me. I know this had to be hard for them. They have never been away from me. I feel so guilty."

"Girl, these kids are fine. Take your crazy butt home and get some rest because when you get back to Louisiana it's on. I want to make love all over the house 'cause I'm shooting blanks. The nurse finally called back after my sixth message. No more frozen peas on these nuts." The two giggled, remembering the two-day recovery after the vasectomy.

"I love you," Dexter replied with a little sadness in his voice, before hanging up the phone.

"Love you too," she mimicked, slamming the pink razor shut and bursting into tears. Brown mascara stained her butterscotch-colored skin. "Kelly, let's go. I don't think he's coming." Rage stapled Kelly's temples. "Are you crazy, Shelby? My God is not a liar. I know my Lord is able. Psalm thirty-seven:four says, Delight yourself in the Lord and He will give you the desires of your heart. You go ahead and go with your bourgeois self."

Shelby straightened her auburn hair, with blond highlights out. "Cut it out. I can't leave you. And how in the hell am I suppose to get home?" The pastor woke up from all the commotion. "Miss Kelly, your friend is right. I don't think he's coming."

"What? You call yourself a minister? I know what my Lord told me. He said tonight at this chapel on Seventy-third Street in Chicago." Kelly fumed with anger, mad with the world.

Shelby was still the same selfish brat, now getting my pastor to think I was crazy. How dare her, wanting me to miss out on my man, just because she had warm thighs to go home to every night. Why didn't anyone want me to be happy? I deserved God's blessings. But sometimes things don't come at the exact time we want them to. We have to be patient servants, Kelly thought to herself.

Kelly threw her bouquet at Shelby. "Just leave. I need time alone. Time with just me and my God. I want all negative spirits out of her," Kelly sobbed.

Shelby dodged the flowers being thrown at her and tried to approach her friend. Kelly extended her arm and placed her hand out. "Please, I need to do this alone. Just go."

"Okay, but you really need psychological help. I hope you call the therapist I referred you to," Shelby said with agitation in her voice. "I'll just get a cab and get out of here. I could be home with my husband and kids. Instead, I'm sitting up here at five in the morning with you. I need my butt kicked for being so stupid," Shelby ranted.

The minister passed Shelby a number and she exited the church without a good-bye. Upset because she let Kelly talk her into believing a man would show up and marry her. Mad because she had to leave her precious kids and loving husband for the first time.

Thoughts ran through Kelly's head as she sat waiting for her husband to show up and watching her close friend walk out of the chapel doors. *What a selfish friend she was. I still couldn't see why she was married with two kids anyway. She was so mean to all of the boys in high school. Shouldn't I be married before her? After all, I was the nice one. Gave the guys anything and everything they wanted . . .*

NINE

Shelby stood outside of the small church. Raindrops hit her pink umbrella like falling stickpins.

"Need a ride?" the cabdriver asked as Shelby stepped to the yellow car.

"That was quick. I've only been waiting five minutes."

"Well, I've been waiting six years," the cabdriver replied.

"Excuse me?"

"Shelby, it's me," he replied pulling the baseball cap off of his head. Shelby's heart dropped the minute she recognized her old friend. It was Joel, her best friend, roommate, and lover. The two were friends in high school and had become very close. Joel was like a brother to Shelby, but when Dexter ended things with her and moved to California, she leaned on him for fulfillment. The two crossed boundaries and became more than friends. Joel performed oral sex on Shelby daily and she never returned the favor or slept with him.

Shelby didn't want to believe what her eyes were seeing. "I can't believe it's you. You still look nineteen. Looking just like Tyrese." He exited the running cab and reached to embrace her, his strong masculine biceps lifting her body off the ground. The rain didn't seem to bother the two as they squeezed each other tight.

"Ma, what you doing in Chicago? And on this side of town," he asked, mystified. He had thought of her every day for the past six years, regretted not chasing her and making her his wife.

"Crazy story, but to make a long story short, Kelly's wedding." He stared at her with an intense gaze. "Girl, you don't know how much I've missed you."

"I've missed you too," Shelby replied out of courtesy, backing up from his black, intriguing body. "We were best friends."

"Yeah? Well, friends keep in touch. It's been six years since I've seen or spoken to you," Joel grumbled as his eyes assessed Shelby's body. "You look good." He sucked his teeth and looked down at her legs. "And them legs still sexy. Got you some muscles."

"Gained a little weight," Shelby said, patting her thighs.

"What? You look fine, curves in all the right places. I mean no disrespect, but you a bad bitch." He rubbed his chin and gazed at her again. "I can't believe I'm standing here with you. It's like a dream." He paused. "Can't believe we lost touch."

She remained silent, stunned by his forwardness. Not able to believe he thought she was so sexy. Her husband told her that all the time, but there was something about another man's comments.

Joel touched her hand lightly. "So why haven't I heard from you?"

"You know why we couldn't keep in touch. You're the reason Dexter left me in the first place. He assumed we were messing around and you didn't make it any better,"

Shelby told Joel as her mind drifted off, thinking about the ancient event. *"You two are a little too close."* Dexter stated. *"Who? Joel? We are only friends,"* I said defensively. Dexter stood up. Then he looked down at me and raised his voice. *"You in this bitch naked and shit. Nigga walks up in here with his shirt off. Swolled up like Fifty Cent . . . What? Y'all trying to play me? I ain't down for all the game-playin' and bullshit."*

"What? You don't trust me? I gave you a key. Do you think I would risk you walking in on us?" I retorted. *"What am I supposed to think?"* he said, sounding frustrated. I sat up in the bed after I realized he was serious. My heart started to beat fast. I had never seen Dexter so mad before. *"Well, I don't have time for your insecurities,"* I replied.

"You must be fucking him," Dexter stated firmly with plenty of attitude. I paused for a moment. That comment stung. It felt as if I had been punched in the stomach. I couldn't believe Dexter thought I'd do something like that. I thought about the statement again. Since I did mess around with him, knowing he was Max's best friend; did he respect me, or was I just another whore in his book? Was the truth finally coming out?

"What? I have never slept with Joel. How could you say that?" I questioned the man who I thought loved me.

"Easy. Look at the damn picture. You have two bedrooms in this motherfucka and his shit is always in your room," Dexter responded taking a look around my room.

"Don't you trust me? You told me you loved me. Nothing is going on between Joel and me," I pleaded, trying to grab his hand, but Dexter brushed me off swiftly as he stood up and walked toward the hallway.

"You know what? If you ain't fucking him, I'm goin to give y'all the opportunity to. I'm out this motherfucka," he roared.

"You can't be serious. Stop tripping. Nothing happened," I testified, wanting him to believe me. A frustrated Dexter replied, *"Even if ain't nothing happened. You got that charge anyway. I'm a man and I deserve respect around this bitch."* The tears were brewing inside of me. I wanted to get on my knees and beg him to stay, but I refused to submit to him. I wasn't going to let him see me break down, so my cool side stepped in. He was being ghetto with me; therefore, it was only fitting that I return the favor. *"Bitch, give me my damn key. I don't want you to walk in on Joel and me fucking."*

Dexter gave me a heated look. *"I got yo bitch,"* he mumbled. *"Take your muthafucking key."* Dexter lightly placed the key on my dresser and walked down the stairs. When I heard the door slam, I closed my eyes tight. My face tensed up. Tears couldn't be controlled. I loved Dexter, but I wasn't going into another depression. I stomped down the stairs and placed the double lock on the door. Then I stared out the window, hoping Dexter would return.

"Stop daydreaming about the past and get in out of this cold rain," Joel insisted, holding the passenger door of the cab open. "I had nothing to do with Dexter leaving you back then."

"No, I was thinking about something else," Shelby lied, not wanting Joel to believe she was a little perturbed with him about something that happened ages ago. An incident that should've never happened if she'd set boundaries and kept Joel out of her room. Months she missed being with Dexter because of Joel's plot to have her, him deliberately placing his belongings in her room and flaunting around almost naked. A fling that would have never happened if Dexter hadn't left her.

"What you thinking about anyway?" Joel asked as he turned the cab meter off and drove down South Shore Drive.

"Oh, nothing . . . well, just thinking about crazy Kelly. She has drained me mentally and physically with this husband-sent-by-God wedding ordeal. She's histrionic, always doing things for attention. I bet her dumb tail is still at the church waiting for her husband-to-be to show up."

"Shawty, you still the same, always worried about your no-good-ass girlfriends. Don't nobody want Kellyanna Swanson as a wife. You can't turn a ho into a housewife. I don't know when you're gonna see that broad is jealous of you."

"And Joel, you haven't changed a bit. Always willing to tell the truth no matter how it may hurt," Shelby admitted in a soft tone. "But what are you doing driving cabs?"

"My brother and I own this cab and limousine service."

"Oh, that's what's up. I'm happy for you. It's so good to see black males do something with their lives. The man expects our men to stay statistics, in jail, selling drugs, or dead. There was an article on CNN's Web site that stated that was the reason more sistas were dating white men."

"Ma, that's deep. I'd beat my sisters' ass if they thought about dating a white boy. There are some good brothas left." Joel smiled, still in shock that he was actually with Shelby. "Let me return this cab and get my truck. I want to take you somewhere."

Shelby didn't refuse. She rode with Joel back to his business garage and jumped into his black Avalanche truck, decorated with expensive gaudy rims and chrome.

When the car stopped on Lake Michigan in a very familiar spot, right near Hyde Park on Fifty-ninth Street, this didn't startle Shelby one bit. She wanted to enjoy the sun rising over Lake Michigan, even if it was pouring down rain and snow in the month of April. Her mind needed a break. A break from being a wife, mother, professional, and friend. Shelby just wanted to forget about everyone else's problems and focus on her. And Joel reminded her of her youth; he made her feel young and powerful again. He gave her an identity, she was somebody, an attractive individual with personal goals and dreams.

The cold wind was lashing out in quick, rapid movements as the foamy waves busted out of the ice beating against the rocks. Sleet hammered against Joel's front window, ruining Shelby's view.

"I'm sorry. I wanted to surprise you. You seemed a little down and I know how much you used to enjoy this spot."

"You remembered?" she asked, shocked by his attentiveness.

"Shelby, I remember everything about you. Your favorite color is pink. Favorite number is seven. You love Chinese food and pizza. You prefer curls versus wearing your hair straight. You have one dimple that pops outs whenever you laugh and you love diagnosing people with histrionic personality disorder." He held Shelby's hand and shook his head. "I even remember the outfit you were wearing when we first met."

Shelby blushed. "I bet you don't." She glided her hands through his hair, realizing in all their years of friendship she had never noticed the beautiful grade of hair he had, mainly because he always kept his hair bald or in a low fade.

"You had on that yellow and black—"

"Spandex skirt," Shelby blurted out with excitement, finishing Joel's sentence. "I loved spandex back in the day, looking like a bumblebee," she continued, playing in his black, fine hair, really loving how it felt between her fingers. Joel reciprocated and ran his fingers through her hair.

"It's not weave. I see all the women here have major stock in weave and tattoos."

"Yeah, you see that shit. I like a woman that's not fake," Joel stated, gazing directly into Shelby's eyes.

"What you staring at?"

"You. I can't believe I'm sitting here with you after all these years." He paused. "And to think you married that busta. That shit really hurt me. Didn't you know I was in love with you?"

"In love with me? You made it clear you were marrying Chloe."

"Yeah, you made me make that big mistake." She couldn't reply and Joel continued to speak. "I've been in and out of jail since you stepped out of my life and the only thing that kept me going was thoughts of you." He nodded his head, his eyes never leaving hers. "I never got in trouble when you were around. I needed you."

"So you married Miss Ghetto?"

"Yeah shawty, I married Chloe and we have five boys."

Shelby hesitated. Ignoring the fact that Joel just admitted to having five kids and he was only twenty-nine. "That's wonderful, I'm sure you make a great father. I didn't think you would go through with the marriage, though."

"I regret it; for years I've hated her for not being you."

"Then why did you marry her?" Shelby asked in a subtle, dwindling tone.

"You hurt me. I was there for you through all your bullshit with them other niggas. I even waited after Dexter broke up with you and when I thought we had something, you flipped out, saying we could only be friends." Shelby glanced away and stared out of the window. The sleet had dissipated, leaving raindrops. Joel turned Shelby's face toward his and spoke with a soothing, deep masculine voice. "Ma, what happen to you and me?"

"We were friends," Shelby answered before he could complete his sentence.

"Friends don't do what we did."

"Huh?"

"You heard me. When yo nigga left you I became yo man. I made that clit sang."

"Excuse me, I am a happily married women. Do not talk to me like that."

"Are you? I felt your nipples turn hard when we embraced outside of the church and I know you felt that brick in my pants."

"My nipples were hard because of the cold rain."

"Shelby, you know I know you. We lived together for almost a year. Just admit you want some of this," he said, lifting up on his penis through his black loose-fit jeans.

Tears rolled down her cheeks. They stared into each other's eyes. Feelings from the past emerged with no words spoken, only long, steady gazes and heavy sighs. Her panties moistened at just the thought of his full, juicy lips between her thighs. His lips captured hers and his tongue glided in her mouth. "Is this lust?" he said after a minute.

"Stop! Why did you do that?" Shelby asked, slapping Joel away from her lips, the stench of his cigar breath pissing her off more than anything. He ignored his stinging cheek. "I love you." Shelby sat up straight. "I told you I'm happily married. I thought you wanted to talk about old times." Joel sucked his teeth. "Old times? I remember sitting yo big fine ass on top of my face. Yeah, I fantasize about that all the time. You'd have multiple orgasms dripping in my mouth. Do you remember the way yo legs would shake?" Shelby began to breathe hard. Joel continued to speak. "I've always imagined and dreamed how it would feel to be inside of you." He unzipped his jeans and forced Shelby's hand on his private part. "Do you see what you've missed? You can't tell me you ain't curious."

Chills went up Shelby's arm. Bumps popped out. She was confused. Her body was reacting to touch and the delicate sounds of the rain falling didn't make things any better.

"Please, let my hand go!" she moaned as her body stiffened and her eyes shut tight. Joel ignored her whining as he moved her hand up and down the huge, vein-throbbing vehicle. Her curious hand didn't move. Another man was turning her on and she liked it. She thought about living on the wild side and taking a chance; making love to Joel for the first time. The car shifted and Shelby opened her eyes, instantly remembering her family. "Oh my God, I'm going to have to scrub my hand," she spat out, yanking her hand off of his penis. "What am I doing? Just take me to my parents! I told you I was married," Shelby panted, her voice full of paranoia.

"So what, you were supposed to be my wife. I should've met your ass in Jamaica on Dunn River Falls. Would you have married me instead of Dex?" Joel exclaimed, hitting the steering wheel.

"No, God brought Dexter and me together. I love him. Not you."

Joel sucked his bottom lip in and let out a heavy sigh. He was angered by her rejection. He always felt Shelby thought he wasn't good enough for her. Good enough to eat her out, but not meeting the high standards to be her man.

Joel pressed his foot down on the accelerator and headed south, not saying one word to her. And from his expression she knew he was ticked off. Shelby ignored his rage and concentrated on her own. After all, she was the one who was damn near raped by him. However, her mind ignored the fury, wandering back to the days Joel used to make her happy. As they traveled down 57 south, she thought about their close friendship and the way he made her laugh. She fought hard, but a warm tingling sensation overcame her body as she recalled their old sexual encounters. The way her body exploded with triple orgasms after Joel magically licked between her legs. The way he sent her legs shaking into a wild seizure. Those were the days, she reminisced as they pulled into her parents' driveway and she fought with the idea of sneaking him in for old time's sake.

TEN

The young Caucasian doctor pulled his latex gloves off of his tan-colored hands, traced with blond hair. He looked down at his patient and smiled. "Mrs. Myru, you haven't dilated, but your cervix is very soft, which is a good sign."

"How do you know I haven't dilated?" Megan asked as she jittered from side to side with a frown on her face. "I'm ready to get this baby out of me."

"When I examined you, your insides felt like the inside of your mouth. Take your tongue and roll it around the inside of your mouth. Do you feel how soft that is? That's where you are now. Now touch the tip of your nose. That's how the inside of your vagina used to feel last month. That baby may arrive early." Megan looked over at Victor, who was still rolling his tongue inside his mouth. The doctor turned to Victor. "Getting turned on, daddy-to-be? Go home and give this man some. Poor thing acts like he's been deprived for months."

"Doctor, do not start. I am dying for sex. The little woman is on strike. I was trying to engage in a little relations a few weeks ago when you e-mailed her about an appointment. That put an end to my nookie," Victor snorted with a loud chuckle.

"Look, forget what he's talking about. I want this baby out. I'm tired of being fat and pregnant. Can we induce or schedule a C-section today?" Megan pleaded with the good-looking gynecologist.

"No, not yet. Let's let nature take its course. Now, I'll see you two crazy kids next week or before. Call us if you experience any bleeding or extended contractions. And don't forget to hook my man up," Dr. LeBlanc preached as he grabbed his clipboard. Megan looked down at his size twelve Gucci shoes and hunched her shoulders up. Then she shot him a quick wink as he walked toward the door. "Now, don't forget to wash your hands before you leave out of here. . . . And I want a complimentary tummy tuck when I deliver this baby," she uttered as he exited the examination room.

Megan and Victor walked hand in hand out of the doctor's office, both excited about the up-and-coming birth of their child.

"We have the most comical doctor alive," Victor said, kissing his wife's cheek. "Did you hear what he said about sexual relations?"

"I look like a blimp. How am I supposed to have sex? You can't crawl on top of me with all of this belly. That is just disgusting. Too close for comfort."

"You said we could not have sex, but the good Dr. LeBlanc said we could," Victor teased, swaying his index finger from side to side.

"Remember, you don't believe in the forbidden doggystyle position. And anyway, you already used your one-sex coupon for the month," Megan grunted, squeezing antibacterial gel in her hands as they exited the elevator.

"Oh no, I did not, that was six weeks ago. I am overdue for some good, sanctified loving. And I will take it doggy-style or any other fashion since your stomach is in the way."

"You're such a hypocrite. I thought it was a sin and against the law," Megan scolded her husband as they giggled down the gray hallway swinging hands.

"Megan, Megan Cole, my baby's mama," a lady yelled from the end of the hallway. Megan turned her head and placed her hand in front of her face as the rapid clicking of stilettos traveled toward her and Victor. It was Sapphire.

Sapphire was a girl that Blair, Kelly, and Shelby went to high school with. Her and Blair were roommates at one time and quite close, but the rest of them just dealt with her when they had to. Sapphire was attractive, flamboyant, aggressive, bold, and proud to be bisexual. She left nothing to the imagination when she dressed or wanted something. Her words were like ice and fire, either you loved or hated her, there was no in-between.

"Hey sexy, when were you going to tell me about the baby?"

Megan gave her old friend a dirty look, "don't disrespect my husband."

"Little Africa knows me and he knows you and I go way back. Way back when your nose was small."

Victor laughed and Megan pinched the side of his argyle sweater, managing to grasp some of his skin. "Ouch! Baby, your nose has expanded, quite wide, I have to admit." Megan didn't laugh. She couldn't believe the two were clowning her in the middle of the medical plaza. "Most black women experience nose bloating when they're expecting," Megan muttered as she rubbed her belly. She prayed they didn't start on her swollen feet that looked like loaves of honey-wheat bread.

"Well, Dark and Lovely . . . have you heard from those other stuck-up ass bitches you love up on?" Sapphire asked with a steady gaze into Megan's oval eyes.

"Blair, Kelly, and Shelby are fine," Megan said with a firm voice.

"Are they as fine as you? I have to admit you still look good, twelve months pregnant and five years later."

Megan wiggled her fingers through her long, black bouncy hair, which was past her shoulder. "Thank you and they said you had no taste. And the answer is no. No one is as fine as me."

Sapphire rubbed her diamond nose ring. "I know that's right. That ass is tight," she uttered, raping Megan's bottom with her eyes.

"Watch your mouth, Rhinestone. My husband is a man of God." Her nostrils flared open and her arm extended out. "And would you like some hand sanitizer while you touching all on your face?"

"Humm . . ." Sapphire sighed, looking down at the tattoo on her hand that read *fire*. Because fire is exactly what she wanted to slap from Megan. "Naw, my hands clean."

"Uhh . . . If you say so. The hands are the dirtiest part on your body," Megan grunted, tooting her nose up as she read the tattoo across the back of Sapphire's neck—a heart and a burning flame and the word *pussy*. "I see you haven't changed."

"I see you haven't either, you still the same bourgeois-ass Megan I remember. Look at you with all those diamonds," Sapphire blurted out, while she stood with her hands in the pockets of her tight hip-hugging blue jeans, which were barely covering the top of her pelvic area.

"Stop looking at my wrist and fingers. You're the one wearing two-hundred-fifty-dollar Dolce and Gabbana jeans, diamond earrings, and that new thousand-dollar Fendi purse," Megan answered, but wondering at the same time how someone like Sapphire could afford the finer things in life.

"How do you know these aren't knockoffs?" Sapphire asked with a chuckle.

"Oh! I know real stuff when I see it. An amateur can spot knockoffs. You are definitely wearing the real thing."

"Yeah, Megan, you still a gold digger," Sapphire retorted, shaking her head in approval as she moved closer. "Do I smell Juicy Couture on your sweet neck and passion fruit lip gloss on your full, luscious lips?" Megan backed away, but Sapphire was not offended. She caressed her own chest, rolling circles between her breasts, arousing Victor with the ever-sensual movement she made. His eyes protruded out, lusting over *fire* with the large size-D breasts and the tattoo of two women entwined.

"All right Rev., watch your eyes," Megan told her husband.

"Down boy, these triple D's are for Megan," Sapphire told Victor, who was drooling like a dog.

"Yeah, down boy. You just lost your pussy coupon for the month," Megan taunted Victor, then turned to her friend. "What type of work are you doing now?" she asked Sapphire in an attempt to break the monotony that was stirring up among them.

Sapphire handed Megan a business card. "I'm a model and an actress. You'll have to look up my Web site so you can see my nude pictures." She fondled the sapphire gem on her belly button. "Make sure you tell Blair I asked about her. I miss her," she said with a kissing sound. Megan wanted to ask Sapphire what she meant by that comment. It made her wonder about her close friend. Had her thinking what really went on between Blair and the Fire. Inquiring minds really did want to know, especially her.

Sapphire's facial expression changed. A sense of gloom covered her appearance. "Just tell Blair I want to see the kids, especially the new baby, Bryanna. I heard she looks just like Bryan."

"She does . . . she's the cutest little red baby. You have to see her. I'll be sure to tell Blair I saw you when we meet for lunch again." Megan yawned, then rubbed her back. "Well, it was nice seeing you, but I must retire, these feet are killing me."

Sapphire pointed to Megan's feet with her mouth wide open. "I see those Flintstones throbbing. Go home and get some rest with your fine, pregnant ass."

Megan grinned. "You are so crazy. But then again, I am stunning, fine, gorgeous, and strikingly beautiful wrapped up into one expensive body."

"Call me after you have the baby. We'll have to go on a shopping date for old time's sake. I'll buy you some pink diamonds, David Yurman jewelry, and some Jimmy Choo shoes for a small price if that's all it takes." With that said, Sapphire sucked her teeth, gave Megan another flirty body scan, and pranced off.

ELEVEN

Kelly sat in her white wicker bed and cried. She had been a faithful servant to God and had prayed for a husband. He promised her. But no part of a man showed up to marry her. She felt embarrassed, humiliated, and worthless. It appeared that everyone around her had a man and didn't know how to treat them. They didn't appreciate their good thing, but she would have.

"Lord, why is Shelby Lynn Denise Tate happily married to Dexter. And I'm sitting here in this dump of a house with a dope-fiend mother." Her eyes looked down from the ceiling. "I still can't believe she's married with two kids. She was so mean to all of the guys in high school." Tears crowded her face. "Jesus, why me? Why didn't my husband show up? You promised me, Lord." Kelly wailed as she raised up out of her bed. "Lord, where is this jealousy coming from?" she screamed aloud. "I am blessed. I am blessed. Jealousy is not of God. Lord, forgive me. I love my sisters. Devil flee, you are not going to take away my joy. Blessed be his name," she prayed as she pulled a yellow fuzz-ball-covered sweater over her head. "I'm on my way, Lord. I know I was rude to Shelby the other night. I'm on my way to Shelby's house to apologize," Kelly cried aloud.

"Sit on my face like you used to back in the day," Joel stated, pulling on Shelby's arm several times as he laid his head on the plush, round Oriental rug in her parents' living room.

"Shit . . . you don't know how long I've waited to feel your thick, long tongue inside of me again," Shelby replied with a smile plastered to her while sliding her panties down and pulling her dress up.

"Shawty, you should of married me instead of Dexter. I would have served you proper every night."

"Look bitch, we've talked enough. My parents will be home soon," Shelby snapped as she approached Joel's face.

"That's what I'm talking about. My dirty-mouthed girl is back with a phatter ass and a wetter pussy. Pimp me like you use to," Joel said as Shelby's smooth morsel greeted his face.

Shelby relaxed her body on top of Joel's face and gyrated like she was twenty-three again. Nothing had changed between her best friend and her except a few extra pounds and six years of life. Joel still had the magic tongue that Shelby's clit loved. His tongue delved deep into her insides and his hands massaged her luscious cheeks.

"Oh God! This feels so good." Shelby shouted as she bounced on Joel's mouth, eyes never leaving his huge, rock-hard vessel.

Her mouth watered as she fantasized about swallowing down the dark chocolate treat.

"Why didn't I give this pussy to you?" Shelby asked, bouncing up and down Joel's face with a huge smile.

Kelly walked in, outraged by the two. She couldn't fathom the idea that God was having her apologize to someone who was cheating on her husband.

" 'Cause you're a selfish bitch. You let all of that big, long black dick go to waste. Joel, I would have fucked you every night and gave you the world's best blow job, which I know you've heard about," Kelly exclaimed, waiting for Joel to remove his tasty lips from between Shelby's legs. "Oh no, you were Shelby's best friend, her little slave. Eating on her and getting nothing in return. And what did she do? I'll tell you, she married Dexter. He should've been mine too."

"Kelly, get out of here. Shouldn't you be waiting on your husband to arrive? Go pray for a man because Joel is all mine," Shelby shouted, still mounted on Joel's mouth. "K-e-l-l-y, please l-e-a-v-e!" she stuttered.

"If you're getting pleased, then I am too. I haven't had sex in five years," Kelly stated, licking her lips. She kept on licking and wouldn't stop until she approached Joel's big, long black penis. "I'm the one who got stood up at the altar. I deserve a treat like this one," she protested as she pulled up the tight black nun dress and pushed the long black veil out of her face.

Shelby closed her eyes and bit down on her lip as Joel devoured her. Kelly placed her hands on the long, wide, solid dark treat. Her hands twisted and turned his aroused penis. With a watery mouth, she muttered, "You are a very greedy boy. Two women? You're greedy. You're greedy. Greed is a sin, you naughty boy." She inched her head down. Her wet lips moistened the tip of his head. She engulfed his girth, taking him deep inside her throat.

Joel's torso flopped and flipped like a fish taken out of

water as Kelly implanted herself on top of his tall erection, body facing Shelby, whose eyes were still closed. "My Lord, forgive me. My body needs this," Kelly screamed, meshing her hands on her breasts with great force, while devouring him with her insides.

TWELVE

The sound of Kelly's alarm clock awakened her from her sinful dream of Shelby and Joel. She leaped up, frazzled by the sudden noise and moisture between her thighs. She tried not to dream about sex, but sometimes the devil slipped it in. "Jesus, thank you for waking me up this morning. I repent for those lustful thoughts. Nothing is going to stop me from receiving what you have for me. Now, I have a plane to catch," she sang in her gospel-choir voice as she headed out to catch the bus.

Bryan looked in the rearview mirror of his car as he sped down Cicero. "Mane, that was Kelly?" he said aloud, and made a U-turn. Kelly was sitting under the bus-stop awning singing to the Lord.

"Hey, kid. You need a ride?" Bryan asked through the rolled-down window.

"Yes, I'm headed to Midway. I have a man to marry."

Bryan popped the trunk, got out the car, opened the passenger door for Kelly, and placed her luggage in the trunk.

"Keep the faith, kid. God is good. You know we have to go through storms to get where we need to be." He exhaled noisily and thought about his own life, reflecting on his marriage to Blair. He was trying hard to weather the bad times—after all, he had created them.

"That's right. I know God loves me. You see, I had some unfinished business. I didn't do right by my mother. God told me to take care of her and I didn't. I ignored everything that was going on in my mother's house. But this morning I took control and checked my mom into rehab. Now God can bless me with a husband. You see, I'm doing things right. You can't get what the Lord has for you if you don't obey him when he speaks," Kelly said with a smile.

Bryan nodded. Shelby had told Megan and Blair all about Miss Estelle Swanson's condition and Kelly's. She urged the girls to come to the wedding, even if they didn't believe, because Kelly was on the verge of losing it. But Bryan said nothing, he just listened.

Minutes later, sounds from a honking car invaded the street. "She's following us," Bryan said, biting on his short fingernails. "Who's following us?" Kelly asked as she turned around. Blair was directly behind them in her red Hummer. "Oh Jesus, she was the last person I wanted to see us. Bryan, just pull over," Kelly pleaded, wringing her shaky hands like an old dishrag.

"Naw, Blair will kill you and me. I'm telling you. You don't know your girl, she ain't wrapped too tight. She promised to go to counseling and ain't went yet." He pointed to his forehead. "You see this cut up here. Your girl put it there."

Kelly looked at Bryan. He was really stressing. Sweat beads were popping off of his forehead and fear was written all over his face.

"Yeah, Blair can be pretty violent. She used to beat up my boyfriends back in the day. But let me tell you some-

thing . . . fear is not of God. The devil wants us to be
scared. Just pull over when we get to Seventy-ninth and
Cicero, by White Castle. There is no reason for us to
sneak around. She saw us; it's too late," Kelly said in a
panicky voice, contradicting her statement about fear.

Bryan pulled the car over. Sounds from his wife's screech-
ing tires were heard from behind as she rammed into the
back of the car. Kelly's head jerked from the bang. Seconds later, Blair and her cigarette were marching over to
the car like Sophia in *The Color Purple* when she stated,
"you told Harpo to beat me." She had a fried chicken leg
in her hand, a lit cigarette in her mouth, and a facial expression similar to the Grinch. Bryan dashed out of the
car like a track star, meeting his wife before she made it
to his car.

"Where the fuck were you going? And who is that sun-
glass-wearing bitch? Don't lie. I followed you all the way
down Cicero," she screamed before socking Bryan in the
eye with her fist. "I'm not going to ask you again. Who the
fuck do you have in the car?"

Bryan couldn't speak. His eye was stinging from the un-
expected blow he had taken a second ago and things were
only going to get worst. How could he tell his wife one of
her best friends was in the car with him, especially Kelly.
She wouldn't understand.

"You bastard, I have your daughter in this car with me
and you're out fucking around. Let's see if she'll take care
of a two-year-old," she cried as she beat on his chest.

"Now come on, Blair, I'm not fucking around. I can explain," Bryan stuttered, short of breath from the heavy
blows to his chest.

"No, yo bitch is about to explain," she ranted and raved,
walking to the passenger side of the car with Bryan right
on her heels.

When her eyes met with Kelly's her soul boiled with hatred. Betrayal floated in the air. "That's Kelly in the car." She shook her head in disbelief. "The same Kelly you took to the Keith Sweat concert when we first met." Her voice began to crack. "My close friend, who put all the passion marks on your neck? Even gave you a blow job and some free pussy before I did." Blair took the lit cigarette out of her mouth and poked it up and down Bryan's arm. "Remember that?" she asked, then throw the cigarette on the ground.

Bryan cracked a smile, remembering the wild, exciting night he spent with Kelly. "Girl, come on now. That was almost seven years ago," he said, hopping about, finally feeling the heat on his arm. "Girl, you den burned me."

Blair's long fingernails dug into Bryan's skin. Grease prints embossed his arm. "Yeah, I'ma do more than that to you since you think that shit was so funny? I know you fucking that two-dollar ho now. 'Cause I heard that smart-ass Bible verse you quoted to her after that fake, crank wedding of hers."

"Come on, Blair. I'm your husband and Kelly is your friend. Stop acting like this," he argued as he pulled away from her grip, blood dripping from his arm. "I saw her at the bus stop with three suitcases so I stopped. She was on her way to Midway Airport."

Blair knocked on the car window with all her might; grease smeared over the window. "Get yo ass up outta this car and tell me what's going on!"

Kelly clicked the doors to lock, refusing to let Blair in. She banged harder and harder with more force each time. "What in the hell are you so afraid of if you're not screwing my husband?" she yelled. "Bryan, open that damn car up now. I'ma fuck this bitch up."

"Blair, leave that there girl alone. She has enough problems. I told you there is nothing going on."

"Oh, you taking up for her? You taking up for her?" she asked, pulling her gat from the back of her pants. Blair hammered the car window with the gun. Glass flew everywhere. Kelly swung her face to the left, allowing the shattered glass to miss her face. Sharp pieces of glass pierced her arm in two places. Dark red blood trickled down her arm, afraid to pour out.

Crazy Blair is on a rampage. Lord knows, all I want to do is get to Los Angeles to find my husband. I don't need this drama in my life. You know you try to live right and it seems like your past always haunts you. If I could take back sucking Bryan's dick at that Keith Sweat concert in 2000, I would.

"Devil, flee from my friend. We've been girls too long to be having this misunderstanding," Kelly chanted in a subdued tone as she eased the door open to greet Blair. "Look Blair, I thought we were better than this," Kelly continued, holding her arm with a McDonald's napkin she found in the car door. Blair grabbed Kelly by the neck and yanked her to her feet. The bloody napkin fell to the ground like a parachute landing.

"You are a filthy ho, a fuckin' hypocrite. You wanted a husband so damn bad you thought you'd steal mine."

"Bryan saw me with my things and he gave me a ride. I'm moving to be with my husband. I didn't want you guys to know because I knew you'd make fun of me after I was faked out at the pulpit." Kelly strained, wiggling out of Blair's grasp.

"Faked out? Kelly, the man never knew anything about a wedding. He hasn't seen or spoken to you in months. What you need to do is check your crazy ass into a mental institution. And stay the fuck away from my husband,"

Blair shouted, poking her long, decorated fingernail into Kelly's forehead.

"Jesus! Jesus! Blessed be your name," Kelly screamed and hopped about. "To be wise you must first have respect for the Lord. If you know our Lord and Savior, you have understanding. Honest people are safe and secure, but the dishonest will be caught. . . . Bryan and I didn't do anything wrong. He loves you. You have a spirit-filled man, take care of him," Kelly cried as she beckoned for Bryan to take her suitcases out of the trunk.

Blair stood with her eyes focused on her shoes, unable to look into Kelly's eyes as she placed the gun back in her pants. What was wrong with her? She was out of control. Blair had lost her baby and Bryan had done the unthinkable, but she stayed with him. He hadn't given her any reason not to trust him, she knew Kelly was right. Bryan loved her.

Kelly isn't the crazy one, I am. She believes in love and will do whatever it takes to get her husband. Here I am with a wonderful husband who is trying his best to make me happy again and I won't allow him. I'm going to get back on my medication and seek him before I lose my husband, Blair thought to herself as she walked back to her car.

Bryan reached Kelly the luggage, shaking his head. His wife was psychotic and it was his fault. She attacked one of her best friends, all because of him. His actions in the past had torn poor Blair apart, leaving her insecure and irate. A side of her no one had ever seen but him. The Blair everyone knew wasn't insecure and savage. She was bold, sociable, humorous, and fun, but nothing like this. Blair was in pain, a miscarriage at eight months, and her husband cheating on her a month later.

"Thank you. I'll continue to lift you up in prayer," Kelly

mouthed to Bryan in a solemn tone and walked off with her luggage to another covered bus stop blocks from the airport. Bryan put his head down and vowed to keep on pampering his wife until she was completely healed from all the havoc he caused.

THIRTEEN

Shelby sat on the airplane thinking about her last conversation with Joel. *"If you ever come to Chicago again, I'm going to fuck you and get you pregnant,"* he said, wearing a serious expression on his face. *"Then your wife would leave you,"* she replied to his insane comment. *"I know. Your husband would divorce you and we could be together."* Shelby shuddered between her legs, just thinking about having sex with Joel. She didn't want to have those feelings but the craziness and boldness of his words electrified her. *"Only in your dreams,"* she whispered with a warm, seductive tone as she exited his truck. The door closed in Joel's face, not giving him a chance to reply. He rolled the window down to respond, but she was too quick. She had already made it to the front porch. *"Think about me when you're fucking your wife tonight. Give her seven hard pumps in remembrance of me,"* Shelby called out to Joel in a sassy manner before prancing into the front door.

When Shelby landed in New Orleans and headed out on

10-West, she smirked to herself, scrolling to her contacts and pressing send.

"I made it home safe. I mean to New Orleans," she stuttered. "I still have a few more miles before I make it home," she muttered into the cell phone.

"Yeah, that's what's up," Joel replied, surprised that Shelby took the time to think about his request for her to call when she landed safely. They had exchanged cell numbers the night before and decided to be friends again, but Joel wasn't crazy about the friend crap. He had played that role for years. In 2008 he wanted more than her friendship. "Think about what we talked about. I promise I can be a better husband to you than Dexter could imagine." Shelby ignored Joel's words and hung up without a good-bye.

Confusion mapped her weary mind and by the time she arrived in Baton Rouge her body was ready to collapse from the two-hour flight from Chicago and all the crazy information she had obtained. She exited 10-West and ventured down Highland Road, passing the country club, Smarty Pants Village, and her church. Shelby looked to the right and noticed her home nestled on top of the hill with a WELCOME HOME sign written in black next to a hot pink Harley-Davidson with a huge red bow on top. The car crept up the steep, winding driveway and Shelby began to beep her horn several times, overwhelmed that her husband paid attention to something she wanted. Ever since she started her motorcycle lessons she had dreamed of owning a pink Harley. Signals were always thrown out to him in an attempt for him to catch on and as she could see, he had taken the bait.

Before she could park and check out her new toy she spotted Dexter and her two children rushing out of the twelve-foot doors to greet her. She looked at her family and smiled, tears forming in the corner of both her eyes. Shelby stared at Dexter. He hadn't changed a smidgen since the day they met. His big brown eyes and deep, caramel-colored skin with a few brown freckles still glistened with no signs of aging. And his full black, wavy hair didn't own a strand of gray. Her husband was gorgeous and just seeing him sent chills through her spine. She wanted to lick his lips and kiss all over his low-cut beard. He had finally taken her advice, letting his beard grow in, tracing the side of his face, mouth, and chin. "Welcome home, Mommy. We missed you," Dexter stated with the most beautiful grin as he embraced Shelby. She showered her husband and kids with kisses. "I was only gone three days."

"Baby, three days without you is like eternity," Dexter confessed while grabbing her suitcases out of the car. Savannah hugged her leg tight as she said, "Welcome home, Mommy."

"That's not your mommy, that's my mommy," Dexter Junior, who was his father's mirror image, stated.

"D.J. hit me."

"I did not hit her. She's bad."

"What are you guys still doing up?" Shelby asked as she picked up her little girl.

"We were waiting for you, Mama. How you like your new bike Dad ordered for you in pink?" Dexter Junior asked, leaping around in circles. Shelby jumped up and down. "Honey, I love it." She sat on the seat and pretended to start the engine. "I'd love to take it for a spin if I wasn't so tired," she told her family, grabbing her son's hand and following Dexter into their home after he parked her new bike in the garage.

They walked into the entrance. The ceilings were twenty feet tall. The living room was painted in bronze and the ten-inch crown molding was painted French vanilla.

"A clean house? Wow!" Shelby stated with glee as she checked out the house.

"Daddy had Miss Ieshia from Heaven Scent came over to clean," her son volunteered.

"Good, 'cause I'm tired."

"Good night, kids. Mommy's tired," Dexter stated, pushing them toward their rooms.

"You just want to have sex, rushing my kids to bed. As long as I have a hole you'll get horny. You shouldn't be having sex this soon after your procedure anyway. Bust your nuts open."

"What? Why are you so snappy?" Dexter asked, following his wife to their bedroom. "We only do it four times a month. If all I wanted was sex I wouldn't be with you. And as far as the vasectomy, the urologist said we could have sex two weeks after my surgery, we just needed to use protection. And it's been six weeks so I am fully healed and ready. I told you that when you were in Chicago."

"Well, four times is good. I read *Journee's Monthly Newsletter* online and a man wrote in saying he only has sex once a month and his wife doesn't work. Dexter, you try working full-time and taking care of two children. I'm tired."

"I know you're tired. But man, it's been weeks." He sighed. "We don't have to do nothing tonight, although I'd love to make love to my wife without a condom."

Shelby knew sex was important and it was her duty to fulfill her husband, but she was too tired to open her legs. Yes, she loved to feel his rawness inside of her but she was exhausted. *Her mother's voice rang.* *"You better make love to your husband or an eighteen-year-old will.*

Look, Shelby, an eighteen-year-old is born every day. There is always someone who looks better than you and is shaped better. Those young girls will do whatever a man wants them to do. They'll cook and run the bathwater too. Keep yourself looking good and you better have sex with your husband before someone else does."

Shelby let her mind go, forgetting all about her meeting with Joel. Allowed her conscience to be free, feeling her thoughts with her husband. There was no need to think about any other man and could-have-beens. She let go of all her skeletons and accepted the love her husband was giving. "I belong to you, Dexter, body, mind, and spirit. You are my husband, my everything, and I love you." She sighed softly.

FOURTEEN

Sunday came expeditiously with no warning. And Kelly was prepared to meet her husband and his huge congregation. She had no time for negative thoughts. "What if he doesn't like me? Do I fit the preacher's wife-to-be mold? The devil is a liar. Karl is going to see me and instantly fulfill God's plan." With those positive words of encouragement, she pulled out her wardrobe that was donated by Megan: a navy blue Dana Buchman suit and a blue and gold pair of Stuart Weitzman heels, then she marched out of the hotel to meet her husband-to-be.

The white Ford Focus she rented pulled into the church parking area and Kelly was in awe when she viewed all the expensive cars parked in the lot. Nothing but Mercedeses, BMWs, and Jaguars were parked in one area, titled *church staff*.

"Are you a visitor or member?" a church officer asked, at the same time tapping on the window of the rented car.

"Visitor," Kelly said with conviction.

"Okay, the visitor parking area is to your right." His eyes stayed glued to hers. "Can I tell you something?"

"Sure," she replied, wondering what the tall man could possible tell her.

"You have beautiful gray eyes. Are you married?"

"No, not yet. I'm Reverend Hughes's fiancée." He coughed, "Oh, I'm so sorry for offending you. I just think you're beautiful, I couldn't help myself," he chuckled. "Don't tell Rev."

"Thank you for the compliment and I won't tell Pastor Hughes." His voice turned professional, deep, and assertive. "If you turn to the left and drive near the entrance of the church there's a sign that fits your title."

Kelly turned the compact car like he told her to. The sign read FIRST LADY. She grinned at the thought of being called "first lady" and glided into the parking spot without any problems.

As Kelly sat in her car patting her makeup, members were busy gawking at her like she was the devil in the flesh. She could see their heads turning and their mouths moving fast. Everyone wanted to know who was the strange woman parked in front of the FIRST LADY sign. But the attention didn't bother Kellyanna Swanson, it actually flattered her as she waved at the crowd of people walking in the sanctuary. "Okay Lord, what does she want?" she asked when she noticed a middle-aged woman around fifty rushing over to her car. The lady pointed to the sign. A second later, she knocked on the car window with her long, pearl-colored fingernails. Kelly cracked her window to hear the urgent message.

"Precious, you're in the wrong spot." She pointed across the parking lot. "Visitors park to your right."

Kelly turned the car off and inched the door opened,

trying not to hit the woman because she was standing
very close to the vehicle. The lady situated her hands on
her full hips and batted her eyes. "Miss, what are you
doing? You cannot park here!"

"Bless you for being so concerned, but I am in the right
spot. I will be the pastor's wife very soon and first lady of
this church." On that note Kelly stepped out of the car,
swung her long black hair, and slammed the Ford Focus
door shut. She placed her right hand on her chin, making
sure the lady got a good look at the huge diamond engagement ring, courtesy of cubic zirconia and the local
thrift shop.

"Oh, I'm sorry," the lady voiced with no sincerity, standing there, stuffed in a loud purple dress trimmed in gold
with her ass on top of her back. Not to mention the too-
small purple and gold high-heel sandals with her heel
hanging off the back. Kelly smiled to stop herself from
laughing. "It was a pleasure meeting you. God bless," she
said with a cute little sneer and pranced to the entrance
without looking back.

"Nice meeting you too. I didn't catch your name," the
lady yelled back.

"You'll catch it during the service." Kelly snickered, giving Barney a cute little wave good-bye.

The drama was starting already and Kelly hadn't stepped
into the church good. She had been interrogated and almost searched, just for demanding to sit in the VIP sec-
tion behind the pulpit.

"Lord, forgive these people. They don't know who I am,
yet. But they will know very soon," Kelly stated aloud.

"Excuse me, were you talking to someone?" an attractive woman who looked around twenty-nine asked.

"Just talking to my Lord and Savior."

The lady stood with her white Bible in her hand wearing a red, fitted, above the knee, low-cut suit. Her face was glowing and her matching diamond earrings and necklace were sparkling bright. Kelly looked at the young lady's lovely bronze-colored skin and became jealous.

Flashbacks from my childhood evolved. I dreamed of having brown skin like my father, instead of light skin like my Caucasian mother. I hated my color and my white-girl name. I used to tell people who didn't know me my name was Tanika. In the summer, I'd load my skin up with tanning oil, hoping I'd change ten shades darker.

I was tired of all the foreign stares people gave when my father and I were in public. When I started middle school things didn't change. I experienced more racism. The kids would call me cruel names like, Half-breed, Oreo, White B, Hunky-Nigga, Pepe LaPew, Zebra Girl, and Pale Rider. Being biracial was no fun and I wished that curse on no one. I didn't fit in with the blacks because I was too light and the whites thought I was too dark. You know the old saying, if you have 1 percent black in you, you're black. That's why I promised myself I would never date a white man or a light-skin African American man. My motto was a dark-skinned man is always in.

"Hello! Hello! Is anyone there?" The bronze-colored lady extended her hand and waved it in front of Kelly. "Welcome, sister, I'm Bronze," she said, snapping her fingers in front of Kelly.

"I'm sorry, I was daydreaming. I'm Kelly, Reverend Hughes's fiancée."

Bronze embraced Kelly and kissed her cheek. Kelly could have fallen out of her seat when she told her name. It matched her exterior; her perfect creamy bronze skin.

"I didn't know the pastor was engaged."

"Well, it's a secret. We haven't told anyone yet," Kelly said in a sneaky voice, hoping the lady wouldn't question the minister.

"Oh, okay. Well . . . you have a good man, but I'm telling you, you better keep him close to your heart because these southern California women are vultures." Before Kelly could reply, Bronze and her huge behind pranced off.

The last service ended at two and Kelly was ready for another. The day was perfect and the Holy Spirit was present at all three services. She thought Karl was incredible and she loved what the Lord was doing with him. Kelly believed her husband-to-be was a true minister, ordained by God. He brought the word to the congregation directly from the Bible, never straying away from it. And that's what she loved about him.

After church a loud thump greeted Kelly's car window. A familiar face greeted her and she welcomed the visitor right away. She swung the car door open and rested her eyes on Karl, who was kneeling down at the seat of her car.

"Miss Kelly, I'm honored to have you in my presence. God is so good. I was just telling the good Lord how much I missed Chicago. And he brought Chicago to me," Karl said with a laugh. "I was so shocked to see you. Why did you run out so quickly? I hope my sermon didn't drive you out."

Kelly blushed. "No, I was coming to move my car."

Karl looked up at the sign and extended his hand to help her out of the car. "You don't have to move. There is no first lady." He patted Kelly's hand. "What brings you to L.A., anyway?" he inquired with a huge grin.

"Well, I missed my study partner." She winked. "The Lord sent me here on a mission to find you. I want to preach."

"Praise God, isn't that grand? But preaching is an anointing from God. It is not something you chose to do on your own," he said, motioning for her to get out of the car again.

Kelly exited the car this time and the two embraced. Her limp legs dangled as Karl's strong biceps held her body in the air. The two were clinched together, a perfect form for husband and wife.

"Just like old times. Didn't you hear me tell you the Lord sent me," she chanted in his ear. "You haven't changed a bit. When we sat next to each other in class we'd debate about this."

Karl released Kelly. "Yeah, you're right. We didn't agree on a lot of things concerning women being equal to men. . . . So where are you staying? I'd love for you and I to get acquainted. Maybe do dinner or coffee like we use to after class. You need a little more weight on those bones," he stated after he took a good look at her.

"I'm staying at the Motel Six on LaCienega until I find a place." She pulled at her suit. "And the weight loss comes from fasting. But my prayers have been answered. So I'm free for dinner, whenever."

"Why are you staying at that sleezy hotel?"

"Well, that's all my church-secretary salary could afford."

"Don't fret. No sister of mine will stay at a Motel Six. Pack your stuff. I have an eight-bedroom mansion in Brentwood."

"Hallelujah. My Lord is good, even though I am not worthy. He keeps on blessing me. Thank you, Karl."

"No, thank God. I have nothing. All of this is God's," Karl replied as he stood up and beckoned for Kelly to get back in her car.

She let the window down as he was walking away. "Wait, Pastor, you need my number."

He winked. "Oh sweetheart, I have your number and I will be putting it to use. You'll see when the church limo picks you up to move your things. You won't have to spend a dime. The Lord has blessed me and I you."

FIFTEEN

Megan stepped into the doctor's peach-colored office. She smiled as she viewed all the exquisite paintings on the wall, admiring the artists' work.

K. Graves. I need to get her number. Her paintings are so elegant and beautiful, she thought to herself.

"Mrs. Myru, have a seat, the masseuse will service you while you wait."

The tranquil sounds of ocean waves saturated the waiting area. Megan was in heaven. She had done her research. This was the only gynecologist on her side of town that had this type of elegant service. Her stress had dissipated in seconds as the masseuse kneaded on her shoulders.

"You can come back," the tall, blond nurse announced.

Megan made herself comfortable in the examining room after she washed her hands three times and sprayed the room with Lysol. She pulled off her underwear and sat down on the examining table. Dr. LeBlanc toddled in the room and washed his hands. His platinum ring shimmered. The diamonds were a nice cut and very pleasing to the eye. Megan had always found her doctor sexy, but today his skin was glowing. He was more handsome than before. His new beard accentuated his good looks and Megan could hardly control the temptation stirring up inside of her.

"So, Megan, how are you? Where is Mr. Myru?" the young doctor asked with a cute grin.

She corrected him. "Dr. Myru had to work." She pointed toward her waist. "And I'm having a problem down there."

"Where?"

"Between my legs. Have I dilated? I don't want to have my water break in public."

"Take off your underpants and place your feet in the stirrups."

"Oh! My panties are off," Megan said, blushing and dangling her panties as she stared at his deep dimples.

Dr. LeBlanc washed his hands again, placed gloves on and squeezed lubricant on them. Megan quickly took notice at the diamond Gucci cuff links he was wearing.

That must have set him back ten thousand dollars.

"Let's see what we have here," Dr. LeBlanc stated, rubbing his gloved hands together. "Un-huh . . . Okay . . . Megan, you feel real good. You are very soft this time. You've dilated two centimeters. Your cervix is wide open. Your little girl will be here very soon."

Megan licked her lips as she backed away from the edge of the table. "Can you just break my water bag and induce me today?" Dr. LeBlanc looked down at Megan, pulled her body to the end of the exam table and placed her feet back in the stirrups.

"I guess I can. I'll be right back."

The doctor returned, washed his hands, positioned her body to the end of the exam table, and repositioned her feet back in the stirrups. His muscular frame eased toward the exam table. Half of Megan's bottom hung off the table with her labia exposed. Dr. Jackson LeBlanc's white lab jacket swung open, exposing his nude body, as he placed his foot on the first step of the exam table and rolled a condom on.

"I'm going to break your water bag like this."

Megan had no complaints about that. She let out a comforting sigh the minute his girth connected. Her insides hadn't felt his tantalizing touch in months. He was bountiful and fulfilling, nothing like the old can of Vienna sausages she was used to getting at home. Each stroke was given with care and concern, her insides melting with pleasure. "Are you okay?" he asked as he shifted in and out of her. "Am I being gentle enough?"

"Oh, yeah, you're making Megan real happy. Whoa. Whoa," she panted, full of ecstasy as orgasms attacked her body just like their last time together at the Ritz-Carlton in New Orleans.

When the two finished their sexual encounter, Jackson cleaned Megan off and set her up for another appointment the next day. "Come back tomorrow afternoon and I'll check you out again to see if our baby is ready to come out," the doctor announced as he helped Megan get dressed.

Elation was written all over Megan's face. Dr. Jackson LeBlanc pleased her sexually. She thought she could stay away from him and she did for a few months. But her body just couldn't fight the lust and temptation that drew her near him. Victor hadn't excited her in years, and an orgasm in their home was unheard of. She had meet Jackson two years ago on the Internet and he was everything she had ever prayed for in a man, which included stamina, size, status, and millions. Megan would do anything to be Mrs. Jackson LeBlanc and after she had his baby or her husband's maybe she would.

SIXTEEN

Kelly and Karl left the city limits of Los Angeles and arrived in Brentwood. The town was south of Westwood between Bel Air and Beverly Hills. Brentwood was a small, wealthy community, it wasn't polluted like Los Angeles, way less smog covered the sky. And that pleased Kelly as she peered out of the window and saw how the rich and famous were living.

They entered a secluded neighborhood, which teased and amazed Kelly at the same time. She had no idea how exquisite the houses were up close. Her mouth was wide open as they passed the mini-mansions lined with palm trees.

"Slow down, we're approaching the cul-de-sac," Karl communicated to the new church driver.

"Who lives here?" Kelly asked, stunned by the grand palace that stood before her.

"Someone very special."

"God has blessed them. They have a beautiful house," she said in awe.

Karl handed her a key. "No, we have a beautiful house. Driver, pull in that driveway."

Kelly was so frantic. His house was right around the corner from the movie stars.

"Oh Jesus, I can't wait to see the inside. Boy, God has been blessing you." She gasped, trying to cover her excitement as the limo charged into the cobblestone driveway. There was no hiding her happiness.

"Rev. Hughes, are you kidding me? You rich like Job."

"Kellyanna Swanson, this is your house for now."

She clutched her husband-to-be hands' tight and jittered in her seat. "Oh my, God is good. You are incredible. This is a big, big upgrade from the Motel Six. Thank you, Jesus."

He stroked her hand gently and looked at her with a silly expression. "I am a man of Christ. When you are in his favor, you are blessed and lack nothing."

She looked into his dark brown eyes with tears streaming down her face. Seconds later, kisses covered his lips, "I love you so much!" Awkwardness covered her body when Karl did not reciprocate the affection. "I'm just grateful to you. Sorry for being so forthcoming." She began to stutter. "I just wanted to thank you for sharing with me what God has blessed you with."

Karl let her hand go, ignoring the words that she'd just spoken. He couldn't believe someone as gorgeous as Kelly had kissed him. Furthermore, he didn't like the warm, tingling, lustful feeling that implanted itself in his groin area. Karl and Kelly were very close in theology school. They sat next to each other in class, studied, ate lunch together, and went for coffee on a regular basis, but they had never kissed.

"Karl, did you hear me? I said thank you."

"Oh, oh, you're welcome. Go ahead, the driver is trying

to help you out," he said, trying to rush Kelly out of the car before she noticed the slight bump in his pants. But Kelly didn't notice a thing. The house had her full attention.

Lord, I know pride is a sin but I wish my girls could see me now. Thought I wasn't going to get my man? Look at me now, I'm in his lavish house and I'm going to live it up. I will be Mrs. Karl Hughes very soon. Blessed be your name. Blessed be your name.

The grand entrance of Karl's house was mind-blowing. Kelly wondered how a man could have such an immaculate home.

"I love your home. It's dazzling, very impressive. Who decorated for you?"

"One of my church members is an interior decorator. She did all of this for free. We network at my church. There's a directory with all the church members' profession in it. Our congregation supports one another. We have members who own landscaping businesses, beauty salons, barbershops, doctor offices, car dealers, and many more businesses. That's what I love about my congregation, that fact that we pull together and help one another. We'll get rich together. Blacks have to learn to support one another to prosper."

"You are so right." She stared down at the jewelry on his fingers. "How many members do you have?"

"We have over six thousand as of last Sunday. Membership is increasing fast."

"What? It didn't look that big. Why didn't you tell me? I can help you preach."

"Look Kellyanna, I don't know why God sent you to Los Angeles, but like I told you earlier, leave the preaching to me. You just sit on that front row and look pretty. You may be an ordained minister, but only a few are called to preach." Karl clutched both of her hands as he placed his head down to touch her nose with his. "I hope you like the house. Enjoy this place like it's yours." Karl situated himself in his pants. "It's time for me to go."

"You don't have to leave. I won't bite."

"Yes, I do. I couldn't possibly stay here. That's disrespectful. I'll live at the church house." He looked into her gray eyes. "There is just too much temptation and chemistry between us. I am a man of God and you are a very, very, very sexy, single woman and the two just don't match." He patted her on the shoulders. "We'll play catch-up one day," he said sternly and turned away.

Kelly rubbed her huge breasts on his back, trying to get him to loosen up, but he ignored her gestures.

She whispered in his ear. "Let's go upstairs. I can't wait to feel you inside of me." Karl turned around quick. "What?" He shook his head in a disapproving way. "Kelly, are you willing to fall to lust this quick? Don't act like you don't know the word. Are you preaching from the book of Kelly now?"

His words burned her soul as she stared into his eyes. Embarrassment painted her face red. She could no longer hold the stare. Her eyes looked down and away. "I'm sorry."

Karl caressed her hand and spoke softly into her ear. "Dear sister, I was only trying to be nice to you. L.A. is expensive and I didn't want you living out of a motel, especially since you said you were already on limited funds. I'm here to help you get on your feet. Find a job and a place. But that's it. Right now you need to pray for that lust demon. You are not acting like a minister. We went to the same theology school so I know you know the word. You have to resist temptation." He kissed her chin and walked toward the front door. "I respect you, so please respect me," Karl verbalized as he closed the door leaving Kelly all alone in the state of California.

SEVENTEEN

Weeks passed. Kelly glanced at the clock. She thought Karl would've surprised her with a visit, but no such luck. The house was quiet and deserted and she just didn't know how much more isolation she could take.

Lord, you said he was the one. He hasn't made one move. I'm trusting and believing in you, God. Don't let me down. I'm patient and waiting for your will to be done.

The phone rang, snapping her out of her gloomy mood. "Hello," she said drily. It was Shelby and Megan. Kelly had been so busy with her own life that she hadn't spoken with her girls in weeks.

"We have some great news. Megan had the baby!"

"When?"

"Two hours ago," Shelby said into the phone, checking her text message from Joel. All signs of excitement were disappearing. She was sick of his constant calling, voice messages, texts, and e-mails. She regretted giving him her number. There was no way they could remain friends with the strong feelings he had for her. He had no respect for her or her marriage and his either; calling drunk all times of the nights, two in the morning and sometimes five. She wondered what kind of arrangement Chloe and him had. There was no way no husband of hers would be out that late on a consistent basis. Like her grandmother always said *"there is nothing open after two in the morning, but legs."*

"Congratulations. To God be the glory. Megan, how do you feel?" Kelly said with more perk.

"Actually, I'm miserable. Can you believe that. Me, Megan. The most beautiful one of them all." Tears poured out of Megan's eyes. "I'm still fatherless. My mom and Victor are working close with a detective, but no news yet and I've been searching for a year."

"Megan, sweetie, pray about it. God will send your father to you." Kelly wanted to comfort Megan. If she could have reached through the phone to snatch away her pain she would have. "I'll pray for your family too, but I want to be your backup. A prayer doesn't work as well when the leading vessel is not in agreement. And don't you worry. They'll find your dad." An awkward pause dominated the phone line. "So girls, what's the baby's name?" Kelly asked, breaking the silence.

"Macy Victoria Myru. She's six pounds and twelve ounces and fourteen inches long. She looks just like Megan," Shelby told Kelly, because Megan was in no mood to talk about her brand-new daughter. Megan's baby came out looking just like her and Victor. There was no chance the little princess belonged to Dr. Jackson LeBlanc. There wasn't an ounce of white in little Macy. She came right out of Megan's stomach with dark ears and fingertips, and coarse hair. Her African features were very apparent and Megan was mad about that. She had prayed that her baby belonged to the rich white doctor so that they could escape, get married, and be one happy, wealthy family.

"Shelby, when did you get there?"

"Dexter, Brooklyn, and I drove down yesterday. Blair's having a party for Bryan tomorrow."

I knew nothing about a party. I guess I was no longer on Blair's invite list. Hadn't heard from her since the day she busted up my arm and threw me out on the curve. That psycho bitch was going to pay for slicing up my perfect arm and belittling me! Kelly thought to herself.

Megan found her phone and began to text Jackson. *I'm depressed. I need some medicine and a kiss. Where are you?* Tears rolled down her eyes. "Oh, my God. Oh, my God." She wept. "I wanted my baby to be lighter."

"Megan, calm down, it's okay," Shelby replied, rubbing the top of Megan's hair.

"What's wrong?" Kelly asked through the speakerphone.

Shelby took the phone off of speaker. "Megan is a drama queen. She hasn't stopped crying since Macy was born."

Seconds later, Dr. LeBlanc showed up at Megan's hospital bed and her whole demeanor changed as he planted soft kisses on her cheek. The whimpering halted. Shelby looked amazed at how fast her friend's irrational behavior changed. She shook her head in dismay, but smirked at the idea of Megan dating her white gynecologist. The exciting rendezvous between Megan and her doctor thrilled Shelby, making her think about being with Joel.

"I'll check on you later," Dr. LeBlanc announced.

"Kelly, hold on," Shelby conveyed, focusing in on Dr. LeBlanc and Megan's unethical behavior.

"I love you," Megan replied with a rejuvenated voice full of energy.

"You too, beautiful," Dr. LeBlanc told her as he walked out of the room.

Megan snatched the phone from Shelby. "So Kelly, when are you coming home? I know you should've run out of cash by now."

"No, I have plenty of cash. I'm living in Karl's mansion," Kelly stated in a fake voice.

"But he never comes over. He leaves me in this big house by myself. He hasn't thought about looking at me or coming close to asking me to marry him. He is too holy," she whimpered.

"Kelly, I never thought I'd see the day that you called someone too holy. Remember when you first became saved. You were so radical, cramming the scriptures down everyone's throat. I hated you back then, especially when we went to Jamaica," Megan hollered cheerfully, glad Jackson still loved her, even if Macy wasn't his. "Maybe he's gay."

Shelby grabbed the phone back from Megan.

Kelly's whimpers turned into loud cries. "He's not gay. He's just not attracted to me. Maybe my vision was wrong."

"Stop crying. Megan was just playing," Shelby told Kelly.

"No, its not that. I want to be married."

"He's just waiting until the two of you are married. You are a beautiful woman and he probably feels sexually tempted every time he sees you. He's trying to be obedient to God," Shelby stated, looking down at her cell phone at Joel's second text message. She rolled her eyes and typed back, *I cannot meet u. R u drunk again? I think u need help.*

"Don't worry about it, Kelly, as long as he keeps your Gucci purse filled with platinum cards and green," Megan echoed through the speakerphone.

Her weeps decreased and she managed to giggle at Megan's last comment. "I try to be obedient too. It's just hard when you're in an unfamiliar town. Everyone here is so fake. Fake eyes, hair, and everyone owns a BMW . . . You guys don't understand. I have nothing, not even the love of Karl. He has given me everything and I want to give him something. But he doesn't know I exist in that way. He deserves my body. I want to make love to him so bad." She paused. "It's hard to play the sit-back-and-wait game. I want to get married now. I'm ready for my vision to become reality," Kelly said in a quick, raspy voice.

"Kelly, you don't have to have sex with a man to show him that you love him. Did you ever go to that therapist I referred you to?" Shelby asked, thinking she'd need her own therapist after she received a picture text from Joel of his dick. She found the act repulsive, but yet fun and exciting. *Does my dick look drunk?* his text read.

"No, Shelby! God is the only therapist I need."

"Megan, how did you and Victor manage to wait?"

"Girl, I didn't wait. Victor and I dated three months. I was still having sex with other men because I had to get paid. And you know there was no way I could go without sex for three months. I was out on the prowl back then. I didn't change until we got married, but all of that may modify itsself in the future." Megan snickered, thinking about her handsome white doctor. Shelby took the phone off of speaker and snatched it from Megan and shook her head, not wanting to judge Megan for lying or cheating on her husband.

Megan echoed in the background. "Tell her to seduce him. Seduce him. If he hasn't had pussy in ten years, he'll marry her ass when he gets a little dip of that tight-ass nun pussy that hasn't been touched in five years."

"Hush up, Megan. That pain medicine has you cutting

up," Shelby taunted, fingers typing on her phone to Joel: *Ur dick looks very drunk. Alcoholic!*

She giggled and start fantasizing about the nice picture of Joel's big, black penis with the cut on his abs.

"Kiss the baby for me. I'll fly down soon," Kelly said in a low, sad voice.

She put the phone down and took off the rest of her clothing, ran hot water into the Jacuzzi, then added lavender bubble bath and bath beads. She lit the lavender candles that lined the back of her tub and glided into the roaring water, then laid her head on the bath pillow and closed her eyes. Thoughts of Karl entered her mind; he still hadn't called. She wanted to see him so bad and the urge just couldn't be fought any longer. She reached over toward the Jacuzzi steps and grabbed the cordless phone.

"Hi, I thought you were out," Kelly said, biting on her long fingernails.

"Kelly, where would I be at this time of night?"

"I don't know. Hadn't heard from you," she said in a soft, humble voice.

"You need your privacy. You're staying in my house, but you're free to do whatever you want. Go out and meet some people."

She wanted to tell him she didn't want to meet anyone. Her mission was to marry him, make love, and have babies. "I thought maybe you could show me around like you promised."

"Deal, I'll take you to dinner this week," he said quickly like he didn't want to be bothered.

Just hearing his mature voice sent chills down her spine. She got aroused just thinking about him. "I'll be waiting." She sighed and hung up the phone in a mechanical manner.

And you better be ready for me, Reverend Karl Hughes.

*I'm willing to sacrifice everything to have you as my
man.*

Tears covered her face. "I love Karl so much. Lord, why
can't we get married tonight? I want to make love to him.
It's been weeks and I haven't had sex in five years. I want
to feel him inside of me. I can't wait! I want him now! To
hold me! You promised me, Lord! You promised me!" She
moved the phone away from her side and placed it down
on the Jacuzzi steps.

The Holy Spirit spoke to her. "Just wait patiently. The
Lord will let you know when the time is right." She closed
her eyes and rested her head on the bath pillow. "I receive
it," she screamed aloud, not wanting to be chastised. Not
wanting to hear another sermon about abstinence. She
battled with the Lord and could no longer wait. It was her
turn to please herself.

After Kelly's bath she pulled out her secret pleasure pillow that was filled with naughty toys. Her body lay spread-
eagle across the bed. She inserted the big blue dolphin toy
into the moistness that made her a woman. Her vagina
throbbed as each gentle inch of the amazing toy entered,
allowing the pulsating, energizing object to rob her body
of its fluids and strength. Convulsing as the dolphin mouth
tickler delighted her clit with its vibrating tongue and the
head of the dildo rotated inside of her. Her eyes closed
and she hummed in pleasure to the soothing sound of the
battery-operated instrument.

EIGHTEEN

It was Saturday night, the night of Bryan's surprise birthday party. The theme was throwback and everyone was dressed to the occasion. Blair's home was decorated to match too. Silver disco balls hung from her ceiling and framed pictures decorated her walls. She had a painting of a pit bull playing poker, another portrait was in a velvet print of a Doberman Pinscher shooting pool and a huge portrait like the one on *Good Times* of black people at the club singing and dancing. She also had an array of old school pictures of naked black woman with Afros in black velvet frames. And to top it off she had a record player playing albums.

"Come along and ride on a fantastic voyage," Willie, Bryan's cousin from Natchez, Mississippi sang aloud with the Lakeside Band's song, as he gawked at Bryan's birthday cake. "Man, this cake is somethang. Yawl know how to do it in Chi-town. A butt-naked cake, I be damn. Pat, check out these big titties on this cake."

Pat, Bryan's other cousin from Mississippi, came over

to the cake table and laughed. "Damn, she got a pair of watermelons. And a bush. Mane, I wont me one to take home. I bet she won't talk back."

"Shitt! I'd fuck the hell out of her. I bet that chocolate frosting, moist cake, and creamy filling feel good than a motherfucka!" Willie said, licking his lips.

"Come along, pack your bags. Get on up and jam y'all," blasted from the speakers.

"Yeah, come on and ride on the funk, y'all. Come along and ride on a fantastic voyage. . . . Yeah, that fine-ass red bone, walking in the door, in that short-ass dress, can come ride on this fantastic voyage," Willie sang, wiping sweat from his forehead.

Pat looked at the lady, who he met years ago at the first birthday party Blair did for Bryan years ago. "Boy, that's Shelby. She's married to Bryan's boy Dexter."

Willie held his mouth wide open, eyes glued to Shelby. "Mane, I wouldn't give a mothafuck. That little sweet thang is fine. I'd rock the hell out of that big ass."

"Close your mouth, you're drooling like the dogs on the pictures. And yawl country asses need to make yourself useful," Blair said to Willie and Pat before rushing over to greet Shelby and Dexter.

"Bitch, the theme is throwback. Dexter is dressed in his Houston Rockets jersey, jeans, and Chuck Taylors. Why are you dressed in that short-ass dress, like you going to some bourgeois-ass club?"

"Oh boo, I told you I'm too sexy to dress like a nigga. It's all about me and I'm going to stay on point. I'm a bad bitch and I thought you knew." Shelby pointed to the brown, pink, and orange design on her dress. "Look, the colors I'm wearing are retro and my big hoop earrings." She tugged at her clip-on earrings. "Remember *I need a round-a-way girl* by LL.? I fit the theme."

"Okay. Do your thing. You look good. I need to get like you." Blair expressed indifference to Shelby's new, obnoxious behavior.

"That's right . . . And do something with that cigarette. Don't nobody want to smell that stale smoke. I told you secondhand smoke kills. Fuck around and get lung cancer," Shelby nagged and strutted off in her silver BCBG Maxazaria stilettos. Blair kept on blowing smoke out of her mouth and nose. She shook her head at her friend who had been preaching to her about not smoking since high school. She turned to Bryan's cousins and pointed to the door. "Get the basement door. More guests are coming."

Max, five feet four inches, chestnut brown skin, one hundred fifty pounds, and a smile that made any woman or gay man blush, stepped in. On his fine gold decorated arm was his wife Sidney, his high school sweetheart and the mother of his children. Shelby sprinted over to greet the both of them. She embraced Sidney and Max like they were the best of friends. "Everyone, this is Sidney. And all of you know Maxtin Brooks, the owner of a Gentlemen's Touch," Shelby announced like a game-show host.

"Yeah, can't nobody forget big Max. I'm the realist nigga around," Max yelled, slapping his chest.

"I remember you. You use to work at the bar for Max. I think you were the only one he wasn't sleeping with." Sidney laughed nervously, shaking Brooklyn's hand.

"Mr. and Mrs. Brooks. I'm so glad to see you two here in one piece." Blair turned to Max. "How are you, big businessman of the year?"

Max replied, "I'm fine. I see you're doing well. You've put on some weight. You're wearing loose clothes too." He nodded his head in approval, scanning her black Afro wig with the black-plastic fist pick stuck in the back of her head and the New York Yankees jersey she was wearing. "Damn, I didn't know they had two-toned jeans in your size," Max joked.

Blair's face turned upside down. She sucked her teeth hard and clutched her fist shut tight. "Don't have me slap the black off of you, Max. And add some height to your little munchkin ass," she cursed discreetly so none of her guests could hear. "Still trying to clown? Looking like *little man.*" She looked over his head. "An old fool, damn near thirty-one with French braids in your head. Nigga, you on death row?" Blair rolled her eyes again. "Oh yeah, congratulations, I heard you won the oldest Blackstone gangster award last night."

"Yo mama," Max called out.

"Max, stop harassing people. You don't tell women they've gained weight. You can be so rude sometimes," Sidney scolded, but changed the subject. "Blair, how is . . . the one that used to bartend topless at the club?"

"Oh, Kelly. I guess she's fine. I haven't spoken with her since she got faked-out at the altar."

"I heard. I just knew she'd be here. I wanted her to talk to Max about his evil ways. The nigga been baptized six times and needs to be dunked again."

The girls looked. Their eyes shot open wide, in awe that young, timid, shy, submissive baby mama no longer existed.

Dexter hit Max's arm with his fist in a playful manner. "Ya wife been keeping you in check, I see." He hugged Sidney. "We missed you at Shelby's party."

"Oh, I missed you guys too. Max was already down there and with these high fuel costs I couldn't afford to fly there."

Dexter took his arm from around Sidney. "You need to

feed Sidney so she can get thick. You see how fine my wife is."

Sidney popped Dexter's arm. "You know what, Dexter, I did like you until today. Kiss my flat butt!" she teased.

Max laughed at his best friend and strutted off. He had noticed how fine Shelby was. He saw that loud and clear at her thirtieth birthday party. Hell, he wasn't blind. Animosity settled in his soul. How could his best friend marry his girl? Dexter knew how he felt about Shelby. The love he had for her was real and special; love that went way back to childhood. Just reminiscing about the past made him want to kick his best friend's ass. That was low-down and scandalous on Shelby and Dexter's part, but Dex was supposed to be his boy. " *'You see how fine my baby is?' Nigga please, Shelby was supposed to be my wife. I loved her then and I still love her. She'll always be mine and I'm gonna get her back,*" Max whispered to himself and stepped over to his favorite place, the bar.

"Big country, where the drinks at? I need about ten shots."

"Max, you still drinking that yak?" Pat asked.

There was liquor lined up at the bar: cognac, Rémy Martin, Belvedere, Crown, Bombay gin, Hennessy, Moët, Hypnotiq, and other brands.

"Yes, sir. Ain't nothing changed but the brand. Give me some of that Rémy VSOP. Straight up." The minute Max received his glass of liquor he swallowed it down in seconds, banged his glass down hard and asked for another.

"Where is the entertainment?" Max yelled out to Blair, who was across the room.

"I wanna see some throwback pussy."

Blair pranced over to Max, her thick rope gold chain with the crown pendent swinging. "Oh Max, I thought you were the entertainment. I told everyone the munchkin that starred in *Willy Wonka* would be here," Blair hollered as she reached over his head for a glass of Moët.

"Blair, I know you ain't trying to crack on me. You standing seven feet tall looking like ghetto Shrek in the NBA." Max laughed aloud, pushing Blair toward the door. "Go say 'surprise.' Yo' husband is coming in."

The basement door creaked open. A husky light-skinned man walked in eating on a burger.

"Surprise! Happy birthday, Bryan!" everyone yelled. He looked stunned, not expecting anything for his thirty-sixth birthday. "This party for me? I know my baby girl did this." He exhaled noisily, bear-hugging Blair then Dexter and his cousins. He had no idea any of them were in town. "Yawl did this shit big. Wow, a house party with real house music. Throwback all the way." The original house music blasted through the sound system. *"We're rocking down the house!"* And on that cue, Pat rolled out a huge five-foot model of a brick house made of cardboard to the middle of the room.

"I haven't had one of these since my seventeenth birthday, when we lived on Seventy-fifth and Crandon. Girl, you did it big. That model house looks just like my old crib," Bryan sang as his body swayed to the music.

Max gave Bryan a quick birthday hug and pushed him out on the dance floor. They started dancing and jumping around to the beats of the house music, allowing the melody to bring back memories. Blair, Shelby, Dexter, Brooklyn, and Sidney joined in when the song, "Jack My Body!" rang out.

About half an hour later the food spread was ready. Blair had everything catered from all of Bryan's favorite food joints: Harold's Chicken, Leon's barbeque (rib slabs and tips), boxes of Italian Fiesta Pizzas, JJ Fish (catfish shrimp, coleslaw, potato salad, bread), and three Eli's cheesecakes.

"It's time to eat. Help yourself," Blair yelled out over the music.

"That's right, we have the ghetto's finest in here, all my favorites," Bryan said, smacking his lips as he looked at his wife. "Baby, fix my plate first." He rubbed his stomach. Blair glared at Bryan. Her lips curled up. She mouthed, "strike one," then fixed his plate and gave it to him with a wide, phony smile.

"The food is delicious. I didn't realize how much I missed the food from home," Shelby raved as her teeth bit down into the hot, fried chicken.

"Yeah, Louisiana ain't got nothang on Chi-town. All yawl eat down there is crawfish and gumbo," Bryan joked with Shelby and Dexter. Then he blushed, wiped the barbeque sauce off of his mouth, and tickled his wife's stomach. "Ain't that right, baby girl."

The sounds of music invaded the room again. "Oh yeah, that's the song, 'Fantasy Girl,'" Dexter shouted, watching the model brick house, in the middle of the floor, rock.

Without notice a girl busted out of the model and shouted "happy birthday" to Bryan. She was wearing old school attire, Gazelle sunglasses, a red, black, and white button-down Chicago Bulls jogging suit, thick, huge braided gold-square earrings, and a Chicago Bulls hat pulled down. No one could see her face.

The stripper pulled a chair to the middle of the floor and sat Bryan down, but he didn't release his plate of food. He just sat there with the chicken in his hand, taking it all in. Her jogging suit disappeared piece by piece as she danced around the chair. Nothing was left on her body except a red and black–net G-string bodysuit. She placed her hands on the seat of his chair and did a handstand in his lap. Her legs spread wide open into a Chinese split; an earring hung from between her legs. When the stripper jumped down and turned around, her sunglasses and hat hit the floor. She bent over and jiggled her cellulite butt in Bryan's face as her hands massaged the floor to the beats of the music. Her arms and head swung up and she began to feel herself. No one could believe their eyes when they figured out who the dancer was. She had aged a bit and gained weight, but everyone knew Sapphire when they saw her.

Bryan didn't appear to care that Sapphire was his private dancer. He appeared comfortable with her and the huge grin plastered on his face displayed that. There was no hiding his excitement while a squatting Sapphire swallowed up a Merlot bottle with her insides. His smile became wider when she inserted a lit cigar in her vagina and blew smoke. The guys were going wild. Ten, twenties, fifties, and a few one-hundred-dollar bills covered the floor where Sapphire performed.

After a short intermission, Sapphire returned, wearing only chocolate frosting on her nipples and morsel. She sat in the empty chair with her legs spread spaciously open with black paw-print tattoos coming from between her legs all the way to her ankle. Willie crawled up to the chair and placed his face in the frosted treat. He lifted her butt cheeks up and shoved twenty dollars under her. Sapphire yanked Willie's head from between her legs and stuck his head on her breast. "Take it slow, Jethro and don't swallow my nipple ring." Then Max rushed over to eat the frosting off of the other breast. "You too, Mighty Mouse." After the frosting was gone Sapphire slapped the guys away.

"That's what I'm talking about," the guys yelled.

"I'm gonna pay that bitch to get some of that," Willie bellowed.

"Oh yeah, this pussy doesn't come cheap," Sapphire called out with a bold stance as she bent over, clapping her oil-downed booty cheeks in Bryan's face.

"Clap it baby," Bryan yelled out, as he took delight in her big butt, licking his tongue up and down her crack. "Remember our agreement. You did not want her," he said several times between licks.

Blair saw everything, standing in the corner taking it all in, evil brewing in her eyes, thinking of a punishment for her disobedient spouse. She fixed her eyes on Bryan. "Strike two, motherfucka!"

"Blair, get out of the corner with all that hating. You're the one who wanted to get Bryan a stripper. Chill out, Sapphire use to be your girl. Let's go get a drink," Shelby demanded in a bossy way.

"Did you see how uncomfortable we made the guys?" Sidney questioned.

Blair rolled her eyes. "Yeah, I saw. But Sapphire is no threat. She loves pussy. I'm trippin' on that fact that Bryan licked that nasty whore's butt crack enough to catch a disease."

"Yeah, that HIV is running rapid among African-American women," Shelby replied.

"Fuck the statistics," a drunken Brooklyn stuttered.

Sidney studied Sapphire. "I'm not gay, but she has skills," she said, trying to wiggle her hips. "I'm glad I came. I want to learn how to clap my butt."

"Sapphire will teach you. That used to be Blair's girl," Shelby answered.

"Like the old women always say, you better be a freak in the bedroom for your husband before somebody else will," Brooklyn added.

"Amen," Sidney hollered out, slapping Brooklyn's hand.

Minutes later, Sapphire appeared with Joel. "Look who I found outside while I was taking a blow," Sapphire yelled out. Her face was glowing, almost matching her platinum-blond Afro. She was wearing a sheer robe with nothing on under it and heading directly toward Blair, and Joel toward Shelby.

"What are you drinking, Blair?" Sapphire asked as she bumped into Blair's backside, breathing hard on her neck, then taking the glass of liquor out of Blair's hand and sipping from it. After she finished tasting from Blair's glass she gave it back to her and took her cigarette. Sapphire licked the filter of the cigarette, placed it in her own mouth and took a long puff. Then she exhaled the smoke into Blair's face.

"I was so surprised when I saw Bryan. I didn't know he was the lucky birthday boy. And I definitely didn't expect to see you here." She licked her lips. "I asked Megan about you. Did she tell you?"

"Yeah, she gave me your business card." Blair coughed from the smoke.

"Blair, I've missed you and Blairson so much and I'm dying to see Bryanna. Why didn't you call me?"

Blair scratched her eyebrow. "I couldn't. Bryan is very controlling and you know how he feels about you. I stay submissive to my husband. I don't want any confusion."

"Oh really?" Sapphire said sarcastically, allowing her robe to grace the floor. "Are the kids here now? I want to meet Bryanna."

"No, they are at his grandmother's," Blair said, scanning Sapphire's body, which was a piece of work. She had added more piercings and tattoos. And Blair was captivated by her natural beauty. Sapphire was standing completely nude, allowing Blair to take it all in. When she saw how hypnotized Blair was she turned for her to get a good look at her graciously sized behind. Sapphire knew all women were curious by nature and women always noticed a beautiful woman, minutes before their men did.

"What's up, shawty?" Joel said as he approached Shelby with a lustful grin. The smile was not mutual; an expression of hatred covered Shelby's face. She looked like she wanted to kill him, but played it safe as he reached to hug her above the waist.

"I didn't know you were coming," Shelby stated softly, looking away from her husband into Joel's dark brown eyes.

"Man, I had to come. I wanted to see you so bad. Shawty, you know I got mad love for you."

Shelby nodded, then rolled her eyes. "You're here with her?" she asked, looking at Sapphire.

"No, Blair invited me. I saw her at the café the other night. Sapphire just let me in the door." He rubbed Shelby's elbow and whispered into her ear, sneaking kisses in when no one was looking. "Have you thought about what I asked you over the phone?"

Shelby couldn't believe how bold Joel was. He didn't care that Dexter was around, he wanted her and that's all his little mind could compute. She, on the other hand, felt different. It was like being stalked. He called every day, e-mailed, and texted her. Now showing up at Bryan's party, enough was enough. Things were getting scary and it was time for the charade to end. There was no way he was going to ruin her marriage. He had already disrespected it by coming to the party and approaching her.

Shelby rolled her eyes and spoke in a soft tone, barely audible. "Joel, I told you no. I thought something was there, but it's not. I think it's best if we never talk again. Now chill out, my husband is here," she stated in an ag-

gravated manner as she broke away from Joel's grip,
blending in with Sapphire and the other women.

"Hello, Shelby. I haven't seen you tramps in years," Sapphire hissed. Shelby looked away like Sapphire couldn't
possibly be calling her a tramp. Her eyes met Joel's again.
He looked bruised and confused, hurt stamped all over
his dark skin. She wanted to caress her old best friend,
wanted to make the pain go away, but deep down in her
heart she knew that would only make things worst.

*It was better this way. Hell, Joel could have HIV, Her-
pes, HPV, meningitis, hepatitis C or B, as many women
as he screwed. And with his prison history, somebody
had to hit that sexy, black ass while he was locked up,*
she thought to herself as she watched Joel leave Blair's
house through the basement door.

Never being an adventurous type or a free spirit, she
felt comfortable with her decision to remain faithful to
her spouse. After all, he was caring, compassionate, intelligent, and her soul mate. She loved him and he loved her
more than life. She couldn't dream of breaking his heart
or destroying the history they had. Love like theirs was
hard to come by and rare.

"I love your eyebrow piercing," Brooklyn said, mesmerized by Sapphire's beauty and skills.

"And who is this sexy little flower?" Sapphire questioned as she rubbed Brooklyn's shoulder, staring intently
at the tattoo of Nefertiti on Brooklyn's left breast.

"Pish-posh! I'm Brooklyn and you have to teach me
how to make my ass jump like that," she rambled quick,
chugging down her glass of gin and juice between words.

Sapphire raped Brooklyn with her eyes as she gawked
at the spine of her back, admiring the butterfly tattoo out-
lined in black filled with colors of pink, purple, and yellow.

"I can teach you more than that. Can't I, Blair?" Sapphire asked, now caressing the small of Blair's back, winking at Brooklyn.

Blair shrugged her shoulders and moved away from Sapphire's wandering hands.

Shelby stood in front of Sapphire. "No one is down with the down-low. Go mess with the men. That's what you were paid to do."

"I prefer women. And you know I've always wanted you, I like all that ass you got out of layaway," Sapphire taunted, examining Shelby's firm thighs, which were barely covered by the fashionable multicolored short dress she was wearing, which stopped at her butt cheeks.

"I'm glad you like all this ass, but guess what . . . you'll never get it. Feel free to look all you want. Fantasize about it tonight when your head is between some thighs," Shelby chanted in a sarcastic manner.

"You always did have a mouth on you. Hmm . . . Let me finish my show. I'll show you what this tongue can do between some thighs," Sapphire answered back with a cunning twist.

Blair hadn't said much, but her ears listened to every word that escaped Sapphire's mouth. She had always been curious about Sapphire. And a little attracted to her, she had to admit. But didn't all women have thoughts of making love to a woman?

Sapphire sat on the pool table. "Does anyone like to play pool? I need two volunteers." Dexter and Max rushed to the table. "Stick that pool stick in me!" Sapphire yelled.

Dexter did as he was ordered. Sapphire pulled it out real slow and licked up and down the pole. Max was instructed to grab three pool balls and put them inside of her. And he obeyed her order. He licked the pool balls and inserted each one.

"Get back every one!" Sapphire bellowed.

A black eight ball exploded from between her legs, then the red three solid ball and the five orange solid ball. The three balls all flew in separate directions.

"That girl has some powerful muscles between her legs." Willie rushed over to Sapphire's opening. "Baby, you can have all my money."

"Go ahead big boy, give me all your money."

Willie pulled out a rolled twenty-dollar bill and inserted it in. "Damn mane she even has diamonds on her puttnanny."

Max pulled a hundred-dollar bill out. "Shit, she deserves a big tip. That pussy is like a slot machine, the more money you put in the bigger the jackpot," he announced as he trotted to the pool table.

Sidney grabbed the money. "You can stick that money in this slot. We have three mouths at home to feed."

"What? Who in the fuck do you think you talking to? I make the money around this bitch," Max checked Sidney, snatching his money back. "I'll kick yo ass all over this place. Now get your funky butt up them stairs."

The men started shouting, "get the women out of here. Get the women out of here." Bryan stood up. "Baby, you and your friends need to go upstairs."

Blair stood tall with her arms folded, rolling her eyes at Bryan. "I don't think so," she said firmly, but too low for anyone to hear.

Clapping was filling the room. "Go Sapphire! Go Sapphire!" Bryan stepped up to Blair and snatched her arms, unfolding them quickly. "Please go upstairs."

"You are out of strikes, busta," Blair sneered and hauled Bryan into the bathroom when no one was looking. "Don't you ever try to check me in my house. I'm paying, so I'm staying," Blair scoffed, staring at the golden hot curling iron that was plugged into the wall near the sink. "Nasty ass licking on her butt crack."

"Mane, you paid for the stripper. Why can't I lick a little ass?" Bryan slurred.

"What? You den lost your mind," Blair hollered.

Bryan replied in a slurred, drunken voice. "You seem to like the show better than me, anyway. Just go ahead and stay."

"What? You striked out tonight." She boiled with rage, attacking him with the smoky, hot curling iron. The iron beat across Bryan's neck, arm, and back several times. "Fuckin' licking that nasty ho's ass! Nigga, you striked out," she fumed, pinning the iron on the back of his neck.

"Aaaagh! Ooooch! I'm gon' get you." Bryan yelled in agony, but too drunk to move and the music was so loud, affording no one the pleasure in eavesdropping.

Blair slithered back in the wild shindig, eyes fixated on Sapphire's gyrating ass, rage overshadowing her mood. She had taken care of Bryan for his indiscretions, now it was time for Sapphire to pay. Revenge was like sweet and sour potato chips, tangy and fulfilling, yet bitter and tempting.

"Stick your hands in my deep, wet, hollow tunnel," Sapphire ordered Max. He obliged. His hand sunk inside of her deepness. "Withdraw," she demanded. Scarves were attached to his hand. The more he pulled the more colors popped out.

"I wanna hit that tonight! Come on, Sapphire. Can I buy some?" Willie hollered.

"Bryan, get them women out! It's time to start the real party!" Max shrieked, looking around for Bryan. "Where is Bryan?"

"I don't know," Dexter grumbled as he walked over to Shelby. "Baby, you trust me, don't you?" She nodded. "Go upstairs and take your girls with you. These niggas are getting ready to clown. You ladies don't need to be down here because Willie is ready to snap," Dexter explained in a nonnegotiable manner.

"Okay, have your fun with your boys. It's late, I'm tired, and Sapphire loves women anyway," Shelby teased, feeling guilty for her whole ordeal with Joel.

Shelby headed toward the stairs. And footsteps followed directly behind her, inspecting her round bottom and creamy caramel thighs as she hiked up the basement stairs. The glittery pink thong she was wearing was a tease as it rubbed against her plump, juicy behind. Quick hands had a mind of their own and eased up between Shelby's butt cheeks, fingers dipping into her moist vagina.

"Ohh," Shelby sighed and wiggled her bottom even more. She loved the way her husband got freaky with her in public.

"You like that?" he asked.

"What?" Shelby asked in a high-pitched tone when she noticed the voice didn't belong to her husband. She turned around, caught off guard by his bold behavior. "What the fuck is your problem? You been outside smoking that shit."

"Calm down. Yo man didn't see me. He's too busy looking at other ass." Joel smacked his lips as he licked on his wet finger that was drenched with Shelby's juices. "Don't act like I ain't never fingered your ass before."

Shelby swung at him. "You're drunk and high."

He smiled in his drunken state and pinned Shelby in the corner at the top of the stairs.

"Shelby, I still love you and I always will. So are we going to fuck or what?" an impatient Joel questioned.

Shelby backed up, legs shaking. "Aren't you being the perfect gentleman."

"I'm being straight up. I know what I want," Joel stated, moving closer to Shelby, grabbing her crotch. "Come on, bend over and let me fuck you."

Shelby pushed Joel's hands away. "Look, Joel. I don't like you like that. We are friends now and that's all we should've ever been. Respect me and my husband and just stay the hell away from me."

"Why you telling me this shit now? Why weren't you one hundred with me in the first place?"

"Because," Shelby yelled, growing scared and tired of Joel's antics.

Rapid footsteps darted up the basement stairs. When Dexter reached the top his eyes locked in on his wife and Joel. "What's going on?"

Joel smiled. "Nothing man, just playing around with Shelby."

Dexter looked at his wife. "You wanna tell me what the hell is going on?"

"Nothing," Shelby sobbed.

"Are you sure? What you crying for?" Dexter asked, looking at the awkward expressions on his wife and Joel's face.

"He touched me, but it was nothing," Shelby said in very fast motion. "I shouldn't worn this short dress."

"Naw, you with me. You can wear whatever the fuck you wanna wear." Dexter's nose flared, his body moving closer to Joel. "You put your hands on my wife?"

"Man, don't even step to me like that."

"Come on, Dexter. Let's go. I said it was nothing. I handled him," Shelby bargained.

"Naw, fuck that, we ain't goin' nowhere until this bitch-ass nigga tell me why he put his hands on you. Hell, I see the way he's been all up on you tonight. I should of whipped his ass proper when you two were living together," Dexter cursed.

Shelby's hands became moist. Dexter never cursed unless he was extremely mad. She looked at Joel's devilish beady eyes and knew he was about to lash back.

"Man, you need to check your wife. For months, she's been contemplating giving me the pussy."

Dexter pushed Joel in his chest. Anger polished his body. His fist connected with Joel's eye.

"Oh nigga, you wanna box?" Joel reached behind his back. "Well, nigga, I'm riding dirty. I don't fight anymore, I throw bullets. I'm a Blackstone for life."

"If you man enough to pull a gun out, you better use it," Dexter shouted, not backing down.

"Ahhh! Dexter, let's go. It's not worth losing your life over. Joel is still with that gang shit," Shelby preached, seizing her husband's arm.

"Baby, let me go, if I have to kill this motherfucker then that's what I'll do. If not, I'll die for you," Dexter replied, shaking his wife off of his arm.

"You know what, Dex, I don't even need this gat for yo punk ass," Joel answered back with a swift punch to Dexter's shoulder.

Dexter swung back, knocking Joel down the stairs. Joel tumbled, but grabbed Dexter leg. The two slid down ten stairs. When they reached the bottom Dexter was on top of Joel choking him. "If you ever touch my wife again I'll kill your slimy ass."

Joel was rolling from side to side, trying to get Dexter off of his neck, but Dexter's grasp was tight. His punches were like mosquito bites to Dexter's swollen biceps.

"Man, yawl, it's my birthday." Bryan intercepted, trying to pull Dexter off of Joel.

He was so loaded himself, he couldn't budge Dexter's hands from Joel's neck.

"Baby, let go. Joel ain't worth it. He's a hater."

Dexter listened to his wife, loosening the grip on Joel's neck. With that leverage Joel eased up, kicking his knee into Dexter's scrotum. Dexter let out a piercing cry, releasing his hands and balling over. Joel regained his composure, eye bulging with blood. He stood up and started kicking Dexter with his high-top Converse. Dexter snatched Joel's foot and slung him to the ground. He pinned him down with his arm and elbow. "Nigga, if you every think about saying my wife's name again or looking at her I'll kill yo punk ass again," Dexter panted as he rose up with a busted crimson lip. Joel stood up with blood drizzling down his chin. He straightened his stiff, starched jeans out and looked at Shelby and then Dexter. "You tell your wife not to scream my name either. You know she has a habit of doing that when I'm sucking that clit," Joel replied and walked toward the door. Shelby's heart skipped a beat. Her knees became weak and her entire body felt like jelly. She saw her life blowing up in her face. But Dexter was not impressed one bit. He gave her a long, steady gaze, nodded his head, and walked away too.

NINETEEN

Karl invited Kelly to dinner in Pasadena, at Jennifer Lopez's restaurant. She leaped to the closet like a fairy princess in search of something sexy and alluring. Megan had put something on her mind and she was anxious to put Rev. Hughes to the test.

The dress Kelly picked out was very seductive looking. It wasn't her ordinary thrift store special. This was an expensive, Hollywood piece. Her freshly bathed body glided into the fine, red designer dress by Marc Jacobs. It had the Marilyn Monroe look, a low-cut halter dress with the flowing bottom. What really made the dress sexy was the low-cut halter front, which reached her waist. "My God-blessed breasts are sure to grab his attention. If I have nothing else I have breasts," Kelly repeated to herself in her brass-framed mirror as she sprinkled edible sparkling honey dust with pheromones on her chest. "God, you promised me Karl Hughes, but you're moving too slow. I figure this sexy number will give us a helping hand. Tempt the good reverend with the grand blessings you've bestowed on me." She licked her index finger and caressed her breasts. "My old faithful body, my trademark, the deed that got me put on the map, this *liquid mouth*," Kelly said, puckering in the mirror after applying a thick glossy coat of red lipstick.

The doorbell rang. Karl arrived, prompt as promised. He parked in the driveway with the engine running, as he stood in front of his house. Kelly peeped out of the window from upstairs. He was dressed in a tan linen suit and his platinum cuff links were sparkling.

She sprayed sweet perfume behind her ears and a hint between her thighs, took one more glance at herself in the mirror and shook her head in approval. The lady in red was ready for a nice, seductive romantic evening. When she opened the door the aroma of his cologne was enough to turn her flame into a blaze. The man aroused her with just the sight of him. She couldn't stop imagining the things they could do together.

Karl kissed her hand. His thick mustache pricked her. "You look gorgeous. I've never seen you in so much red. Your nails and toes are even polished in red. Wow!" Kelly brushed into him on their way out the door, allowing him to view her almost exposed breasts, wanting him to smell the pheromones and see the sparkling dust and maybe taste a nipple. She thought she would drench her panties because the smallest things turned her on and his touch had definitely accomplished that.

Karl's presence gave her chills as she moved a little closer. He couldn't ignore her beauty. His consistent stares at her cleavage verified that. "That dress is very low-cut. Maybe you should change."

"What's wrong with me showing a little cleavage?" she said with an erotic pitch. "Don't I look beautiful?"

"Yes, you look extraordinary. Just think it's a bit much

for our date. You should wear something like that for your man, not me. I'm your pastor and friend."

"Can't you control yourself?"

"Oh yes. Don't change your clothes. I can show you better than I can tell you. Sexy women try tempting me every day." He giggled.

"Oh do they? Well, none of them are as sexy as me."

He looked at her with a guarded air. "When did you turn so worldly? You're not the same Kelly I went to theology school with. The plain, homely, humble young lady that was on fire for the Lord."

She winked. "Oh, I'm the same Kelly."

He opened the car door. Her body slid onto the leather seat, exposing smooth, well-defined legs. Karl picked her feet up and placed them into the car with care. He nodded his head. "You are making it very hard for me. I'm a man of God and you need to respect me."

"Loosen up. I respect you. Can't I feel and look sexy? Is that a sin?" she asked as they drove off and headed to Pasadena.

He rubbed his forehead like he wanted to speak, words stolen by lust. He was feeling her and it was very apparent. The huge locomotive of his was starting to smoke. She was finally making progress and there was no holding back. Time was running out and Kelly needed a husband. She traced her delicate nipple with her index finger, placing her finger in her mouth, opening her legs wide, gliding the pointing finger in, working herself out, right in the car. "Want to taste? Come on, place your hands on my blessed breasts. Put this flame out," she moaned as she drove her cum-soaked finger out of her vagina and into her mouth.

Karl fixed his head to the right. "Come on, Kelly, don't do this to me. Why do you want to tempt me into doing something we'll both regret? I want you, in the flesh, because I am a man. But we both know it's not right to have sex without being married. You know about my first marriage. I cheated on her and lived a double life. One woman was not good enough for me. I had an addiction, no different than crack or cocaine. That stronghold ruined my life. I lost my wife, my businesses, and my house. But God saved me from it all. He forgave me and helped me heal. I received favor, and *In the name of Jesus*, I will not forsake my Lord."

Karl's testimony meant nothing to Kelly. She had heard it several times before. "Taste this lust. Come on, you know you want me." Kelly carried on for over ten minutes; dipping inside, teasing and taunting.

"Jesus, give me strength." He battled with himself, but couldn't stop imagining making love to her.

TWENTY

Months had gone past and Karl and Kelly were still unmarried. Her plot to seduce him on the way to dinner had failed drastically. She ended up wet, embarrassed, and unfulfilled. Before they made it to the restaurant Karl pulled over and prayed for her after her uncultured attempt to entice him. That night he rebuked every lust demon that Kelly owned and then referred her to counseling. From that moment she was aware that getting Karl Hughes to be her husband was going to be harder than she thought. The man was grounded in the word and no matter how hard she flirted, prayed, or fasted for him nothing worked.

Kelly studied the bridal shower invitation on the counter. She was a little depressed and Bronze was her only friend in town. The other women at church and her just did not click. She believed the other ladies were all phony and a little jealous of her. Bronze was different. She was down-to-earth and straight-up about everything.

The bridal shower was at Bronze's sister's house in the

hills of Santa Monica. Her home was beautiful, overlooking the ocean. The view was worth a million dollars, not to mention the accommodations of her extravagant home. The party was set up outside along the pool, lit with red lights and cream-colored, heart-shaped floating candles. Jazz instrumentals played through the pool speakers. Small cocktail tables with cream linen and hurricane lamps were arranged along the pool and palm trees. The tables were also covered with red rose petals and confetti hearts. Two long tables with cream linen were situated near the front of the pool under a cream canopy with chiffon bows draping the corners. One table had food on it and the other was for gifts.

The gift table was overflowing. Gifts were on the table and laced around the bottom. The chocolate-covered strawberries were placed around the two champagne fountains on a mirror platter and three strawberry and cream cakes in the shape of hearts were sitting on a three-tier cascading platter with vines and lights wrapped around it. The sterling-silver serving trays were placed on top of red and cream linen clouds with glass hurricane candles placed strategically on the table.

A young woman, around thirty-five, with a loose red two-piece business suit on approached the podium. "I'm Madam Cherry and I'll be your Lust Shoppe hostess tonight. I hope all of you are enjoying your food. I'm going to tell and show all of you how to get married like Bronze or keep the man you already have. Sit back and enjoy the show."

She clapped her hands three times and lingerie models came out, a male and a female. They were wearing white satin honeymoon lingerie, strutting around the pool showing everyone their fashion. When the models finished, they stopped in front of Bronze. Madam Cherry stepped to the bride and presented her with two garment bags, one with *His* on it and the other with *Hers*. A duplicate of the two outfits modeled were given to Bronze. "Thank you," she mouthed as Madam Cherry and the models pranced to the back.

"Now let's give the bride an outfit to keep that man," Madam Cherry shouted to the sex-craved group. The female model strutted out with a red sheer robe on. She tossed the robe to Madam Cherry to reveal her provocative lace crotchless, nippleless one-piece suit. Her furry boa was draped across her neck and her long legs were housed in red thigh highs and heels. Ooh's and aah's were heard across the pool.

"Oh, child, you will definitely keep him with that outfit. You don't have to take nothing off," a lady yelled aloud.

Madam Cherry walked up to Bronze and presented her with a duplicate of that outfit. "Now I have something for you ladies in the audience."

The male model walked out with no shirt on, displaying nothing but abs and a G-string with a heart-shaped pouch in the front. Kelly's eyes were focused on the plush heart. She tried to imagine Karl's sexy body in the dainty getup. Would she ever get a chance to see his body? At the rate they were going it didn't look like it. And that saddened Kelly.

"Ladies, look under your chairs. If you find a red heart-shaped envelope with *hers* on it, you win that sexy lingerie. If your heart says *his*, you win the male G-string."

They all reached under the chairs, grabbing and searching. Kelly couldn't feel anything under her chair, but that didn't stop her from sweeping her hand under the chair again. "I have the *hers* heart envelope," she yelled as she danced in her seat.

Bronze's mother leaped up. "I have the *his* heart envelope. My man is going to give me a strip dance tonight."

The male model walked over to Bronze's mother and ripped off his underwear. "Here you go."

Bronze's mother gazed at the man in amazement. "Do I get to try Mr. Long Chestnut Brown?" she asked, gawking at the long penis the man employed.

The model whispered in her ear. "For a small price you can try all of me." Bronze's mother smiled and took the man's number.

Kelly didn't know what she was going to do with her outfit, but the unknown excited her. Karl would get to see her in it sooner or later and sooner was her plan.

"All right ladies, this jar I have in my hand is some powerful stuff. It will get you in the mood in a matter of seconds. I need three volunteers to go to the bathroom and try this."

Three ladies popped up. Madam Cherry had three Q-tips. She dipped each one in the jar of Cleopatra's Secret Response mint cream and gave each lady a sample. "Apply this to your clitoris." The women rushed to the bathroom to try the product. And while they were gone a male model walked out, wearing an elephant G-string. The long elephant trunk played music as the guy danced around.

"No, don't lick on the back of my ankle." Kelly squirmed about, trying to get away from the dancer's wet tongue that had slithered up the back of her thigh. She jumped up like the Holy Ghost had entered her body. Old feelings were coming back. Desires that she locked up years ago were beginning to emerge.

"Lord, give me strength. I know it's time for me to get out of here anytime I'm letting a stripper turn me on," Kelly chanted to herself, fanning away imaginary spirits with her hand.

"Ooh, girl, it's okay. We sell toys to fulfill that urge," Madam Cherry expressed with a grin big as Texas to an anxious Kelly before handing her a strawberry gift bag with a pair of glow dice in them. "You are lucky tonight."

"I guess I am," she stated, reaching for the bag, not following the Holy Spirit's advice about leaving the party.

The ladies who had just sampled the response cream pranced from the house. They were smiling and walking kind of weird. "This stuff is off the hook. My cat is hot and ready for some."

One lady grabbed her purse and headed for the exit. "Congratulations, Bronze. I got to go. I'm about to get my freak on. This shit has me on fire."

"Wait," Madam Cherry screamed. "Here's your gift bag of Cleopatra's Secret Response cream."

The other two women also received their gift bags. Their faces displayed excitement as they reached in the bag to read the label.

"Ladies, tell the rest of us how good the cream feels," Madam Cherry announced.

The lady giggled. "If you use this cream you better have a man. I don't have one, that's the only reason I'm still sitting here," she murmured low. "Hoping to buy me one after this show."

"The next product is used to keep him erect longer, gives it a pleasant taste, tantalize him, and reduces the gag reflex. You will be able to deep throat with no interruptions. Can you guess the name of the product?"

Women shouted aloud, "Erector, Big Penis, Gag Man, Tasty Pete."

"No, that's not the name."

A lady stood up and waved her red napkin in the air. "Head Job."

"You've got it. Pass her this gift bag of mint-flavored Head Job."

They all laughed, but Kelly sniggered to herself. She

could've used something like that back in the day because blow jobs were her specialty before she found the Lord.

The male model stood in front of the women with jungle-print satin boxers on. He stood next to an empty chair, searching through the crowd until he found Bronze's sister, Cinnamon. "Come on, pretty girl," he said. licking his full brown lips. She ran to the chair so fast you would have thought she was on *The Price Is Right* and the host was saying "come on down."

"Close your legs," he ordered while placing a silver object that looked like a small egg at the end of her knees. The power button was pressed and the silver object shot up to her vagina in one second.

"Oh shit!" Cinnamon yelped. "I got to have this. This object is amazing."

"It's yours," Madam Cherry said, wearing a game-show host face, passing Cinnamon a strawberry bag with the object inside.

A young woman dressed in a red tube-top dress with a panther tattoo on her ankle blurted out, "place that bullet inside of your cat and let him come in behind you. Baby, you ain't felt nothing till you experience that shit. That bullet is the bomb. Hell, and the double bullet is even better because you both get a thrill."

Bronze stood up and fanned herself. "Little cousin, TMI, that is too much information. You and Black Panther keep your bedroom secrets to yourself."

Cinnamon rose up out of the chair and walked over to Bronze. "Speak for yourself, me and Steven will be trying that tonight." She slapped her cousin's hand. "Thank you, Angele."

A female model sashayed out, wearing glow-in-the-dark body paint and glass high heels. She was carrying two big chocolate-colored dildos with balls in her hand. "My name is Candy and I like Mr. Dependable." Candy glided the dildos into her mouth and her jaw jiggled. "These babies feel real." She twisted over to Angele. "Touch Mr. Dependable."

Angele clutched the dildos in her hand. She caressed her neck.

"Oh, hell yeah! I can use this when the Panther is in desperate need of some loving. I'll slap this joker on the wall and tear it up." She squatted down and pretended to ride Mr. Dependable. "I'm going to stick this on the bottom of the tub and go to town. These motherfuckas feel like the real thang. I don't need a man."

Madam Cherry handed Angele a gift bag. Then she passed out prize tickets to all of the women at the shower. "Let me know how y'all like this." She pulled out a big purple vibrator with a huge hole in the middle of the tip. Madam Cherry turned the power on and water shot out of the head of the vibrator that was twisted around. "They have finally made the dildo that can replace your man. This baby cums." The women started clapping, stomping their feet and yelling. They were really impressed with the gadget. Kelly wasn't; she needed the real thing. That toy could not hold her tight at night, pray with her or give her a baby. She was already having thoughts about tricking Karl into bed before marriage. Now she was determined.

The jazz music ceased. Usher's song, "Yeah" blared out of the pool speakers, followed by a splash into the pool. A second later another male in Burberry bikinis, who resembled Prince, dived into the pool. The third male wearing Gucci G-strings did a backward flip into the water. And Kelly's eyes followed the dark chocolate treat's every move, right down to his big cock.

The guys exited the pool. Their strong, masculine bodies were covered with dripping water. The women were going crazy and Bronze was really having a good time as

she waved her five-dollar bill in the air. She winked at
Kelly. "Girl, enjoy yourself. You better get you one of
these fine brothers to hook you up. I'm not going to tell
Karl and none of the sisters from church will."

Kelly opened her mouth to reply, not believing her
church members were off the chain. She knew the Bible
was right when it talked about hypocrites in the syna-
gogue. But she was right along with them.

Bronze was swept away by all four strippers. They held
her high up in the air like she was a goddess. When the
men reached the hammock they gently placed her body
down and pulled off her high heels. Gucci rubbed his
hands together and rolled them in circles. He grasped
Bronze's foot as Burberry poured massage oil onto her
feet. Gucci massaged her feet like a baker kneading dough
then he placed her feet in his mouth. She let out a light
yelp each time he repeated the act. After the men finished
pampering Bronze and feeding her chocolate-covered
strawberries, Gucci zipped the hammock up with a tent
cover and joined Bronze.

"Oh my God. Yes, it feels so good," Bronze screamed.
The sheet moved up and down and the hammock swayed
slowly.

Kelly watched from afar and analyzed the scene. *What
the heck was my church member doing under that sheet
in front of everyone? There was no way I was letting
any man put his filthy hands on me.*

Cinnamon walked over to the moving hammock. "What
are you doing in there? Are you guys having sex?" She received no reply. "Open this hammock up!" Cinnamon
banged on the hammock like she was LAPD, but stopped
when she heard Angele behind her, yelling at a stripper.

"Hey, sexy. Baby, I got tips for yo fine ass. Come to
Mama. I am ready to pay."

The stripper wearing the Burberry bikinis picked up
Angele and placed her on his neck. He raised her dress up
and rotated his head between her legs. She raised her
hand in the air. "Eat it up. Slide my panties to the side."

Burberry placed Angele on her feet. She threw her dress
up and started rolling her bottom into the male dancer's
groin. Her bare bottom was mooning the world as she rotated clockwise. It appeared she wasn't wearing underwear but when Kelly looked close she saw the thin row of
diamonds between her butt cheeks as the dancer started
smacking her cheeks. Her butt jiggled like green Jell-O
just taken out of the fridge. The stripper mashed his body
into hers, mimicking the doggystyle position.

Mr. Burberry could not keep up with Angele's wild animal moves. She flipped over on her back and extended
her legs wide as she pulled him into her web. She seized
his bottom and pressed his eighteen-wheeler into her tunnel. Kelly thought she was watching a porno movie. The
two were really exciting her. They were so sensual, every
movement made was perfectly calculated and on beat.
Kelly's eyes were like magnets attracted to their bodies.
She kept on imagining that being her and Reverend Hughes.
If only she could get a taste of lust, she thought to herself
as she wiggled in her chair.

"My God, what am I doing? In the mighty name of
Jesus, Lord forgive me," Kelly cried out when a heavy
woman bumped into her. She thanked God for the dis-
traction, realizing she had to get away from the hypocrites among her. "Excuse me," she stated, trying to
wiggle past the bent-over plus-sized woman. "God, why
did I come here? Are you trying to test me?" she mumbled
as she pushed her way through the madness.

"Come on. Right this way," Madam Cherry exclaimed

when she saw Kelly and escorted her in her private showing room.

Bronze walked in the house and collapsed on the couch
as Madam Cherry and Kelly were walking out of the private room. "Kelly, why didn't you stay outside with the
live entertainment?"

"Huh?" she replied, shocked by Bronze's statement.

"With your past, I know there's no way in hell you can
stay away from sex. I can pay two of the guys to hook you
up real good just the way you used to like it."

"Bronze, I told you I don't do those things anymore. I
am saved and I only want one man and that's Karl."

"Is that why you have that gift bag of goodies in your
hand?"

"What I have in my bag is none of your business. Just
because I'm a minister doesn't mean I'm dead." Kelly
smirked, feeling guilty about buying more toys. She always questioned herself about that. Was it a sin to use
toys? The articles in *Essence* didn't think so and she didn't
either.

Bronze licked her red lipstick and her eyes focused in
on Kelly. "As women, we have needs. It's about time you
learn how to please your body. Keep on waiting for Karl
Hughes and you'll need surgery to open your vagina back
up. Just like the earring holes in your ear, if you don't use
them they'll close up. I'm telling you. You need to get you
somebody else to fuck and Pastor will still think you're
saving it for him. That's how I do it and my fiancé doesn't
know the difference. Shit, you can even get a woman on
the side." Bronze laughed like a possessed demon, moving closer to Kelly.

The guy with the Gucci bikinis entered the room. He
looked down at Kelly's bag. "Did you buy that prickly pear
gizmo? That's the best product the Lust Shoppe has."

"Kelly may not be ready for that yet. She'll need a companion for that one and Pastor isn't having that until they're married," Bronze stated as she backed away from Kelly, allowing the half-dressed man to move closer to her.

"Would you like for me to demonstrate the prickly pear?" he asked Kelly as his hands caressed her tense shoulders.

"No, thank you," she said in a quick, computerized tone. "I'm fine with the peaches and cream body butter I have."

"I can demonstrate the prickly pear for you. It feels really good when I stick it on my big cock and hit it from the back. That damn pear vibrates the clit and those orgasms never stop. You can take all of this big, long dick doggystyle or riding," he said, rubbing his erect penis.

Kelly glared at the blessed piece of meat. Her insides pulsated. Panties filled with liquid. The temptation was too strong. She hadn't seen a penis in years. Her eyes and feet were glued in place.

"No one has to know," the male stripper told Kelly as one hand stroked his penis and the other her neck. Bronze shifted closer. "Kelly, I will not tell anyone if you let me join in."

The devil knew Kelly's weakness. She had struggled with the sin of oral sex most of her life. And tonight was just too tempting. Her mouth watered at just the thought of tasting him. Tasting the clear liquid that dripped from the tip of his penis. She closed her eyes and her head inched down. Mouth opened wide.

TWENTY-ONE

Weeks had passed and Megan was back in stride. She had her figure back and was on a mission, a mission to find bigger and better things.

"Mrs. Myru, your time is up. It has been twelve long weeks. We can have relations now," Victor announced to his wife, who was more beautiful to him now than before the birth of their daughter.

"Don't you see me on this damn laptop?" Megan vexed, trying to minimize the Millionaires page, but had no luck.

"Megan Myru, do not use that category of language with me. I do not want to engage in a difference of opinion. I yearn to make love to my wife."

"Please, you can't even afford this priceless pussy anymore," Megan rattled and moved her hands to the left, singing Beyoncé's song, "Irreplaceable."

"Oh! I have money. Do not get it twisted. Isn't that what you guys say here?" her husband responded, mocking the American slang.

A comment posted to her page. *Your twelve weeks are*

up. Are you ready to make love to me? I want to pamper you with all of my love. I've waited an awful long time for you, Mrs. Myru. Megan replied within seconds, typing faster then a court reporter. *Yes, I'm wet and ready. My clit is calling your name and has been for weeks. The cyber sex was good, and the office visits were great, but I'm ready for the real deal again. I'll call you later. This jerk wants to have sex.*

"Can we have sexual relations?" Victor asked in stern voice, approaching the laptop.

"All right, get the condoms." Megan replied, slamming the screen down.

Megan shut her eyes as the familiar routine began; holding Victor's head down tight as his mouth explored the mound between her thighs. However, her senses were not reacting to touch. The delicate vaginal opening remained dry and pleasure free.

Think about you and Dr. Jackson LeBlanc. Imagine your husband is Dr. LeBlanc.

Megan's hips gyrated. She moaned aloud and fondled her perfect C-cup breasts that she had paid over ten thousand dollars for. "Oh, Jackson! This feels so good," she mumbled, but no sound came out. The animal between her hairless legs roared and foamed at the mouth. Hips rotated faster as his tongue dipped in deeper and deeper. Then she thought about her doctor friend again. How his big, white dick dug into her soul, how he'd push her legs back and take care of business, having no mercy. The more she thought about him the more the natural juices crept from her yearning body. "Yes, I love it. It feels so good. Stick it in now."

Victor obeyed her command, sliding his penis right in. "My Sweet Princess, you have never been this saturated before. The baby has exceedingly enhanced our sex life."

She grinned and continued to dream about her and Dr. LeBlanc. "Oh, yeah! Keep it coming, baby. Put it all in. Make love to me harder."

"Thank you, thank you, you feel so good. Daddy loves it." The more he spoke, the madder Megan became. He was wearing himself out and she couldn't feel a thing. Her fantasy was being ruined.

"Shh! Baby, please don't talk. I like it when you're quiet." Victor stopped talking and resumed the long thrusting motion inside of Megan. Her imagination went wild again. "Don't stop until I cum. Oh yeah, that's it! I love it! I love it! Ohh! Ohh!" Victor slowed down and started to jerk. "Don't stop! I'm almost there." He continued the journey. Her body vibrated and tossed about.

I thought about Jackson LeBlanc. How he hit every hot spot accurately. Guilt darted past as I reminisced about him making love to me while I was pregnant with Victor's child, but hell, I was so horny and wet all the time. My hormones were in an uproar and I needed a real man to fulfill me.

Hips gyrated faster this time. The moment of pleasure was near. It was signaled by uncontrollable giggles. "Oh! Oh! Oh, Jackson! Thank you."

Victor rolled off of his wife in one swift motion. "Jackson! Who is Jackson?" he said through clenched teeth.

Megan was still drowning in her glorious orgasm, immobile to the world. She was like a deaf-mute.

"Megan Cole Myru, I said, who is Jackson?"

"Huhh?"

"Jackson? You identified me as Jackson!"

"Oh, I made a mistake," Megan exclaimed without a care in the world.

Yeah, I made a mistake, all right. I meant to say,

"Thank you for giving me an orgasm, Dr. Jackson LeBlanc.

"That was an enormous oversight, Mrs. Myru," Victor yelled, pointing his index finger.

"Oh well, deal with it."

"Oh well, I will deal it," Victor taunted before rushing off to the shower.

Megan knew he was upset because he usually wiped her off with a warm washcloth following their lovemaking. This time was different. He didn't grumble a word.

When Victor returned to the bedroom he was fully clothed and had a strange air about himself. "Here's a washcloth."

"This thing is ice-cold. What happened to you catering to me first? I don't appreciate how I'm being treated. You let me sit here all nasty and sticky while you freshened up. I'm a lady, not a tramp." She covered her eyes up. "Oh, my God. Oh, my God," Megan cried aloud.

"A lady doesn't call her husband another man's name."

"I—I—I—made a mistake," she said, bursting into more tears.

Victor sprayed cologne on his neck. "No, I believe I made some mistakes. I've been spoiling you, but not anymore. It's time for you to go to work. Nurses make excellent money and they have flexible hours. You can pay some of these hospital bills." He threw a stack of hospital bills at her. "Here, you have to pay them ten thousand by next month."

"What do you mean? I refuse to work. This is my first child and you expect me to work? You must be crazy," she said in a shaky, hysterical voice.

"I thought I could foot the bills, but I can't. It's getting tight. You can work on the weekends. Now that's what's up." He twisted his mouth. "Yeah, I can be hip when I want to."

"Oh, my God. My God . . . How am I supposed to leave my brand-new baby?" Megan pleaded, tears running down her cheeks.

"American women do it every day."

"Victor, there has to be another way," she begged between hyperventilating gasps.

"You can sell your car, get a smaller house and pawn your diamonds . . . because guess what?"

"What? What?" Megan asked between weeps, stunned by her husband's rebellious behavior. "What?"

"I can't afford the pussy. Maybe Jackson can," Victor retorted with perfect diction and then stormed out of the house.

TWENTY-TWO

Bryan and the kids made it home at eleven-thirty. He had spent the whole day catering to them. They went to the ESPN sports center downtown and later that night to Navy Pier for a ride on the Ferris wheel.

Things had been going well in their home and Bryan wanted to keep it that way. Blair was pleasant, kept her hands to herself and even cooked a night or two. All she wanted from him and the kids was space. Time, as she stated, to get her thoughts together, without medication and counseling. So every spare moment Bryan was off, he spent it away from home with the kids.

The black-gated door inched open. Blairson and Bryanna crept in, trying not to awaken their mother. They scattered upstairs to their bedrooms like mice in the night, leaving the front door of the house partly opened for their dad to enter.

"Where in the fuck you been?" Blair snarled, creeping from behind the huge door. "You know this is the anniversary of my miscarriage," she said through teary eyes.

"No, honey, I didn't know. I took the kids to get something to eat and then we went to Navy Pier, knowing how much you wanted to be alone," Bryan stuttered.

"Bitch, it's almost midnight. My kids are too young to be out this late." A loud whack sent vibrating sounds throughout the living room. "Ohh! Wee!" Bryan howled, grasping the back of his neck. "Chill! That's where you burned me. It's still healing," he whined, remembering the night of his birthday when she burned him with her hot curling iron.

"I will beat yo motherfucken ass!" Tears drowned Blair's face. Her body trembled as she gazed into her husband's eyes. "I lost my baby and you cheated on me a month later. How can I forget that? And to make matters worse, I'm sitting here with herpes blisters between my legs because of yo worthless ass. Yeah, all of this shit hit me today, an outbreak and the death of our child."

Muffled words came from his mouth. "Baby, I'm sorry. I'll continue to wait on you hand and foot to make it up to you. I love you."

Blair yelled louder. "Yeah bitch, I feel the love. And look at ya? Your eyes red. You high on something, either crack or pussy."

She leaped up the stairs like the Hulk, flipped the light on in her son's room, and pulled the covers off of him. "Where have you guys been?" Blairson had his headphones on, his mind in another world. "Beat it like a cop," he sang. She pulled the headphones off his ears. "What's up with your dad?"

"Mama, cool out. Dad's straight. He's been good to me and I ain't even his son. He'd never disrespect you and that's on everythang."

"I hope you're not lying to me, boy," she shrieked, rushing back downstairs to interrogate Bryan further. "Pull your drawers down! I said drop 'em!"

Bryan loosened his belt. "You ain't said nothing but a thang. But I want some of that there sweet juicy stuff after this," he replied, handing Blair his drawers.

She snatched the underwear off and smelled them, then she pointed to the crotch. "Why do you have cum stains in your drawers? You didn't even have enough respect for me to wash your funky dick. Who were you with?" Blair bellowed, yanking on her husband's lengthy penis. "I can't stop picturing you licking her nasty, crusty crack," she moaned, wringing her hands. "Bryan, I love you. I would never cheat on you," Blair cried, smacking her husband across the head repeatedly with his underwear.

"Calm down. I love you too. We goin' make it through this." Bryan grasped her face with a gentle touch. "But I'm not cheating," he communicated in a catatonic manner.

Blair inhaled and relaxed her body when she exhaled. "You really hurt me in the past, but I forgave you."

"Did you? You go off weekly 'bout my slip-ups. You say you forgave me, but you keep on throwing it back in my face. And you haven't been to no counselor or taken a pill. How long do ya think we can go on like this? I'ma tell you it's getting hard for me to refrain from hitting you back."

Her voice escalated. "How long? Bitch, I'll have this shit for the rest of my life from your dirty-dick ass. And the other for eighteen years." She paused. "You got your nerves. I hate you sometimes for doing that shit to me. I just want to hurt you like you hurt me. I want you to continuously feel the pain that I feel," Blair screamed, beating her fist into Bryan's arm.

"Is there anything I can do to make it up to you," Bryan stuttered. "I want you to be happy again."

A cute smirk skated across Blair's high cheekbones. "I'll do anything if you'll just forgive me."

"Anything?" she asked, still grinning.

Bryan shook his head up and down with slow nods. None of the locks in his head moved. Uncertainty written all over his face; he loved Blair and was willing to do whatever it took to keep her.

"I'll be right back then." She ran up the stairs like a track star, her arms moving back and forward, relay style.

Bryan stood there wearing his Coogi shirt. He looked on the ground at his underwear and jeans, dick hanging and mind wandering. His life was falling apart and he didn't know how to glue it back together again.

Blair came back down the stairs wearing a red wife beater, red heart-covered boxers, and red and black high-top Jordans. Her long weaved hair was pulled back into a ponytail and her hands were covered with weight-training gloves.

"Mane, don't tell me we about to box?" Bryan asked his wife as he reached in his jean pocket.

"Yeah, we about to box all right. And you don't need those clothes, so put the jeans down. You said anything," she said, punching her fist into the palm of her other hand. "Let's go downstairs to the basement. I don't want nobody to hear you screaming," she giggled with a happy, giddy grin, wanting to humiliate and punish him.

Bryan looked at the back of his wife's head as she jogged to the basement. *Oh, you want to have rough sex. I'm down with that,* he chanted in his mind as he took his car key and dug it into a little plastic bag that was in his jean pocket.

Bryan headed to the basement in a trance; snorting the white powder off of the brass door key. His footsteps were slow and staggered. This was the vice that helped him deal with his wife's erratic behavior. He tried church, Bible study, and counseling, but nothing numbed him like the white horse.

"I see you finally made it down here," Blair said, holding a bottle of tequila from the bar. She was standing in front of the pool table. His mind wandered off again. His eyes focused on the red punching bag in the corner that was hanging from the ceiling. "Come on, let's get this party started," Blair teased, grabbing Bryan's hand, pulling his limp body to the pool table where she stood with a strap on. "You said anything."

TWENTY-THREE

Kelly rose from her knees and blew out her prayer candles. Ever day she repented for attending Bronze's wild shower and having those lustful thoughts. She realized it was only him, the Lord Jesus, who saved her from not giving that guy in the Gucci underwear a blow job. The devil was not going to steal her joy and convert her back to the old Kelly. Each day she spent five hours praying in the morning and two hours at night cleansing her mind from temptation.

With all of that said, Kelly's days in sunny California were better. Living alone no longer bothered her. Getting to know herself was a pleasure. She used to beg Karl to visit her after church, but that was no longer an issue. He heard no whining from her. Kelly learned to please herself.

She lay out at the pool, her body glistening with oily tanning lotion, the sun beating on her back, welcoming every stinging ray. Nothing was spoiling her good mood. She was at peace as thoughts of making love to her husband-to-be floated in her mind. The more she reminisced the happier she became.

"Miss Kelly, what are you thinking about?" The pool guy uttered, the words rolling off his tongue in his Hispanic accent. "You're tossing and turning like you're having an unbelievable sexual fantasy."

She rolled over off of her back. "I was just thinking about my man."

José's eyes were glued to her bosom, but he wasn't saying anything. He just stood there with the pool cleaner in his hand. She looked down at his shorts and noticed a small knot.

"What are you looking at? You act like you've never seen a woman with great big breasts before."

José's face turned red. He bobbed his black stringy hair from left to right and pointed at her chest. The knot in his pants was rising.

"What's wrong, José?"

He finally managed to speak. "*Senorita*, your nipple is out!" he voiced loudly with a stronger Hispanic accent. "Your breasts look like *grande*, ripe guavas."

Kelly took a quick look at her chest and fixed her swimming suit top. "Is that all? Why didn't you tell me? If I wasn't saved I'd show your little young butt something that would really get you stirred up. I'd let you taste these juavas."

"*Por favor*, pretend like *tu nada* saved and show me," José yelled out as Kelly was walking toward the patio door.

Let me go before I commit another sin. Yes, I know I've thought about José in a sexual way before. I know it's like having sex if I've lusted for him in my mind. God, work with me. I haven't had any in five years.

"Good night, José. Lock up when you finish," Kelly told the pool boy as she swayed into the house.

"Thank you, Jesus. That little boy almost got me in trouble, but you were here for me. You are an awesome God and I give you all the honor and the glory," Kelly chanted as she marched up the stairs to her room.

The ringing of the phone annoyed her as she tried to pray. On the fourth ring she rose up and looked at the caller ID and saw it was Karl. She picked up the cordless phone with a sly sneer.

"I got your message. Are you okay?" Karl asked, wiping sweat from his head.

"Just a little shook up. . . . I don't want to be alone. He . . . may . . . come . . . back." Kelly trembled, biting her nails.

"I can't believe José tried to attack you."

"Yes, he kept on staring at my breasts. Telling me how juicy and ripe they were. Salivating all over himself, jacking off. I reported everything to the police."

"Oh, I'm so sorry. I should have never left you to live in that house alone."

She exploded, full of nervous energy, acting at its best. "I'm just scared. Please move back over here now. You have to. I can't stay here alone with that pervert on the loose." Loud moans erupted from the pit of her stomach. She cried a river like the one Justin Timberlake sang about in his song. "Lord, protect me. I'm all alone. My dad is gone and my mother's a dope fiend. Everyone tries to hurt me."

Guilt glued itself into Karl's chest. He felt terrible for what happened to Kelly. "I'm on my way," he said into the phone.

As soon as Kelly finished her acting 101 class, it was on.

It would take Karl a good thirty to forty minutes to get to the house. Time she couldn't spare and she raced to her deeply tanned, foreign friend who thought her performance deserved an Emmy. He was sitting right on the bed waiting impatiently for her on the pillow. It appeared he was more excited than she was. The way he jumped about each time they spent time together, every time more anxious than the last. "I can't wait for you to please me, again," Kelly recited like a young girl trying out for a cheerleading team.

Her young friend was ready as she crawled into bed to greet him with her mouth open wide, like a dentist's visit. She begin licking that exotic, new rod like a pro. Kelly welcomed the tip to the back of her throat. The instrument popped out of her mouth. She was ready, wasted no time squatting down on it, getting hers before Karl came to pray with her. Her body sprung up and down the miraculous being, taking pleasure in each motion. It was a shame she had to do this desperate deed to get what she craved for. *A girl has to do what she had to do*, she thought to herself as she lunged up and down. "Oh, Lord Jesus! Oh, Lord Jesus! Help me! Help me! I need help!" she pleaded and begged in a heavy, loud, sensual voice.

Shrill and boisterous sounds ricocheted through the house *the minute Karl opened the front door. Fear graced his body, but he remembered second Timothy 1:7 that stated God gives us a Spirit that does not make us timid, instead his spirit fills us with power and love.* He leaped up the stairs with faith on his side. "Lord, please don't let anything happen to Kellyanna."

He threw his well-built body against the locked door. It didn't move or budge, neither did Kelly or her friend. Her back was toward the door and she was moving swiftly and smoothly up and down the glorious pole. It appeared the sinful activity had taken over her mind. Karl gave the door another heavy heave. A loud sound exited from the door as the wood split. He banged into it again and it caved in. Then the reverend rushed through the frame.

"What are you doing?" His fist hit the wall. "Stop it! Don't hurt her," Karl shouted, almost in tears. Almost in tears, until he opened his eyes and observed what was really going on. Kelly's smile told it all. She wasn't being held hostage. No one was raping her. Pleasure dominated her being as she glided on the glorious amusement ride. She wanted him to see her . . . see what he was missing.

Karl looked down at her with disgust. Then he walked toward the door. A mask of mortification painted on his face mixed with anger. Pictures crashed to the floor as he exited the room with a loud bang.

The reverend stood at the front door of his home, which was still wide open from his panic-stricken entrance. He paced back and forward thinking what to do. Karl kneeled down on his knees and started to pray. Tears were streaming down his face and his temples were throbbing from humiliation. He had violated Kelly's privacy.

Lord, I'm your faithful servant. I'm a pastor over a flock of thousands. I don't need to make any trouble here. It's not worth it. God, please give me strength. I can't go back in that room and face Kelly. I want to do right by you. How could she call herself a woman of God and be doing what she was doing. I guess she has needs, but prayer always helps me, he thought to himself.

The reverend was getting ready to leave his home, the mansion he paid four thousand dollars a month mortgage on, but the devil stepped in and he decided against that. He was only man, a mortal like everyone else. Sin, temptation, and lust did not overlook him. Kelly had weakened him. Her months of seduction attempts had rekindled his sex addiction and he had to have her. There was no fighting the flesh.

The twenty-foot solid cypress wood front door slammed shut and Karl stormed up the stairs. "Kelly, do not do this. I'm going to make it right. I've already made love to you in my mind repeatedly," Karl chanted with perfect English diction as his feet stomped up the stairs. Loud sounds exploded from his footsteps. He made it to the room where he found her flashy, hot naked body in motion. His eyes governed her, scanned her cavity for weapons. The reverend only found delicate, smooth vanilla hands caressing nipples. Legs, bended back toward her head.

Karl's nervous masculine hands snatched the humming chocolate cyber gadget out of Kelly's anus and threw it on the floor. "You don't need these toys anymore. I'm sorry for neglecting you. The sin was already committed when I lusted over you. Let me please you. Masturbation is a sin." He chuckled.

The good reverend dove into her juicy, overflowing insides like a professional diver. His thrusts were full of power and strength. He pinned her legs back further as his immenseness drilled into her saturated wetness. The movement of his hungry body was high-speed and efficient. Kelly loved every intimate hit. She was a target board and he was a dart. His aim was fast, forceful, and accurate, hitting the bull's-eye every time.

"Pastor Hughes is loving this! Oh, Pastor is loving this! This is worth the ten-year wait. Sin never felt this good," he yelped.

"I have to cum! I have to cum! You have to make me cum! Make me cum! I need this. It's been five long years. Please make me cum," she begged and pleaded like a crackhead wanting a hit.

"The good pastor is going to make you have multiple

orgasms," Karl burbled. Without warning Kelly's wet body
was flipped over. "Get on your knees! You've been a bad
girl. It's a sin to lie to your pastor and use fake, inanimate
objects for sex," he stated with a firm smack to her deeply
tanned bottom. His eyes fixed themselves on her shiny,
perfect hole. Her anus was lubricated, throbbing to be
molested. The reverend entered with ease and the tight-
ness of her asshole made him ecstatic. "You feel so
good. . . . Why did you keep this from me? Lord, make her
my wife. This is some good—" Karl panted between
humps.

Kelly enjoyed the anal sex too. The minute he pene-
trated her, her body jolted and jerked with pleasure. Liquid love ran down her thigh.

"I see you like this," he whispered into her ear as he
dipped his finger into Kelly's wetness. "I don't want to
make anyone jealous. Let me satisfy Miss Kitty." Karl
reached down and tasted between her legs.

Their lovemaking went on for hours. The reverend
ejaculated and was able to become erect minutes later.

"Yes, I love it. I love it, Karl. I love it, Karl. Thank you!
Thank you! Jesus! Jesus! Jesus, forgive me! I love you! I
love you so much! Please forgive me." Her words shuddered as the reverend's body pounded inside of her, his
wide girth clenching to the walls of her insides. She had
been called a bottomless pit by many, but Karl was long
and thick, reaching spots in the center of her that had
never been explored. Kelly clutched the comforter tight,
enjoying every bang and the fondling of her jelly-filled
breasts.

"Oh, Goodness! I can't stop quivering!" she hollered
with so much emotion, while her insides pulsated and
trembled with flowing orgasms, three minutes apart.

He nibbled her ear with his mouth. "I didn't know it

would be like this. You're incredible. I can't stay away from you. I . . . love . . . you. Please marry me, Kellyanna Swanson."

The reverend gasped, almost out of breath, as his hot, creamy potion exploded in Kelly and down the back of her thighs.

TWENTY-FOUR

Kellyanna Swanson and Reverend Karl Hughes first time together sexually was outstanding. He confessed his love for Kelly and gave her a huge engagement ring the next day, replacing the fake ring she had bought from Goodwill. He moved back in the house with her and they slept together every night after that lustful act. The reverend was captivating and succulent rolled up tighter than a dipped joint. For Kelly, the whole encounter was like being a virgin all over again, but different because she loved Karl with all her mind, body, and soul. They had a spiritual connection that could never be broken. He was her husband-to-be, selected by God himself.

The moment Kelly experienced the stiff, strong force of his intimate body part inside of her she knew it wouldn't be the last. Her addiction was rekindled. She had been with over a hundred men and none could compare to Karl. Kelly had to have him daily and he had to have her. Some days she'd sneak to the church in the middle of the day, wearing nothing under her knee-length raincoat, just black-strapped stiletto glass heels or she'd schedule to clean the office in her sheer pink and black maid outfit with the booby-free top and the crotchless bottom. Other days she'd walk in the pastor's executive-styled office dressed in a short nun outfit wearing crotchless, fishnet pantyhose and put his mahogany desk to work. Occasionally, Miss Kelly would follow the reverend on his way to work. Then she'd pull him over, dressed in her short police-woman dress, hat, badge, cuffs, and garter with the gun attached. "Sir, you were speeding. That's one thing I don't permit. You rushed out of the house without making love to me this morning. Pull out your dick and let me suck it," she'd tell him. And he would, right there on the side of the road.

Kelly had Karl doing things he would have never dreamed of doing. She made him feel young again. Every day with her was exciting and fun and he couldn't wait to be her husband because he loved every inch of her body and mind. And Rev. Karl Hughes didn't hide it from his church. If God knew it didn't matter what the others thought.

"Reverend, I'm on my way," Kelly whimpered into the phone, her middle finger prodding inside of her. "And I'm wet already," she said as she pulled her finger out, licking the creamy juices surrounding it.

The reverend felt his nature rise. It never failed, just hearing Kelly's sweet voice made him erect. She had whipped him like no other woman had in his fifty years of life.

"I can't wait to taste you," he said, licking at the phone and kissing into the receiver.

She kissed the phone back. "Oh really? Wait until you see what Mother packed for you. I figured we could go to the park for a little picnic." She giggled, thinking about the Little Red Riding Hood costume she was wearing without panties.

She planned to skip to the office with her picnic basket, which was filled with sparkling grape juice, two wineglasses, turkey and cheese croissant sandwiches, fresh strawberries, and potato chips. And for dessert she packed homemade carrot cake, Karl's favorite. He loved the way the cream cheese icing tasted between her thighs.

Kelly figured they'd have a mini-picnic at the park, then christen the playground. Because she couldn't resist riding his long, thick, dark penis on the park swing nor the slide, monkey bars, or the seesaw. They had managed to have sex on almost every object in the park. Her insides were roaring more just thinking about their erotic adventure.

Kelly heard his heavy breathing. She wondered why he hadn't replied. "Hello, Reverend, are you okay?"

He let out a light laugh as he rubbed his naked manhood. "I can't wait to see what you've conjured up. Be careful." His hand moved up and down the long pole in a steady motion. "I love you . . . and Kelly, I can't wait until our wedding." She rubbed her saturated finger on her nipples. "Thank you, Jesus, I can't, either."

When Miss Kelly arrived at the church, no one was there. A car wasn't in sight. The football-sized parking lot was empty. The reverend must have given the secretary and the other staff members the rest of the day off after the heated phone conversation with Kelly, which was common whenever she announced her lunch visit.

Kelly bounced in the vacant office building with her white wicker picnic basket and her Little Red Riding Hood dress without panties, legs covered in white diamond net thigh-highs and feet decorated in seven-inch red pumps. The short, red-ruffled dress with white lace drifted from side to side as she scuttled to the reverend's closed office door. No noise was heard from the room. She placed her ear on the door to make sure, but she didn't hear a peep. "Ooh, I bet he's in there butt naked waiting for me since he knew I was coming. After all that panting and heavy breathing he probably wants to eat me up like the Big Bad Wolf did. Get a little taste of this before we head over to the park," Kelly murmured in a low sound audible to no one but her.

Little Red Riding Hood couldn't wait to get to the Big Bad Wolf. Her hands shook as she rushed to insert her key into the office door. The brass key turned, and the mahogany door crept open. "Reverend, I'm here. I have lunch!" she voiced like a young girl. She crept around the door. Her eyes met with Karl and his guest. The picnic basket crashed to the ground. The sound of broken glass shrieked from the basket. Purple liquid leaked onto the floor from the opened basket. White icing with pecans plastered to the floor. Kelly shut the office door with all of her force and ran out of the office. Her feet would not stop until she made it to her car. She felt like her heart was going to pop out of her chest. Tears found their way to her face within seconds. Soft cries turned into earsplitting sobs. "Why, Karl? Things were so good. Why did you have to do this? I never cheated on you. Lord, what happened?" Kelly wept to herself as forced her foot down on the accelerator with all her strength and skidded out of the parking lot.

TWENTY-FIVE

The heat of Arizona was scorching hot. There wasn't a creature seen for miles and the land was dried-up and lifeless. The only form of life spotted were green prickled cactuses. The flaming rays of the sun appeared to be keeping everyone in. No one was on the highway, not even a trucker.

The air was also noticeably dry as Kelly drove Karl's convertible through the Grand Canyon State. The car's top was down and her body welcomed the torturous climate because it fit her mood at that moment. The desert wind mixed with sand and the searing sun had ruffled and distorted her face and hair in a major way. She looked disheveled, her un-relaxed hair and darkened skin showed no signs of life. Sweat poured down the mystified girl's eyebrows onto the light brown freckles near her high cheekbones. The facial expression she possessed didn't show a care in the world because deep down inside she was feeling the way she looked.

Kelly glanced down at the diamond ring and chuckled.

She stared harder and let out a loud, lengthy laugh. The square-shaped rock still looked exquisite on her beautiful hands and she couldn't believe she was leaving Los Angeles and the man of her dreams. She tapped her hand on the steering wheel with her long fingernail. "Rev. Karl Hughes, I'm going to miss you. . . . I should've never seduced you. Should've waited for God, but I didn't. Now I have to pay the price," she repeated aloud into the hot, dry air.

Miles later, the monotony of the drive tired Kelly as she fought to stay awake. "I need to talk to someone," she screamed into the sky. With that said she picked up the cell phone to call Shelby.

"Thank God you're home. I need someone to help keep me awake. I'm moving from California and I'll be making a slight detour to see you."

"Moving?"

"Yes, I left Karl. A lot has changed since the last time we spoke." Her mind wandered back to the office and tears built up in the corners of her eyes. "It's a long story, I'll tell you about it one day."

"Where are you?" Shelby screamed, noticing the lethargic tone in Kelly's voice.

"Bitch, I'm driving through fucked-up Arizona! This desert is hot as hell! There isn't a mothafuckin' thing to look at! What other questions do you want me to answer? I'll be at your house tomorrow."

"Wait a minute, Kelly. Pull over and get yourself together. I think you're experiencing some type of breakdown."

Kelly's cheek quivered. A lump formed in her throat. Tears escaped from her eyelids and rushed down her freckles. "Duh, I lost my husband-to-be. I've lost everything. I'm moving and I have nothing," she sobbed, rubbing her hand through her wild hair. "Well, I guess I can sell the car Karl gave me because I have nothing. I'll never get married."

"Don't say never. Watch your tongue. Your visions will be coming true. You just needed to be patient and stay positive."

"Well, it's too late for being patient. I slept with Karl, planned everything, manipulated our whole relationship and now it's over. I don't deserve to be happy. I'm an evil person," she recited in a quick, rehearsed manner.

"Kelly, what's really going on? Why do you sound like that? I hear mania in your voice."

Kelly pulled the phone off her ear and looked at it. She yelled into the receiver. "Miss shrink, I am not one of your crazy patients. You're not listening to me. I was not being obedient to God. Me leaving is all a part of my repenting. I am being punished for having sex before marriage. So fuck everything, I'm about to be ten times worse than I was before I became saved."

The phone beeped. It was Karl, calling for the twentieth time. "I wish he would stop calling," she shouted for the world to hear.

"Talk to him. Work things out, don't run away from your problems," Shelby yelled into the phone, trying to reach Kelly's soul.

"I can't . . . Not after seeing him with—" Kelly stopped talking midstream and shook her head. "Just get the guest room ready for me. I'll be in Louisiana tomorrow night."

"Please be careful. Don't go back to your old ways," Shelby muttered into the dial tone.

By the time Kelly made it to the State of New Mexico her little red dress was brown from all the flying dirt and sand in Arizona. She looked down and wiped the sweat from between her breasts without a care in the world. Shoulders shrugged as Kelly took her time peeking at the stranger's face in the visor mirror. The deep beige skin was now the color of brown sugar. The blazing sun in Arizona had tanned her face in a major way.

You finally got your wish. You are brown-skinned. Are you happy now? her alter ego asked.

She was happy about the color of her skin until the sunglasses were pulled off. The reflection of a raccoon appeared. A dimple showed up on her right cheek as the glasses were placed back on her sweating face. She almost laughed at her silly reflection in the mirror. But that was no longer an option. A smile couldn't be housed in her body, were her new thoughts as she closed the camel-leather visor and pressed her foot on the gas pedal. The speedometer went from 75 to 110 in three seconds. Her glasses slipped down to the tip of her nose as she sped through the Land of Enchantment.

Twelve hours had passed without the sounds of music, only the roaring wind keeping Kelly company. She did a mental review of her life and became saddened. The word *lost* was lurking into her vocabulary too much. Her dad crossed her mind. Him dying was the biggest loss she had ever faced.

Thinking back, I was away at cheerleading camp when it all happened.

"Daddy was fine when he dropped me off at camp last week."

"Kelly, darling, things change. Your dad was a sick man."

"Daddy, I'm here. This is your little princess Kelly speaking. Wake up!" My mother tapped my shoulder. "Let's go, darling. He cannot hear you. The man is dying." I looked at my mother. My face and shirt were saturated with tears. "I'm not going anywhere. We can't leave him here by himself."

My mother waddled off. "Look, I have a policy to cash in. He came here alone and he shall die alone."

I sat near his bed and looked down at his frail, eighty-pound body. He was knotted up in the fetal position, not able to talk, eat, or use the bathroom. Cancer had stolen him overnight, turning a handsome, strong man into an infant again. Moans befouled the air. Sound of agony fled from his dry, dehydrated lips. I cried until I couldn't anymore. His pillow had soaked up every tear in my body, leaving me weak and lifeless. The only person that loved me was dying without a good-bye. I glared down at his face. His eyes were glued shut. I tried to pry them open, but they wouldn't budge. "Daddy, get up! Talk to me! I love you! You can't leave me here with her! Don't die! God, please don't take my sunshine away! He's the only person that loves me. Who is going to love me like my daddy. Huh, God? Who is going to protect me?" I rose from the side of the bed, pacing the floor and praying. Begging and pleading for God to heal my dad. Minutes later I returned to the bed. "Daddy, I love you. Can you hear me? I said I love you. Snap out of this. Please, wake up. You're too young to die. You have to see me get married one day. Who's going to walk me down the aisle?"

The car swayed off the road. Piercing, clanking, sounds rung from her tires. Kelly ignored the noise and kept on driving at top speed. She closed her eyes, gazed up at the clouds, took her hands off of the steering wheel and wept. "Daddy, I've lost you, Karl, and most importantly, God. I don't know if I can live without you guys in my life."

TWENTY-SIX

Blair dropped the kids off at Bryan's grandmother's house and charged home. The second she swung open the door her clothes dropped to the floor. She couldn't wait to slip into her sexy, sheer, royal blue lingerie. She and Bryan had scheduled a night of wild sex again, but this time it was Bryan's fantasy.

Their sex life and relationship had sparked up since their encounter in the basement. Blair realized Bryan's love for her was deep. He allowed her to do the unthinkable and she appreciated it in a sick way. Her goal was to disgrace, belittle, and chastise him, but it turned out different. His humbleness made her change. She started seeing her psychiatrist again, taking her antidepressants, and going to therapy.

Blair's body sunk into the king-size bed as she sipped on a glass of Crown Royal and puffed on a fat cigar laced with purple haze. She inhaled the smoke, paused, then blew it up into her nostrils. Blair repeated the ritual several times, often breaking to sip her Crown Royal. "Baby,

I'ma be ready for you. You can fuck me up the ass this time," she stammered in a mellow tone, awaiting her husband and his big surprise.

Thirty minutes later, Blair was passed out. She was so out of it that it took her five minutes to wake up from the sound of her doorbell. Blair sprung out of bed, wiped her face with the palm of her hand and sprinted to the front door, still high and drunk. She opened the door and her eyes were filled with water as she looked into the deep eyes of her friend. "Come in."

Sapphire walked in. "I saw Bryan at the lounge with Max. He told me you were here alone."

Blair shook her head. *Okay, this is Bryan's surprise* she cheered silently.

Sapphire couldn't hide her feelings. She embraced Blair with both arms and kissed her wet cheeks where the tears had fallen.

"You don't know how long I've waited for this moment. It was so hard to keep my hands off of you at the party," Sapphire explained, peering up at Blair.

"I couldn't keep my eyes off of you," Blair admitted with an embarrassed look plastered across her face, not knowing if it was the liquor and weed making her vulnerable and hot. Sapphire held on to Blair tighter. She moved her mouth closer to Blair's lips. Blair inched down and seized Sapphire's tongue.

The two separated and Blair wept more as they approached the bedroom she shared with Bryan. Her breasts were caressed as she was escorted to the cream down comforter on the bed. Sapphire looked up and stared at the family portrait above the bed, her hands exploring Blair's full, round dark nipples. She noticed how big Blairson was, but she couldn't take her eyes off of Blair and Bryan's daughter, Bryanna. The little girl was beautiful. Her essence glowed through the portrait, sending Sapphire into a poignant ambiance, making her feel proud.

"Ooh, you looking mighty sexy in that lingerie. Royal blue has always turned me on. Let me lick on those big-ass titties," Sapphire told Blair before gulping down her triple-D's, which were like putty in Sapphire's mouth. Blair tilted her head back and groaned sounds of pleasure. Sapphire unfastened her lingerie from the bottom and inched her mouth down to the dripping, tingling region of Blair's body.

"No, you can't. I have h—"

"It's okay. I'll use protection," Sapphire replied with a nod as she pulled out a female oral condom.

She inched down toward her lover. And Blair exhaled. She just closed her eyelids tight and screamed aloud when the warm full lips connected with her scorching meat. Her pleasure scale hit ten when Sapphire's tongue ring shuttered her insides.

The lesbian was channeled in on her lover's erogenous zones, their bodies in perfect harmony. No man had ever made Blair feel that good before. It was an unexplainable, magnificent sensation that haunted her body, leaving it hungry and craving more. She thought Bryan had really outdone himself this time.

Five orgasms and three hours later, Sapphire slipped out of the basement door with a sense of accomplishment written all over her face. Her goal to be with Blair was finally achieved and her plan had begun.

"Where you coming from?" Bryan roared into Sapphire's ear, stealing her fantasy moment.

Sapphire was totally caught off guard. She ignored Bryan and continued her journey to her car.

"I said, where the fuck you coming from? We had an agreement," Bryan cursed, snatching at Sapphire's hair.

Her longhaired platinum wig came off in his hand. She swung her fist, but Bryan caught it before it reached his face. "Bitch, you have some explaining to do. I want to know why you're leaving my house at this time of the morning. You didn't want her, remember."

"Bryan, I want to be a part of her life. You can't continue to keep me away from her. She needs to know the truth."

Bryan looked at Sapphire with venom in his spirit. White powder traced his nose as he tightened his hold on her. "You not fucking up my marriage. Me and my family are happy and don't need your drama."

Sapphire wiggled her hand, trying to get out of Bryan's tight grasp. "Nigga, let my hand go. If you were happy and pleasing your wife she would've never let me do your job."

Bryan squeezed her fist tighter. He yanked her body toward his house. "What? Look here bitch, don't start no shit." His eyebrows flickered. "So, I'm not pleasing my wife. I aughta beat yo ass for saying that shit." He dragged her. "Come on, we gon' settle this shit."

Sapphire squirmed and flipped her body, trying to wiggle loose. She grabbed Bryan's braids from the back of his head and pulled down hard. "You better let me go, punk!"

The hair pulling didn't bother him one bit. He continued to drag her fighting body onto his front porch.

Sapphire broke free from Bryan's clasp when her shoe slipped off as they climbed the front stairs. She picked her spiked high heel off of the step and connected it with Bryan's head. He turned around without hesitation and clutched Sapphire's neck. "I see you still have some fight in you. Save it for the bedroom 'cause you two bitches are going to show me what went on." Bryan opened the door and shoved Sapphire to the floor, yelling out to Blair, "I caught your lying ass. Me and yo bitch are on our way to the room."

Sapphire screamed, "Blair, wake up! Get out of here! Run! He's high on that shit."

Bryan whacked Sapphire in the mouth and slammed her into the bed. Blair opened her eyes when she felt Sapphire bang into her. Her eyeballs shot open like she had been hit by electricity.

"Ya shocked to see me. I caught yo little bitch creeping out the back door! Tell me what the fuck is going on?"

Blair chuckled. "This was your doing. You told Sapphire to come over. I thought this was your fantasy."

"Bitch, what?" Bryan cursed, lifting his hand up, scaring his wife. She had never seen Bryan out of control and enraged. And he had never used so many free-flowing, violent curse words before.

"And you call yourself a Christian? Nigga, you a hypocrite." Blair pointed to her husband in amazement.

"Motherfucka, I was a Christian until yo low-down ass started fuckin' with me. You pushed me on some higher shit."

"Look, Bryan, you tell me what the fuck is going on? What are you on? Why you trippin'." Blair shouted, pounding her fist into her husband's chest and stomach. "Furthermore, you told Sapphire to come over."

Bryan raised his voice louder. "She asked me if you were home, that's it." He huffed loud. "The role reversal is over. Someone needs to tell me what the hell is going on. I better hear some words flowing in a few seconds!" he demanded, snatching Blair's fist off of him, spinning her around by her weaved hair, throwing her to the ground in ten seconds flat. Blair didn't know what hit her. She squirmed about trying to lunge back up, but before she could speak

Bryan's foot was in her stomach. She let out a shrilling howl as he extended his leg, kicking her hard and fast.

By the sixth kick Blair was able to grab Bryan's leg. She grasped his leg tight, digging her nails deep into his calves. Her mouth moved closer as he wiggled to be freed. She planted her teeth into his calf, trying her best to tear the meat off of his bone.

"Oh-wee, Bitch! I'ma kill your ass!" Bryan bellowed, dancing about from the pain of her bite. He removed his gun from the front of his jeans and moved it down to Blair. Her mouth uprooted itself as Bryan's 9 mm was shoved in. "You wanna tell me what's going on now? You don't look so big and bad now. Bite my gun like you were doing my leg."

Blair's eyes filled up with water. She wanted to speak, but was too nervous. A huge, loaded gun was in her mouth and she didn't want to take any chances. Bryan crammed the gun deeper into her mouth, almost reaching the back of her throat. Blair mumbled, trying to push the gun out of her mouth. Sapphire moved to the carpet and inched close to Blair and wrapped her arms around her.

"Nigga, take that gun out of her mouth and let me whip this pussy on you. That's what you want? You've always loved this sweet, tangy pussy."

"Bitch, shut the fuck up! Blair, I'ma ask yo ass one more time. What's going on?" Bryan pulled the gun out and stared down at Blair and Sapphire like the devil himself.

The two scattered to the bed to escape his intense, demonic gaze. "I—I—I was waiting on you, sipping Crown and smoking a lil' haze," Blair answered, stuttering for more words, but found none.

He tapped her with the gun on the top of her head. "Fuck this dyke doin' at my house? She said she fucked you! I need to know the goddamn truth!"

Blair cried out with her hand extended. "I thought she was my surprise. Damn, I thought we were doing a threesome."

"Bitch, how you gon' do a threesome with two people. You must think I'ma fool. Now what's up? I'm frustrated and tired, but that won't stop me from whippin' on your ass some more."

"Okay, she comforted me. You haven't been here for me. You cheated on me. Gave me that fucking disease I can't get rid of, and went out and had another baby."

Bryan picked up the bed and tried to flip it over. Sapphire and Blair embraced one another. The heavy weight of the women prevented the bed from flipping over.

Bryan yelled out in rage, "So what. People live normal lives with that shit. It ain't like cancer."

"Bryan, you didn't care enough about me to use protection," Blair whined.

"Blair, fuck you. I should've never married yo ass anyway. You fat and disgusting. With yo sick ass." He paused and stared at the two women. "I knew you were a dyke the minute I met you. How long you been fucking this ho?"

Sapphire rubbed Blair's hand in a smooth, soothing manner. "Bryan, I love Blair. I have always loved her and you knew that. You two should've never met that night at your café. You don't deserve her and I'm sure she realizes that after last night." Blair put her head down and cried, embarrassed by the words that were spoken. But Bryan was furious. He stretched his hand out to slap Sapphire. She grabbed his meaty wrist with her long, sculptured nails. "Don't try to beat me because I satisfied your wife better than you ever have."

He snatched his hand away from Sapphire and slammed her body to the bed, unzipping his pants. "Show me how you pleased my wife."

Sapphire wiggled her tongue and moved toward Blair, tugging on her pussy hairs. "I'll be glad to show you."

"No!" Blair screamed, inching away from Sapphire.

"Don't cry, baby. He was going to find out sooner or later. Let's put on a good show for him."

Tears flooded Blair's face. Humiliation graced her body. She was usually the aggressor and now she was a little punk.

"Go on! Bump pussies!" Bryan yelled, knocking his fists together.

"Honey, I love you. Don't make me do this," Blair pleaded, hoping Bryan would change his mind and go back to his shy, timid self.

Bryan put his gun in Blair's face. "I bet yo big ass wasn't crying earlier. It's showtime baby, you been hanging a nigga by the nuts around this motherfucka. It's time for me to get mine." He chuckled as he climbed into the bed, pulling off his clothes. "I'ma be in on the action this time. Since yo freaky ass then screwed my wife it's only fair that you return the favor to me," Bryan exclaimed as he shoved his penis into Sapphire's mouth before she could put her lips on Blair.

TWENTY-SEVEN

Kelly changed her mind about dying, physically. Because emotionally she was already dead. Her car swerved back on the road and she decided to make everyone else's life miserable. Her objective was to seek, kill, and destroy; the same as the devil's.

When Kelly passed Breaux Bridge, Louisiana she knew she was getting close to Baton Rouge because the long bridge on 10-west stretched miles over vast swampland right before you made it to Shelby's city. Louisiana was full of marshland and she didn't see how anyone could leave Chicago, the third largest city in America, to live there. But Shelby did it. She married Dexter and moved to the south, acquired a country accent too. Kelly just shook her head as she thought about her girl's ridiculous transformation.

Before Kelly made it up the hill, she spotted Shelby and her two children rushing out of the twelve-foot doors to greet her. She looked at her childhood friend and her family. They were gorgeous. Jealous graced her supposed-to-be-holy body. *I can't believe this bitch is married with two kids. She was mean to all the boys in high school.*

Kelly stepped out of the car like a movie star. "Hey girl! Hey kiddies!" The two embraced and her daughter joined in. Her son backed away, afraid to touch Kelly.

"You have beautiful children. D.J. has really grown. I haven't seen him since he was Savannah's age. How old is he now?"

"He's five."

"Girl, he looks just like Dexter. You couldn't name him anything else, but Dexter."

"Kelly, you really look good. California has added beauty to your look. The only change is your hair. When did you kick the perm to the curve?"

"I stopped getting perms when I moved to California. I know it looks a mess. The wind beat it up on the way here. I had my top down. All of that will change. I'm dyeing my head red ASAP. I'm about to be a hot girl again," Kelly told Shelby, motioning with her hands. Shelby shrugged Kelly's silly comment off and entered her home. Her friend needed serious medical attention, but she didn't want to run her away.

"Love your house . . . It's way bigger than it looks outside."

"Thank you. Dexter and I designed it ourselves."

"Where is Mr. Dexter? I can't wait to see him," Kelly said in a much too chipper tone.

"He's playing golf."

"That boy loves golf. Some people never change, but boy did you. I can't believe you're married with two kids. I always thought I'd get married before you. You were always so mean to all the guys in high school."

"Girl, I've been married for six years and I've been a mother five years. Get used to the new me."

"I know, it's just hard to believe." Kelly paused and put her index finger in the middle of her lips. "Have you spoken with Joel? Miss Married Woman."

"No, and I don't plan to ever again. I'm surprised Blair didn't tell you about the fight Joel and Dexter had at Bryan's birthday party."

Kelly perked up and her eyes dashed to Shelby. "You know I don't talk to Blair. But you can tell me."

Shelby looked uncomfortable, not really wanting to discuss the terrible event. But her memory dashed to the past. *"You tell your wife not to scream my name either. You know she has a habit of doing that when I'm sucking that clit," Joel replied and walked toward the door. But before his hand reached the knob Joel was on the floor. Dexter wasted no time kicking Joel's butt again.*

"When you tell me about you and the reverend, I'll tell you about Joel."

"Well, that won't happen. I'm not telling anyone about that freakin' shit that happened in California. But you can tell me about that big-ass dick Joel has."

"Yeah, you have gone crazy. Listen to you, you don't even sound right, trying to curse." Shelby paused and cut her eyes at Kelly. "And for your information, I did not sleep with Joel. My husband has a big-ass dick that I can jump on all day and night if I want to," Shelby expressed, trying to be nonchalant before walking off, the kids following her. "If you're hungry there is food in the fridge."

"Shelby Tate, you can't fool me. I know Joel has your nose wide open. My dreams are never wrong," Kelly whispered to herself as she searched for her black flip-flops with her toes so that she could journey off to the kitchen in search of food.

The fancy doorbell chimed. "Answer the door!" Shelby

yelled from the back to Kelly, who was in the kitchen eating everything she found.

Kelly shoved forkfuls of red beans in her mouth and rushed to the door with a piece of cold fried chicken in her hand.

"Bitch, who the fuck is you? You look like Catwoman on crack with those rings around your eyes."

"Excuse me!" she yelled, shocked by the forty-year-old man's rude behavior.

"Don't pay any attention to Uncle Damon, he's crazy," a young boy around eighteen full of bling bling replied. "I'm Chad, Shelby and Dexter's nephew."

"I'm Kelly, Shelby's friend."

"I don't give a fuck who named you. Where the fuck is my sister-in-law and brother at? Don't tell me Dexter dumped big booty Shelby for a pancake-ass catwoman."

"Man, Unc, chill out. This beautiful young lady deserves respect." Chad kissed Kelly's hand. She snatched it away, thinking he was trying to steal her fried chicken leg. And as hungry as she was she would have killed him before his lips grazed her hand.

"Miss Lady, I was just trying to kiss your hand. Are you married or single?"

"Single"

"Is it possible to interest you in dinner or a movie?" he rambled in one swift breath.

"Huh?"

"Never mind," he replied quicker than his last comment.

"Well, come in," Kelly said with hesitation in her voice, biting into the chicken.

"Come in? When did this here become yo home? I'ma tell Shelby she gotta watch yo cat ass, already tryin to take over," Damon joked, standing at the door, waiting for someone.

Chad, Damon, and a young female walked into the living room and made themselves comfortable on the thick, deep red, leather sectional.

Shelby entered the living room and looked at Damon like he had lost his mind.

"Where is Spring?"

"Hey Auntie, what's going on?" Chad interrupted, trying to hug his aunt.

Damon glared at Shelby. "Who is Spring?"

"Your wife! The lady you married."

"This is Tracy, my new boo. I need a place to knock some pussy walls out tonight. This is young, tight prime pussy, something you and catwoman wish y'all still had."

"Damon, your little short butt couldn't knock down a wall if you hired a crew to help you."

"I ain't talking about the house walls, I'm talking about pussy. I'm gone to tear the bottom out. I'm a drank me some Wild Turkey and pop a Viagra. Ain't that right, Tracy?"

Tracy looked at Shelby and Kelly and blushed. "He is such a fool. By the way, I'm Tracy and you have a very nice house."

"Thank you," Shelby replied and walked off toward the kitchen. "Kelly, I didn't know you were that hungry. I had planned to take you out to dinner." She pulled out the rest of the chicken and placed it in front of her. Kelly tore into the chicken like a homeless dog.

"Girl, this is some shit. Dexter needs to get home to check his brother," Shelby reported to Kelly in a tone that no one else could decipher. But before she could elaborate any further Damon was on her heels.

"Come on, sis, can we spend the night?"

"No, you are not bringing that ghetto superstar into my

house. You are a married man and you'll respect our home."

"Mothafucka, when you get so saved? Stop cockblocking and hook me up with a place to screw this slut. You know all the hotels are booked with people from New Orleans."

Tracy paid no attention to Damon. She giggled, walked up to the kitchen table, looked at Kelly's head and laughed. "Say, boo, what you need is that hair done. Child, your head looks a mess, ya heard me." She put her hands on Kelly's head. "Girl, yeah, I can hook it up some quick. Give you a hella makeover. My hands are like magic, yeah." She looked at Kelly again. "I got all my stuff in the car. I can hook you up like a movie star, yeah."

"Okay." Kelly nodded with a clown smile, unable to speak any further since her mouth was full of chicken.

Shelby walked off and Damon followed her through the house, continuing to beg for a place to stay for the night. He was determined to get her to agree to his offer. However, his journey was short-lived. And from the stupid illustration drawn on his face, Shelby's answer to him was still no.

"Here, hungry-ass girl," he stated as he threw a blanket and pillow at Kelly on the sofa. Chad caught it in the air and wrapped Kelly up fast. The air-conditioning was on sixty, Kelly's belly was full, and she was ready to take a quick nap on the comfortable sectional in front of the seventy-inch plasma television.

Damon looked at his nephew, Chad. "You sweet on this old trifling coon?" He watched Kelly's facial movements and spoke. "And don't you want to wash your ass first?"

"What!"

"Do I have to spell for you? Did yo ass ride the short bus? *Wash your ass!* Toenails long enough to slice bread."

"Shelby! Help me, Keebler the Elf has escaped the cookie factory and is standing in your living room," Kelly sighed in a lazy voice, looking up at Shelby, who had just walked back into the family room.

"Pay no attention to my brother-in-law, he's homeless."

"Naw, this hungry ho is homeless. She cleaned out your house and packed everything in her shopping cart." He picked her feet up. "You better come quick to help me hose this raggedy-head raccoon down and cut these razor blade toenails."

"Damon, please leave her alone," Shelby said as she sat on the other end of the sofa. "You look comfy. You still want to go out and eat?" She asked Kelly. But before the end 'T' sound of *eat* was said, Kelly replied, "that chicken was just a snack. I would be hungry in another thirty minutes. My appetite is like a four-hundred pound man's. I don't know why people underestimated me. Of course, I want to go out and eat. I can't wait to taste this southern Louisiana Creole cooking again. Your little birthday party last year only had tastings. I want a full meal, praise God."

Shelby stared at her friend and shook her head. The old Kelly was back. Saved Kelly wasn't greedy, but the old one was. The preacher named Kelly talked about God in every sentence and this creature before had only mentioned God one time and that was about food. Shelby continued to diagnose Kelly in her mind, wondering what went wrong.

"Earth to Shelby. What the fuck you thinking 'bout? What you need to do is tell yo fresh-ass nephew to leave your girl alone, he up in this bitch acting like T.I or Chis Brown, tryin to mack on a grown-ass woman. I told him to leave that old-ass pussy alone." Damon smacked his nephew's back when he noticed Shelby had zoned him out, a defense mechanism she had learned years ago

when she first met Damon and he asked her in front of his
mother, aunt, and grandparents if she sucked dick.

"Kelly, you see my nephew. He is ruin't, a porn star in
the making. He thought something was wrong with him
last year when that thang sprouted out." Damon turned to
Shelby. "Your nephew is abnormally large like a grown-
ass man on Viagra."

"Man, stop stunting. You don't need to tell the world. I
told you that in confidence," Chad whined, getting up and
pushing his Uncle Damon outside toward the pool house.

"I'll chill out, nephew. I see you a little sensitive about
that big ol' thang between your legs. Boy, feel honored to
house a big dick, it runs in the family," Damon stated,
beckoning for Tracy to follow him, sticking his tongue
through his V-formed fingers. Tracy leaped up quick when
she saw the huge, thick tongue. Kelly's face sparked up
too, wondering how all that mouth Damon had would feel
between her legs.

"Kelly, we'll be in the guest house if you want me to do
your hair," Tracy hollered.

*Dexter's brother was crazy. Not bad on the eye, though.
A little short, but his buff body cancelled that out. Couldn't
help but get excited with all of the conversation about
ruin't dicks, made me wonder if all the Jean Pierre men
were hung,* Kelly thought to herself.

"I can't wait to see how Dexter looks now."

Shelby smirked. "He looks just like Damon, the munchkin, but taller."

"So, Miss Proverbs Thirty-one. I'm so glad you and Dexter are still happy. Some people aren't so lucky. How's
Max? Do you think he's happy that you married his best
friend?"

"The three of us are fine. Max is married to Sidney. We

are all just friends." Max hadn't pushed up on Shelby since her thirtieth birthday party and she was cool with that.

"That's wonderful," Kelly said in a sarcastic way. "The perfect fairy-tale ending after all. Your selfish ass should have told Max how you felt about Dexter. You always playing mind games with people. Just like you led poor Joel on, pretending you didn't know he was in love with you."

"Girl, all that is old news, I'm good. Those guys are out of my life forever and I mean that. Why are you talking like this anyway? Where is all this anger coming from? Don't jump on my ass because you . . . lost your man."

Kelly rushed toward Shelby, giving her the evil eye. She wanted to smack fire from Shelby for being such a smart-ass and she would have but she needed a place to stay for the night.

"You know I'm not in the mood for your bossy ass. You are not ready for the new me; the innovative Kelly who is about to make some major changes," she said while backing away from Shelby, placing her hands to her side. Shelby examined Kelly with her eyes, wondering what the hell was wrong with her. Kelly's behavior was out of control and something had to be done.

"Kelly, I know a good—" Before the word *therapist* entered Shelby's mouth Kelly was out the back door.

I'm going to the guest house with Damon and Tracy, I'm ready to make things happen. Get me a makeover, stiff dick, and a drink too.

TWENTY-EIGHT

The narrow tree-guarded street was very dark and iso-lated. Kelly's blurred vision couldn't adapt to the set-ting. She had no business being out in an unfamiliar town at three in the morning. "I knew I should've gone home with Shelby after we ate at that oyster bar, but no, I had to stay at the bar with that sick-ass bastard named Martin. Drinking that gin and slurping down all those raw oysters, loving the way the slimy sea animal crawled down my throat like cum. Not paying attention to what drug the silly stranger was putting in my drink. Damn, I messed up," Kelly repeated aloud, shaking and trembling. Then her mouth closed and thoughts from her horrible es-capade bombarded her mind. *Martin took me to a motel on Staring Lane, not far from Shelby's house. The hotel wasn't the kind of lodging or atmosphere I was used to, but nothing mattered. The little secluded booty call hole would suffice for the night, I thought to myself.*

He handed me a glass of ice and poured Bombay gin into it until it overflowed. "So how did you like the club?" I shrugged my shoulders. "It was okay. I haven't done the club scene in five years." He rubbed my shoulders. "You drink like a pro and dance like a porn star. I can't believe you're a minister." I looked embarrassed. "Yes, I'm a minister without a congregation. I'm just going through some rocky times now." He kissed my neck. "Why are we here?" I turned around to face him. "I need to be loved."

"I'm the man to love you," he replied. And that's all I needed to hear. My heart had been broken and I needed a man to fix it. So I walked to the restroom and wasted no time slipping off my panties. Returning to the bed, breezy free, guzzled down the gin like it was vitamin water, and stepped to the stranger.

"Come on and bless me, Rev." Martin pulled my dress off and my nipples stood erect. Sat on that bed butt-naked and allowed a stranger to attack my body. He situated his tongue on my melon-sized breasts and licked like a man who hadn't eaten in years. "I love big, juicy titties," he said in a Cookie Monster voice. Little ol' me fell back on the bed, extending my legs wide, hoping he'd inch down to my steamy spot. When his mouth moved down to my belly I almost went into convulsions. His mouth was centimeters from my boiling point. I closed my eyes, preparing myself for the big thrill. To my dismay, my thoughts turned to God and then Karl. My conscience wouldn't let me go any further. I shut my pulsating thighs and sat up. "Martin, I'm leaving. I can't do this. I'm in love."

"What the fuck do you mean? I don't get turned down by no one. Single and married women break their necks for some of this dick!"

"I'll pay you."

"Naw, I don't want your money. I want something else."

My dress was on the floor. I snatched it up and slipped it on while I was walking out of the door. "It was nice meeting you. I'm sorry for the inconvenience, but this is one sin I can't live with. You might want to pick the Sheraton or the Embassy Suites next time."

Martin jolted up and yanked me back on the bed. I fought him. But his strength was too overpowering for a 115-pound woman like me to handle. He fastened the door without delay. My frail body shivered on the small, paper-thin mattress. He gazed down at me and laughed with a mischievous grin. "You ain't going nowhere, Reverend. I slipped something in your drink that will make you very happy."

"You what?"

"Ever heard of blue dolphin?"

If my mother didn't teach me anything she always told me to never leave my drink unattended. Why had I been so trusting of this fool? I closed my eyes and prayed.

"You should've been praying before you came here," he grunted, leaping to the bed, pinning my arms and legs out, holding my wrist with his hands and my legs with his feet. I tried to struggle and squirm to free myself from his confinement. Sadly, the more I moved the tighter his grip became. "Lord, help me!" I cried out, weeping without any pauses in between.

Kelly pulled into the driveway at Shelby and Dexter's home. It was late and she didn't want to wake up their family.

"Good the lights are on in the living room," she muttered, not wanting anyone to see her. With trembling hands and an anxious mind she peered through the huge bay window only to find their young nephew, Chad, sitting on the sofa with his shirt off, watching what looked like a porn movie. "Muscles and a six-pack. Lord, that boy is too young to be so fine," she rambled, tapping on the window. "Why am I lusting over a child?" She knocked on the window again, taking her eyes off of the child's body, redirecting them to the television. "What is he watching? I know that ain't Shelby and Dexter?"

Startled by the pecking noise, Chad jumped up, dashed to the television remote and turned the television off. Then he headed to the door, wearing a mischievous grin.

"I didn't know that was my aunt and uncle on that tape," Chad admitted with guilt stamped all over his face, as he opened the door. Kelly didn't know what he was talking about nor did she care, when her eyes met with his young body, huge jeans hanging with a gigantic silver belt buckle that read *Louisiana*.

Curiosity wouldn't let her remain silent. "What ya got in that belt?" she asked, placing her hand on his well-formed chest. "Is it as big as your Uncle Damon was saying?"

He backed up, choking on his words. "Are you okay, Miss Kelly?"

She pushed her breasts on his naked chest. "You wanna touch?"

"Ma'am."

"Ma'am? Do I look old to you?"

"No, ma'am."

"I told you about that ma'am shit," Kelly replied, pulling her breasts out of her bra, taking turns licking them. "You wanna touch now?"

"No, I was saying I didn't know that was my aunt and uncle on that tape sexing. Don't tell them I was watching it."

"Only if you let me see it," she instructed, holding her

hand out for the tape. "Now, do you want to lick on these big tits of mine?"

A smirk skated across his face like he was contemplating the gesture. Whatever the stranger gave Kelly had her heated and wild. She didn't care if little Chad was eighteen or seventy, he was going to please her tonight.

"I won't tell your aunt," she whispered in his diamond-pierced ear.

"I'm only eighteen," he confessed, testing her morals and sobriety. Age didn't matter to her, especially when she saw that long and treacherous species crawl down his leg, almost to his knee. "Who's your friend? Doesn't look like he's eighteen?"

Embarrassment covered his face.

"Don't be ashamed of what God has blessed you with. Those young girls can't handle what a thirty-year-old woman can."

"They talk all that trash and then they get scared and start running when they see it. They don't know what they be doing, scared to ride and shit." He giggled. "But I can use an older woman."

She stroked the child young enough to be her son. Young enough to have her sent to prison. "Oh no, you are blessed," she replied, shocked and amazed by his size. "I can teach you some things. Where can we go?"

"You serious?"

Kelly nodded her head and pressed her lips against her index finger. Chad snatched her hand and whisked her outside to the roof of the car within seconds. "Yeah, that's what's up, that's what's up. I've always wanted to fuck on top of a Lexus."

"Well, tonight you hit the cat pot. Drop your pants and sit on the hood of my car." He listened to her orders then placed the Magnum condom on.

Had to admit little nephew followed directions well, Shelby would be so proud of him.

"Ooh yeah! Don't stop! It feels so good," he moaned when she placed him into her mouth. "Stop moving," she announced, pinning him down the car. He flopped and tossed. "Grrr . . . Ooh wee . . . grr . . ." he groaned, biting down on his lip. Bobble head was in effect and there was no stopping. It was clear Chad had never experienced anyone even close to her skills. "Stop, Miss Kelly! I'ma bout to—" he screamed and stuttered, with his penis halfway down her esophagus.

"Oh no, I have to get mine. And I'm not afraid to ride," she said gloating, straddling her legs around his thighs as he sat on the car, pointing straight up.

Kelly rode him like an eighteen-wheeler. Switching gears and loving it. No one would've ever guessed Shelby's *little nephew* was only eighteen because he was working with twelve inches. He hammered in and out of her seasoned pussy, sending her into spasms. "Oh God, yes!" she screamed with a roar as her body exploded with double orgasms. Chad extended his hand over her mouth to muffle her ear-splitting howl. But he couldn't restrain her cries. She was enjoying the long strokes and her body was in full motion, gliding up and down with ease, her mouth singing praises for the young dick.

The front door to the house crept open. Dexter stepped out with caution after being startled by the loud noise. Anxiety and a trace of fear blessed his body, but he knew he had a family to protect. He stepped out further into the yard. The sound echoed. His eyes searched the area and landed on their exposed bodies enmeshed in lust. Dexter's tall, six-feet-three frame towered over Chad. He stood there, shaking his head in disapproval, sickened by his nephews' inappropriate behavior.

"Man, I can't believe you. If your aunt comes out here she's going to kill you . . . and this young lady."

Chad locked eyes with his uncle, embarrassment stroking his soul. He tried to pry Kelly off of him, but she wouldn't budge. Her hands were glued to his shoulders and she continued bouncing her pelvic area on him, ignoring Dexter's presence.

"Chad, this time you really fucked up."

"Man, Unc, she won't get off."

And Kelly wouldn't. She wanted Dexter to get a good long look at what she had to offer.

Kelly's back was facing Dexter as he tapped her shoulder. "Excuse me, young lady, you need to get up off of my nephew before I call your parents. You should have a little more respect for yourself and my family."

Kelly swung her head around in slow motion. "I'm grown." Dexter almost fainted when he saw Kellyanna Swanson, his wife's thirty-year-old best friend. When Kelly turned her head to speak she loosened her grip on Chad's shoulder and he lifted her off in one quick motion. He pulled his pants up promptly, put his head down, and evaporated into the house.

"I can't believe you. Chad is a child. He just turned eighteen in August." He looked into Kelly's eyes and inhaled. "And to think your girl was worried about you, had me up waiting on you."

Kelly rubbed her breasts into Dexter's arm and whispered into his ear. "You wanna be next. I hear big, long dicks run in the family."

"You sick. You better hope my sister doesn't press charges on your crazy self." He grabbed her arm. "I want you out of here."

"What? You're supposed to be my husband. This should be our house and our kids in there sleeping."

"Kelly, what are you talking about? Are you drunk? High? Or just stupid?"

"Just *Now and Laters* and gin." She kissed on Dexter's ear. "Wanna fuck? Shelby doesn't have big juicy tits like these. Wouldn't you love to just stick your dick between these girls?" she said, pressing her oversized breasts together.

Dexter pushed her away. "If you touch me one more time I'm going to fuck you up. Treat you like a nigga."

"I see Shelby's dirty-ass mouth rubbed off on you." She rubbed her vagina up then down and across. "Do you want to touch this cross? It's so hot and wet. I know your boy Max told you how good it was. He loved to fuck behind the bar at work."

"Just pull your damn skirt down and button up your shirt. I don't give a fuck about you and Max."

Kelly's gathered her clothes and followed Dexter into the house. But before the front door closed the two were greeted by Shelby. She stopped midstream.

"I don't like what I see." Kelly's heart palpitated at a rapid rate as she scurried to button her shirt up. Shelby's voice was soft and soothing. "Do you two want to tell me something?" Kelly stumbled, trying to reach in the magic hat for an answer. Tried to pull out an explanation, but nothing came out. Shelby searched her husband for an answer. Kelly was praying he wouldn't confess. "Honey, is everything okay?" she asked in a stern, serious tone.

Dexter raised his eyebrows, looked at Kelly and smirked. Nervousness grasped her face. She looked like she wanted to punch Dexter in his jaw. Kelly couldn't believe that her twenty-year lifelong friendship with Shelby was about to end because of Dexter's big mouth.

"Your girl is high. Someone most have slipped her

something. I found her outside half-dressed on top of her car, howling."

"Kelly, when did you start using drugs? I can't believe this shit. You are supposed to be a minister. What the fuck happened to you in California?"

"I'm sorry, Shelby."

"Sorry for what?" Shelby asked with her lips sucked in.

Kelly closed her eyes stiffly. Drops of moisture wet her eyelashes. "I'm sorry that I can't be that perfect Kelly you want me to be. The old me is back."

"What?" Shelby asked with an expression of shock and disgust.

"I'm . . . back . . . You know, the close friend you had that was a whore. The one who slept with every man she could. The old me that slept with two of your boyfriends, Max and Sebastian."

"And you were here tonight to make it three."

"No, Dexter loves you . . . Need to take a bath now. Need to wash up. I was drugged," she repeated in a hypnotic tone, nodding her head from side to side. Not wanting to tell Shelby the truth. *Hell, I wanted her life; career, two kids, and her house. If I could've killed her right then I would have, anything to take away the pain that haunted me. The pain of losing my father at a young age, turning into a whore for any and every man, giving my body to men in return for temporary love; trying to search for that unconditional love that my father gave.*

"Drugged my ass. Please believe, if you ever step up on my husband, I will fuck you up. Bitch, I will kill you and that's on everything. Don't let this psychiatrist shit and the house on the hill fool you. I'm nice, sweet, and polite on the surface, but I still have some scrap in me. Violate my family and your ass is mine." Shelby clutched Kelly's hand tight. "Do you understand me, bitch?"

Dexter looked at his wife with a scolding expression. She released the tight grip, realizing how much she had overreacted. Shelby caressed Kelly's hand with a gentle touch this time.

"It's all good. I know the drug Ecstasy acts as both a stimulant and psychedelic, forming an energizing outcome, as well as deformation in time and perception and increased enjoyment from sexual experiences. The drug is addictive and can be very dangerous to your health. So I think you need to see a doctor in the morning."

"No doctor! There is nothing wrong with me. I just have to sleep this *X* off."

"I understand, but if you change your mind I can refer you to one of my colleagues."

"Shelby, I'm so sorry. I'll be fine. God can deliver me from this. I just need to go to the room and repent," Kelly voiced in a timid, sorrowful manner. Shelby felt terrible for cursing Kelly out. Empathy hit her and she was putty in her best friends' hand. Kelly had been through a lot and who was she to judge her girl, Shelby thought as she followed her friend back to the guest room. The two prayed, hugged, and Shelby tucked Kelly in for bed.

"Good night," Kelly said in a sweet, loving voice. *Oh yeah, Miss Shelby it's payback time. I'm about to watch that porn of you and Dexter, the man that should have been my husband, the two of us should have become one flesh,* Kelly thought to herself as her best friend closed the guest room door.

TWENTY-NINE

At five the next morning Kelly soared up and gathered her belongings. Her mind was replaying everything that went on last night and she couldn't take it. It was time to go. Humiliation beat down on her. How could she disrespect her girl and she still allow her to stay at her home? The guilt was too heavy for her to carry because after Shelby went back to sleep she sprung some pussy on Dexter's older brother Damon. After seeing how big Dexter's dick was on that tape she had to have some. Her first reaction was to go wake Dexter up for some of that well-endowed dick. But she knew that would have been close to impossible with Shelby's watchdog ass. So she gave Damon's short ass some play and they stayed up all night watching the homemade porn and fucking.

Kelly's small fist knocked on Shelby's bedroom door. "I'm leaving. Thank you for your hospitality."

Shelby scurried to the door, wearing Dexter's T-shirt. She wiped her eyes and asked why Kelly was leaving.

"I have to go."

"Kelly, stay, I can get you help here and we can ride to Chicago together next month for Megan's daughter's christening."

"Thank you, baby, but I have to leave now. I'm too nervous to sit in one place. God has some work for me."

Shelby begged Kelly to stay, but Dexter remained silent. Rage painted on his body. He had not forgiven Kelly and probably never would. All the attempts she made to get him in bed had failed. Chad was the missing link, the closest she'd ever get to Dexter. And anyone could see it in Dexter's eyes, he hated Kelly for that.

"I wanna fuck you," she mouthed to Dexter with her arms wrapped around Shelby. The two friends stayed embraced for minutes, swinging from side to side, tears clouding their vision. Dexter looked at the pitiful performance and shook his head.

"I'm so proud of you two. Always remember what God has brought together let no man separate it," Kelly stated aloud. "Not even me," she mumbled in a inaudible tone. Dexter stared at Kelly and walked away without a good-bye.

The car merged on 10-West then 12-East. The moment Kelly saw 55-North, Jackson, her mind was at ease. Cruise control was set and she was on her way. Her body relaxed in the soft leather seat and she repressed the traumatic experience that occurred in Baton Rouge.

Kelly pulled her cell phone out and turned the power on. There were twenty messages from Karl and one from Bronze. She was in no mood to hear from Karl, the wound was still too deep. But curiosity won as she picked up the phone and listened to her voice message. "Kelly, where are you? Karl and I have been worried crazy. I know what you saw, but there is more to the story. You need to speak with him. He didn't do anything wrong. He didn't even preach Sunday. This is really destroying Karl. I feel stupid pouring my guts out to you over the phone. Please call him and don't miss my wedding festivities." She sighed softly. Before Kelly could hit the red end button her phone beeped.

Kelly answered the phone, but didn't speak.

"Sweetheart, I miss you. Why are you doing this to me? Where are you?" Karl was hysterical; he sounded like he had been crying for two days. His voice was hoarse and his tone was low.

She whispered very low. "I saw you."

"Kellyanna, it wasn't what it looked like. I was comforting her. I would never lie to you. Please come home," he pleaded.

"I saw the person in your office. We can never be together," she chanted again in a ghostly voice.

"Why?" he cried aloud. "I love you. I gave you ten years of loving that I was saving for my wife. You are my destiny. God blessed me with you. We can get married today—"

"Our relationship was cursed the moment we slept together. If I'd stayed I would've ruined your entire career. I love you too much to hurt you. Karl, this is good-bye forever."

He begged, "no, I'm dead without you. If you leave I'll never be able to preach again. I'm nothing without you."

"Man, you don't want me. I'm a whore. Do you hear me, a whore. I've already slept with three men since I left you and I plan to sleep with more. I have sexual desires and cravings to pursue. My goal is to be the best whore I can be until the hurt is gone, all gone."

"None of that matters. I love you and I want you to be my wife. Our love was consummated the minute we made love."

"Before I hang up this phone, I want you to know I love

you. God sent me to you. Purified me, five years, you were my first and only true love. God will never bless me with another Karl Hughes because we were destined to be one flesh. That vision was sent to me months ago and I came to California to reveal it." She started to cry. "I tried to play God with you and for that I am sorry. If I die today, I'm glad I was blessed with the opportunity of loving you. Darling, don't stop saving souls just because we stepped off track for a moment. You keep preaching and remember I will always love you."

She hung up the phone with one movement of her thumb and broke down into sobs. Her heart couldn't take the pain, the heavy weight of love. She had to pull over in a mall parking lot in McComb, Mississippi and let go. Weeps were loud, intense, and very torturous. The love of her life was gone forever and so was saved Kelly. "From now on, it is all about me," she sobbed into the rearview mirror. "Life fucked me so now it's my turn to do anybody and everybody. I'm achieving every fantasy that ever swam across my mine. And thanks to Shelby and Dexter I can scratch making love to a eighteen-year-old off my list."

THIRTY

The minute Kelly landed in Chicago she mended things with Blair, Shelby, and Megan. She had to keep her enemies close. There was no way she could pay Blair back if there was animosity about their fight that happened months ago. Kelly was smooth and slipped her way back into Blair's life at her weakest point.

No one knew the pain stirring inside of Blair. Her husband had turned heartless. He forced her to have sex with him and Sapphire and brutal sex with his drug supplier. She wanted to leave him, but she couldn't. Her children, love, and numerous threats of being murdered kept her in check. And things weren't always bad. When Bryan was sober their home was calm and enjoyable.

Kelly mended things with Shelby also. She cried to her and lied. Kelly told Shelby she was diagnosed as bipolar and was seeing a therapist weekly. And Megan was the easiest one of them all. Their friendship didn't need any repairs.

One month had passed and Chicago men were doing Kelly's body justice. Each night she did a different guy.

And they just couldn't get enough of her sweet pussy or throat muscles. With condoms, without condoms—it didn't matter to her. She felt the Lord had thrown her away so she enjoyed life and did whatever her little libido guided her to do.

"Megan, today I woke up with a pain between my legs, a pain for your sideline lover," Kelly mumbled aloud as she stepped into the doctor's fancy office. Hair dyed red, freshly cut and flips bouncing. The aroma of her expensive perfume filled the waiting area and her lips glowed with red gloss. She looked around and no other patients were waiting, which was unusual because Megan told her Dr. Jackson LeBlanc always had between twenty to thirty people waiting.

Five minutes later, she was greeted by Dr. LeBlanc himself. The sight of him made her want to jump out of her G-string. She had never seen a white boy so sexy. His blond hair was short and spiked. His chest was chiseled, triceps pumped, thighs bulged with muscles, and his blue eyes were to die for. Kelly had to calm Miss Kitty down because she was ready to seize her prey.

"Have a seat in examination room five. I'll be with you in a minute," he said in his vibrant professional voice.

Kelly smiled, happy the young doctor was able to fit her in his busy schedule. "Megan didn't lie one bit," Kelly said aloud as she deposited her red panties into her purse. "I'll just pop a love pill and wait."

Minutes had gone by and Kelly was still waiting. She clicked her candied-apple red polished nails on the face of her watch, anticipating Dr. LeBlanc's return.

"Sorry to keep you waiting."

She nearly jumped out of her skin when the young,

white, well-built doctor approached her. Kelly was laying flat, legs spread open wide with a book in between them.

"Did I scare you?" Dr. LeBlanc asked, placing his Palm-Pilot on the desk, stunned by her beautiful nude body and voluminous tits.

She opened her legs wider and popped up. "Yes, you startled me. I was just catching up on some reading."

Characters of Lust by LeBlanc. Interesting title."

"Yes, very interesting, one of the characters reminds me of myself, looking for good sex in all the right places." She placed the book down and shook her head. "But not as interesting as you."

The handsome doctor tripped over the chair, ignoring Kelly's last comment. "Are you ready, Mrs. Swanson?"

"That's Miss Swanson."

The truth was she was more than ready. She had been waiting for this appointment for weeks. Every since Megan mentioned him, it was time he found out what her problem was.

"Place your feet in these and scoot to the end of the table."

Dr. Jackson LeBlanc stood tall, wearing his white lab jacket, leg muscles bulging out, broad chest exposed, and his extensive member gleaming between his tight jeans. Kelly's mouth watered. *Who said white boys ain't packing? The print he left on his leg was undeniable. Letting me know he was ready for some loving.*

"Now let's see what the problem is," he said as he shuffled to the end of the table, putting on his examination gloves. Kelly stuck her index finger into her vagina quick and pulled it out very slow. "The problem is inside of here. Why use your gloves when you can use what's between your legs."

"Excuse me?" he questioned, trampling over his words.

"I have a pain between my legs that only you can attend to. You come highly recommended," she said, gazing down at her dripping wet, spasm-attacked vagina, licking the wet substance from her finger.

"Oh really," he chuckled, blushing with embarrassment, his cheeks crimson red.

"And judging from the bulge in your pants I think I may be able to help you. You see, I'm a doctor as well, a head doctor."

"Oh! So you're a shrink?"

"No, I give the best damn blow jobs in the city of Chicago. Now what's up, doc?"

"Well, that's quite nice, but I'm seeing someone." Jackson replied, peering over at his vibrating BlackBerry.

"You sound like a fool. Let me hook you up. I suck a real good dick," Kelly taunted, opening her mouth wide, wiggling her tongue and licking her plump lips. Jackson looked perplexed. He picked up his BlackBerry, read the message from Megan, *you had too much hair on your cock the last time we met for dinner. Make sure you shave all that hair off by tonight if you want some of this priceless snatch. I despise a man with hair on his crotch.* Jackson slammed the BlackBerry down, angered by his lover's ultimatum. "Hell, I thought married women would've been different. I didn't know I'd encounter so much drama," he said aloud, gazing down at the most beautiful latte-colored black woman he had ever seen. Thoughts kept pouring into his mind. *Her breasts are like two big, juicy ripe cantaloupes, sitting up so perky and vibrant, just waiting to be eaten. Tanned thighs are creamy and inviting. And the treat between these long exotic legs is out of this world. Look at this lovely vagina with Gucci G's etched in the red hairs, standing at attention, purring with cum, just waiting to be stroked. In my eight years of unethical practice I have never seen a piece this heavenly.* Without further hesitation, Dr. LeBlanc locked the exam door, unbuckled his Gucci belt, placed his phone back on the desk, and lowered his Abercrombie jeans. Kelly's eyes popped out in amazement as she viewed the divine artifact before her. The massive monument was surrounded by silky straight blond hair and nice, plump balls. Saliva filled the inside of her mouth as she kneeled down to her knees, anticipating his entrance. But Jackson wasn't having that, he opened a drawer and pulled out a condom, then he lifted his patient off of the marble floor and offered her a chair. Kelly looked at him with a stunned expression, but she followed his lead and sat on the comfortable chair, staring at her next meal.

"Ohh! Damn, you are so amazing," Jackson said before closing his blue eyes. Kelly showed no mercy, swallowing his white chocolaty treat and massaging his hairy testicles. This went on for minutes, minutes that sent her into a wild fit.

"The pain between my legs won't stop throbbing," she yelled after pulling his large penis out of her mouth, massaging herself down there. "Dr. LeBlanc, I need some dick. And I need it now."

"Well, I have just what you need." He pulled his pants and shirt all the way off and put a clean lab jacket on. Then he lifted her body on the examining table and placed her feet in the stirrups, like she was a paying patient. "Come all the way to the end of the table and let me examine you."

Kelly obeyed, awaiting the best fuck of her life, her first time with a white man. It was all about her. She closed her eyes and silently thanked her best friend. *Thanks for the 411, Megan. The next time you won't tell anyone about the good dick you get. You had no business cheating anyway when you had a good husband at home. The Bible states thou shall not commit adultery.* She sniggered.

THIRTY-ONE

Shelby showed up for a girls' weekend of fun in Chicago. And without Dexter, for the second time, which was a big step for Miss Separation Anxiety. None of her friends knew why, but Kelly thought Joel had a lot to do with that. She didn't believe for one minute that Shelby was done with Joel. How could she be? Joel looked just like the actor Tyrese and had the body to go with it. She wasn't fooling anyone. Her nose was wide open after Joel and Kelly needed to know why. So she made a mental note to add Joel on her "to-do" list.

Blair, Megan, Shelby, and Kelly hung out all day with the kids, like they were tourists, which was out of the ordinary for the new Kelly since she was usually somewhere doing drugs or being sexed. But she gave all that up to visit the Shedd Aquarium, Sears Tower, lunch at Gino's East Pizzeria, shopping at Nordstrom on Michigan Avenue, and American Girl.

"It's ten o clock, I almost missed my date messing around with them ghetto bourgeois twins. Had us all up in

Nordstrom like them white folks. Talking about getting
eyebrows done. Hell, that's what the nail shop is for. And
in American Girl carrying around one-hundred-dollar dolls
eating lunch with them and getting their hair done. They
have money to throw away. Ain't no way Savannah would
have got two of those dolls," Kelly said to Blair as the two
were driving home from their girls' day out.

"Girl, naw. Stop hating. Shelby did buy us all a doll that
looked like us. You gotta love Shelby and Megan. What
killed me was them bitches acting like they ain't never
rode the city bus before. Did you see Megan taking pictures? And how about the Sears Towers? Now that was
too much money to spend to stand at the top of the tallest
building in the U.S."

"I thought the Sears Tower was nice. The line was too
long, but the view was pretty. Now the Shedd Aquarium
was the bomb. I can't get over that dolphin show. That has
to be one of the best aquariums in the world. Did you see
how the kids were acting? They loved that shit."

"I guess you're right. We did some shit today we've
never done before and we've lived here all our lives."

"You've lived here all of your life. I just moved back.
I've been in sunny California. I lived the lavish life when I
was with Karl and I could do it again if I made some of
these trifling men pay for the pussy. But would that be
right? Why charge, I am a free, kind giving spirit, sharing
my body with underprivileged men."

Blair looked at Kelly and loved the fact that the old
Kelly was back. She had wondered what happened between her and Karl, but whenever anyone brought it up,
Kelly shot them down. The two were back cool, all was
forgiven and Blair wanted to keep it that way.

"Kell, you ever thought about going back to California
to be with Karl?"

"I could take Karl back. He begged me and still leaves messages for me to return to Cally. I can be just like Megan and Shelby because my man is filthy rich and is sprung on this piece of gold between my legs."

Blair smacked her lips and twisted her mouth. "Yeah, right."

"Oh, don't get it twisted. I know Karl still loves me and wants to marry me, but . . . I just can't go back after I saw what I saw. I could forgive him, but I don't deserve to be happy. I manipulated Karl. I didn't wait for God."

Blair thought about asking more questions but decided not to when she noticed the sad, pitiful, painful look on Kelly's face.

The two ladies and Blair's kids made it back to the house. Blair stuck her keys in the black iron security door. The front door swung open before she could turn the lock.

"Where the fuck have you and Strawberry Shortcake been?" Bryan roared with a glass of Crown in his hand. He was drunk and Kelly could see the rage in his eyes. She gathered Blairson and Bryanna and rushed them into the house and to their bedrooms.

"Bitch, where you been?" Bryan asked, then whacked Blair in her head with the palm of his hand. "I'll beat yo motherfuckin' ass. I know you weren't hanging out with your girls all this time. Who you fucking?" Tears drowned Blair's face. Her body trembled as she tried to speak.

"Baby, I'm not sleeping with anyone."

Bryan yelled louder. "Yeah bitch, you fucking somebody! Ain't those them very words you love to say to me."

Kelly could hear the commotion from upstairs. She was alarmed because this behavior was out of the ordinary for Bryan. "How often does this happen" she asked, looking at Blairson who was bobbing his head, his ears covered with headphones.

"*In this club,*" he sang.

"I said, how often does this happen?" Kelly yelled louder, finally yanking the headphones off his little head.

"Man, what you do that for? Mama's cool. They fight all the time and make up. She told me she didn't need my help. I told her I could get my boys to bust a cap in his fat ass."

Before Kelly could correct Blairson's foul language, she heard her name being yelled out.

"Kelly, get yo half-white, skeleton ass in here now."

She scurried to the living room. And Bryan was waiting. He wasted no time getting in her face, his huge stomach rubbing into her side.

"Girl, who my wife sleeping with?"

"No one, we've been downtown. Please calm down," Kelly begged, wanting to rush to the bathroom to release her bowels.

"Calm down? You calm down on these nuts. Suck 'um like you use to," Bryan said, pushing her head down toward his crotch.

Kelly wrestled her head away from his big, rough hands and scooted next to Blair.

"I think it's time for yo lying ass to go. Get yo shit and get the fuck out of my house. Yo ass popping them beans like candy. Shitting every second, losing all that weight. You need God."

Kelly didn't know how to respond. For once, Bryan was right. She did need God. Her life was empty without him. It was easier being a Christian then a hellion and she couldn't believe how stupid she'd been to separate herself from the Lord. She left the Holy Spirit that dwelled within her in Los Angeles. Right along with her almost perfect relationship with Karl, her husband-to-be, sent by God himself.

Kelly glanced at Blair, who was sitting on her knees, holding her face in her hands. She was waiting for the big bad Blair that she knew to go off on Bryan, looking for her girl to save her, like in high school. But the bold, ruthless Blair was gone; the night her husband crammed his gun down her throat put an end to her violent streak. She feared Bryan and would never put her hands on him again.

"Are you okay? Come on, let's go. We can both get help. We need to get out of here," Kelly pleaded with Blair, trying to shake some sense into her.

"My wife ain't goin anywhere. Get yo shit and go," Bryan bellowed, lifting up on Kelly by the back of her neck.

Her body was shaking as she squirmed away from his grip and sprinted into the room to get her belongings.

"Come get me now," Kelly fumbled into the phone, dissolving a pill under her tongue. "What do you mean you have to perform an emergency surgery?" she shouted into the receiver, listening to Bryan scream at Blair in the living room. "Okay, send the damn limo to pick me up. And make sure it's a red one."

"Pull your panties off! I said pull them off now!" Blair handed Bryan her underwear. He snatched the panties and smelled them, then he pointed to the crotch, like she had done him months ago. The tables were turned and there was no stopping Bryan. "Why you got cum in yo panties? You didn't even have enough respect for me to wash your funky cat."

"That is not cum. All women have a natural discharge. Bryan, I love you. I would never cheat on you," Blair cried. Bryan smacked Blair with the underwear then he stuffed them into her mouth, damn near choking her. Blair pulled the underwear out of her mouth. "Bryan, you the one who stays out two to three nights and don't come home. You on that dope bad and probably cheating too. So don't blame me just because you cheat. I didn't go out in the streets and make a baby. You did. You didn't respect our marriage." Blair started to weep. "You hurt me. Gave me that shit I can't get rid of. That HPV came from you fucking around. Your baby mama probably gave it to you. Now I have to be worried with genital warts and shit." She cried more. Her head drooped. "But I still forgave you. I didn't divorce you or deny your daughter you had by that whore. I accepted her, even after I lost my baby. You knew I was having a hard time coping with the loss of my baby girl. And what do you do? You went out and got another bitch pregnant. But silly me, I treat your daughter like she's my own flesh and blood. I do everything for her. She calls me Mama, not that two-dollar whore you fucked."

"What?" Bryan put his large hands around Blair's neck. "Bitch, I will kill you if you ever talk back to me again! I'm a man, the head of this house, and I can stay away from home if I feel like it. You have rules to follow. Just be glad Kelly's here, you'd be a dead bitch if she wasn't!" Bryan released his hands off of Blair, pulled his thick leather belt off, then he threw her over his lap. He hit her raw bottom with the belt several times, spanking her like she was a disobedient kid. She squirmed about in pain from the stinging whacks, her voice stolen, no oxygen around to provide her with a cry.

When Bryan finished disciplining his wife he picked up the huge antique chair in their living room and crashed it into the wall. Cherrywood pieces scattered to the floor and pictures tumbled off the wall. Kelly thought he had ripped Blair's head off. She was terrified for her girl, but not enough to go check on her. Kelly had always been a big coward and a bit selfish when it meant overextending herself, but when she heard the front door slam, courage appeared. She rushed downstairs to Blair, who was in pretty bad shape. Her eye was purple and red and bigger than an apple. It looked like her bone was protruding out of her skin. Tears flowed from Kelly's eyes, displaying the little compassion she had for her girl. Months ago, Blair had accused her of sleeping with Bryan, damn near kicked her ass, and left her on the street with her suitcases, yet she still cared. That's when Kelly realized God was still in her, trying his best to win her back. *Something I just wasn't ready for,* Kelly thought to herself as she frantically ran to the kitchen to get ice for Blair's swollen eye. "Here, put this on your eye."

"Thank . . . you . . . Pass . . . me . . . my . . . purse." Blair spoke with a wax expression.

Kelly handed Blair the orange patent leather purse. Blair's hand raced inside and pulled out a small plastic bag of weed and a box of cigars. Within seconds she had rolled herself a blunt and lit it.

"When did you pick up that bad habit?"

"The same time you started with them pills and snorting coke with that white boy."

"Low blow."

"Ever since Bryan bought that little girl home," Blair said as she inhaled the smoke. "But that's okay. I found somebody else. Someone who loves me and has always loved me. Bryan can stay gone for all I care. 'Cause my boo is about to come over and rock my world. Gonna eat this cat like no other man has before."

"Don't forget you are married. You need Jesus! Get your life together. Don't let Bryan change who you are. Be the better person, don't fall to sin," Kelly said, astounded by her preaching. She had promised herself she would never mention the Lord again, but the words just flowed from her mouth.

"Kelly, mind your own business. When you do your dirt I don't say nothing, so please return the favor," Blair said, picking up the phone.

Kelly didn't press the issue anymore, instead she went to the bedroom to gather the rest of her belongings and snorted the last lines of coke she had. *This is my last night of doing wrong. I'm giving up all my bad habits very soon if the Lord says the same 'cause I'm starting to experience a little guilt, shame I didn't feel before. Jesus, I guess you still love me. I'm coming home. . . .*

"Minister Kelly, your stretch Hummer limo is here!" Blair hollered.

Kelly rolled her suitcase to the front door and looked back at Blair. "It's never too late to seek the Lord. He's a forgiving God."

Blair ignored her. She was too busy smoking the huge blunt cigar, but the moment the door opened she waved good-bye, almost rushing Kelly out of the door with her vibes. *Blair wasn't going to steal my joy; I rolled my eyes and closed the front door with a hard, swift swing. Just as thrilled to be getting away from her beat-up ass.*

"Hey, Kelly, how you doing? I was wondering where you were," Sapphire asked, licking her fingers then rubbing them up and down the side of Kelly's thighs. "Is Blair okay?"

"Yeah," Kelly stuttered, surprised to see Sapphire on Blair's porch. She had always found her eccentric and alluring and today was no different. Her platinum Afro was fresh and bouncy, blue contacts gleaming, and her diamond piercings were blinging bright.

"Good, I was worried about my suga bear," Sapphire replied, smelling like strawberries and weed. Swinging her arms and ass like her life depended on it, the sound of her jingling bracelets following her as she trotted off to ring the doorbell.

"Blair's in there with Bryan, but I wouldn't go in there if I were you. Want to take a ride with me?" Kelly asked, peering back at the red limo, wanting very much to experience sex with a woman. Not really forgiving Blair for slicing her arm and accusing her of sleeping with Bryan on the way to the airport. Sapphire took one look at Kelly in the red halter dress with the bubble bottom that stopped at the tip of her butt, wiggled her tongue ring, and followed Kelly into the limo without thinking twice.

Their bodies sunk into the plush black leather seats and all of Kelly's worries and concerns vanished. This was definitely the life she wanted to live. To hell with Blair and all of her problems, tonight it was all about Kelly. Her need to accomplish all of the whorish goals she'd set for herself and sleeping with a woman was about to be achieved. Not just any woman, Blair's woman.

"Grr . . ." Sapphire roared at Kelly's zebra-print belt as she pulled off her red pumps with zebra print on the heels. Then she unfastened Kelly's belt with her teeth. The two women nestled in the seat and Sapphire's journey began with soft, supple kisses to Kelly's toes. Her legs eased open from all of the delightful stimulation, exposing her panty-free pussy in which the dyed red hairs were shaved into an ice cream cone. Kelly found it to be a hoot to shave her pubic hairs into different shapes and styles weekly, giving her various lovers something to vibe on.

"Oh, Kelly, strawberry, my favorite," Sapphire moaned, licking her way up her lover's legs and to her thighs like a panther on the prowl. Kelly looked at Sapphire's healthy, paw-print tattooed muscular thighs stretching across the seat and her pussy became wet and juicy. Sapphire's tongue was flip-flopping about, centimeters from Kelly's red ice cream cone and Kelly thought she would depart this life. She couldn't believe how gentle, sensual, warm, delicate, and passionate the touch of a woman was.

Kelly exhaled but remained silent, trying to remain calm as the tongue ring sizzled inside of her. But she couldn't contain her sanity. Sapphire grabbed at the huge breasts and begin licking them to muffle Kelly's cries. The electrifying strokes she demonstrated sent volts through her lover's clit. Kelly's hands went wild, reaching for Fires's plump ass, hurriedly spreading her cheeks and dipping her candy-red coated nails inside of her tunnel. Sapphire let out a sharp moan as Kelly's two fingers gravitated about in a seesaw motion, Fire's lips suctioning on to Kelly's clit even tighter. The ex-nun fought hard to keep quiet, but couldn't. "Ahh!" she screamed. "Ahh."

The driver slid the window down and Kelly nearly fainted as she pulled her fingers out of Sapphire's ass. Fire never lifted her head up from between Kelly's legs, tongue enthralled in battle. "Well, hello, Joel Cullin. Have you spoken to Shelby lately?" Kelly asked with a mischievous grin, wanting to know the truth about him and Miss Morally Right.

"No," he replied, slow and lethargic. "Not since I kicked her husband's ass," Joel answered back, his eyes glued to the two women.

"All right, you were just the person I was looking for. I'll do what Shelby wouldn't."

"Hmmm . . . you will," he said, full of excitement, gawking down at the women. "I see you're still wild," he said, shaking his head.

Kelly grabbed Sapphire's luscious cheeks and massaged them with both of her hands. "Why don't you come back here and join us, see how wild I can get. Give me some of that big, long black dick I've heard so much about."

"Oh, she told you about this dick. I find that funny when she never gave me the pussy." He rubbed his knuckles. "If I ever see her and her husband again I'm gonna fuck them both up."

"I don't want to talk about Shelby and Dexter. Let's talk about us."

Joel pulled the limo over at Fifty-fifth and Lake Shore Drive and leaped into the back with the two women. Sapphire had eaten Kelly up very well, but the ex-nun wanted some dick, some dick that Shelby was too square to divulge in. She tried to ease off of Sapphire's mouth, but Fire wasn't having that. Her mouth was glued to Kelly's insides. "Come on. Let me please you," the ex-nun begged Sapphire, watching Joel's dick grow harder by the second, his hand gliding up and down his lengthy dick. Fire didn't budge. Kelly settled her face between Sapphire's cheeks and dug her tongue deep into Fire's ass. Joel's hand moved faster and faster. Kelly lifted her head up and pushed Sapphire back, whose mouth was sticky and wet. The ex-nun looked at Joel. "Come on, fuck me like a rock star in yo bitch favorite spot." Kelly got on all fours, lashed her tongue onto Sapphire's pierced cunt and swallowed all she had to offer. Joel stuck his fingers in Kelly's butt three times then he rammed all twelve inches of his juicy black dick inside of her. Sapphire reached three of her fingers inside of the ex-nun's pussy and clawed in and out. Kelly's ass was on fire as Joel sped through the wet tunnels. Spasms invaded her body with each thrust and turn; the crook in his dick causing so much pain, yet pleasure.

"Stick that shit in my pussy now," Kelly demanded, inching up off of Sapphire for a split second. She couldn't see letting a good crooked-ass dick go to waste. Kelly felt that shit was curved to the right just for her pussy's G-spot.

Joel laid his back down on the seats and the ex-nun hopped on top of him, easing her cum-drenched pussy onto his penis. The head slipped in without difficulty and she slithered her pussy down his black greasy shaft. Kelly's ass pumping harder and harder as she swiveled his girth in and out of her dripping wet cunt. His strong hands on the side of her ass directing the flow. "Damn, your dick curves to my spot. Shit, this feels so good. You are blessed. Oh God, you did it with this one. Oh, I love it."

Sapphire watched them for a while, tossing her clit ring through her fingers, fondling her stiff labia. She had been with Joel in high school so he was no big deal to her, but when Fire saw the facial expression on Kelly's face it made her want to indulge a little further. Because seconds later, she soared on top of Joel's face and his hungry tongue plunged up in her. Her huge breasts bounced about like she was riding a horse naked and free. Kelly couldn't keep her mouth off of them, suckling like a newborn on her full brown nipples.

They rode Joel simultaneously, Fire had his mouth and Kelly his penis. Their lips and arms tangled together, the perfect threesome for Kelly, but this time with two women instead of two men. Another goal achieved, an accomplishment to be scratched off Kelly's list of lusts.

THIRTY-TWO

It was a bright, sunny day in July and the weather was gorgeous. The girls had chosen a great day to go down to Grant Park to partake in the Taste of Chicago, a favorite Chicago tradition that offered cuisine from more than seventy restaurants, plus entertainment and activities for the entire family. The event was free, but to eat you had to buy tickets that looked like bingo boards to sample everything from the restaurants the Taste of Chicago had to offer: fresh buttery corn on the cob, chicken, barbeque, Chinese food, Greek food, soul food, Italian Food, deep dish pizza, seafood, steak, hot dogs, you name it. They had it.

Megan looked away from her purse-sized mirror and stole a glance at Blair and her kids from the platform.

"Come on! Run faster, you're going to miss the train!" Megan yelled as she stood at the Metra train station in Flossmoor, not far from her $450,000-dollar home. Blair, Sapphire, Blairson, and Bryanna ran as fast as they could to catch the orange and silver train. Crowds of people were getting off the locomotive so they made it aboard with a second to spare.

"We thought y'all were going to miss the train. Moving all slow," Shelby teased as they all climbed up the stairs to the upper deck of the Metra train.

"I can move fast," Sapphire replied to Shelby, wiggling her tongue ring.

Shelby twisted her lips and ignored Sapphire without blinking her eye. "Megan, hide those diamonds. I don't want to get robbed again. I don't know why you get all dressed up in your two-thousand-dollar outfits and your diamonds to go downtown with all that dust, smoke, and a million sweaty folks at the Taste of Chicago," Shelby ranted before they could sit down on the orange and brown plastic seats.

"You can't even get on the train good and you're already bitchin'," Blair snapped back.

"Darling, don't worry about me. This is the Metra, not the subway. You do you, country girl. And I'm goin' to do me, 'cause I'm just so sexy," Megan chanted. "And Blair, mind your business."

"Shelby, you lay off of Blair. She's been through a lot," Sapphire said in Blair's defense. "Have you looked at your girl?" Sapphire pulled Blair's hater-blocker sunglasses off. Silence dominated the area. Blair's eyes were covered with purplish blue bruises. Sapphire grinned like a movie star getting an Oscar. "Go ahead baby," she said, nudging Blair.

Blair put her head down. Tears dropped in her lap. She spoke slow and soft. "Bryan is beating me."

"Oh my God," Shelby sighed and started to cry.

"No . . . your face is the most beautiful thing on your body. How could he?" Megan replied, shaking her head.

"Now y'all know I ain't no punk. I've been kicking his

ass for the past two years and he's been letting me. You know how that guilt shit is. I mean, I was knocking him in the head with bottles, burning him, punching him, stabbing him, you name it."

Kelly spoke up. "Yeah, she jumped on me too. Thought Bryan and I were messing around, but I wasn't the one cheating," she said jokingly, melting three pills under her tongue without any one noticing her.

Megan and Shelby were speechless. No words came from their mouths.

Blair rolled her eyes at Kelly. "And I'm bisexual. . . ." She paused, then spoke in a rapid manner. "Sapphire and I are lovers."

Not a sound was heard from the top of the train. Eyes focused in on Blair and Sapphire.

"So what made you feel so angry that you had to beat Bryan?" Shelby asked, playing the role of psychiatrist, trying to cut the tension.

"When I lost my baby I went into a depression. I think Bryan did too because this was his first child. The next thing I know he's staying out late, drinking every night, and screwing. Because a year later a bold-ass woman knocked on my door and handed me a three-week-old baby girl and told me to get checked for HPV."

"You said Bryanna was your great-niece? I thought you said you guys adopted her from your niece who lived in Mississippi," Megan asked, stunned by this whole ordeal. But not too stunned to clean and spray the train rail with sanitizers and Lysol.

"Megan, I lied. I was embarrassed. What would you girls have thought of me if I stayed with a man who went out cheated on me and had a baby by another woman? And I'm taking care of her like she's my own."

"I would have admired you. You took vows and there is

nothing wrong with forgiving. Don't mess your whole life up based on this. You and Bryan should just get some help." Shelby passed Blair a card. "I think you're bipolar too."

Blair stuck her middle finger up. "I wish it were that easy. I have Sapphire now. I think I've been lying to myself for years. There is nothing more gentle or passionate than being kissed by a woman in all the right places. No one knows more about a woman than another woman."

Sapphire blushed and kissed Blair on the cheek. Then she looked at Shelby and Megan. "You girls should try it."

"Oh, you have lost your mind," Shelby answered quick.

"Sapphire, you don't have enough money for this good, expensive kat of mine." Megan turned to Blair. "I'm still trippin' on that dirty husband of yours giving you the human papillomavirus. Blair, you can't get rid of that. Why didn't you use protection?"

"Megan, she thought she could trust her husband," Shelby added.

"Oh my God, I don't trust anyone. I make Dr. LeBlanc use a condom all the time, even when he's eating this sweet treat of mine. You have to. You have to check a man out. The HPV virus can be spread by nonsexual activity. Meaning just grinding, if that unsanitary dirtbag has a wart on his balls you can get that shit. You have to examine these disgusting, dirty men before you jump in bed with them. Search their bodies for warts and moles," Megan lectured, frowning up, squeezing more sanitizer on her hands.

"That's why you should've been with me years ago," Sapphire told Blair while rubbing her thighs. "Men carry that virus and give it to women. Blair, I would've never never hurt you like your husband did."

Blair listened to every word that came out of Sapphire's

mouth. And when no more words exited her lips, Blair planted soft kisses onto her lover. Sapphire reciprocated, and the two sat in their chairs side by side playing tag with their kisses.

Kelly's ears started burning. She had never been with a woman before last night. And just looking at the two made her tingle between her legs, wanting to make love to Sapphire again. "Lord, help me fight these feelings. I want to be with you," she chanted to herself. Not wanting the demons in her head to win.

Meagan put her mirror down. "Blair, let's cut the lesbian shit. If you want to be gay that's on you, but I don't want to here about your disgusting-ass lifestyle or see it. Letting a bitch lick on you, that shit just ain't normal," Megan snapped. "Unless she's loaded," she chuckled.

Sapphire winked at Megan, her left pierced eyebrow arching up. "Why, Megan? You don't want to hear about how I eat a mean pussy?" Sapphire taunted, wiggling her pierced tongue and caressing her breasts inside her shirt, inching toward Blair's seat. Her arms reached between Blair's legs. Hands planted firmly on her thighs. She stuck her tongue out and nestled her face between Blair's legs. Intense giggles filled with joy exited Blair's mouth and Kelly couldn't do anything but stare as her own pussy became moist.

Kelly was mesmerized as she gazed at Sapphire's size Ds in her multicolored deep-cut shirt, eyes fixed on her chest tattoo of two women making love. The ex-nun's lips drooled over Sapphire's paw-print tattoos on her ankle leading to her twat, making her want to cum in her panties. She looked away to control the impure thoughts. Being a saint again was going to be hard and separating herself from her friends was the only way.

Shelby changed the subject quickly, trying to get Sapphire to stop her public sex show. "Look, Maze is performing later on," she uttered as she read the Taste map. But that didn't stop Sapphire. "So Megan, tell us about your trip. How was it meeting your father for the first time?" Shelby asked, hoping that would spark an interest.

Blair pushed Sapphire away. "Wait boo, I got to hear this."

"No, you can listen while I make you feel good," Sapphire answered back, moving back down between Blair's legs.

Megan motioned with one finger. She was applying her lipstick again. She put her mirror down. "Girls, my trip to California was wonderful, thanks to my mom. She went to L.A. and met my dad a few months ago. She cried to him, telling him all about me and Macy." Tears formed in the corner of her eyes. "My father and I look just alike, it's so scary . . . And he's really nice. We hit things off immediately. When we arrived he had gifts for all three of us. The man has expensive taste like his daughter." Megan threw her hands in the air and gave a light giggle. "He drives a Jaguar. If I wasn't his daughter, I'd marry him. I think he makes more money than Victor." The friends laughed, but short cackles, anxious to hear the about the rest of her trip. "Well, my father's a pastor of a huge church. He's not married and is currently single." Megan licked her tongue out. "I'm his only child and he's too old to have any more now. So guess what? All that money is mine when he kicks the bucket."

"Child please, a man can have kids until he's seventy," Blair taunted.

"My father is in his late forties and has no plans to make any more babies out of wedlock. He is really deep into his religion and takes his job serious. My father isn't like a lot of those preachers you read about." She closed her eyes, twisted her head, and swallowed before she spoke. "I finally have the rich father I've waited all of my life to have and he's perfect," Megan told her friends with tears in her eyes.

Blair lifted Sapphire's head up. "Baby, I said that's enough. You can't be showing off all your talents in public. Plus, that's rude, Megan was telling us her story."

"Just trying to show Megan what she's missing. Ain't that right, Kelly?" Sapphire whispered in a low monotone, then winked at Megan. "I'm going to get a piece of that bourgeois-ass kitty cat sooner or later. And Miss Shelby, you can join us."

"What do you mean, ain't that right, Kelly?" Blair asked in a serious tone.

"Oh, I fucked the shit out of Kelly last night," Sapphire told Blair, wiggling her tongue. "With this."

Blair held her chest and begin to hyperventilate. No words exited her mouth. "What," finally came out and tears formed in her eyes. "Sapphire, you said you loved me."

"Blair, just chill out, stop being a fuckin' drama queen. You are still married to Bryan and I'm free to sex anyone," Sapphire shouted and kept on wiggling her tongue at the other girls.

"Kelly, how could you?" Blair paused. "And you call yourself a Christian. You just told me you were trying to live right again."

"I am. I'm done with the devil's work. I can't straddle the fence any longer. Either I'm for him or against him. And I'm with him. I'm doing his work again. That was yesterday. Today I'm a new person in Christ."

"I didn't think I'd ever see the day when Kellyanna Swanson gave up on God. I'm glad you're over whatever you were going through. I felt so sorry for you," Megan said with plenty of sympathy as she rubbed more sanitizer on her hands.

"You what?" asked Kelly. "Hell, I felt sorry for yo' gold-digging ass. You look for love inside of every man's wallet. We should feel sorry for you . . . 'Cause Jackson and I had a good time last night. What? Huhh? Yeah, rich bitch, I fucked the shit out of yo' white boy. Yeah, while you thinking your stale-ass pussy is the bomb."

"Umm, I like it like that," Kelly sang and gyrated, trying her best to ignore her friends.

"Kelly, look at you. You're a minister. I don't know if you noticed, but I've been quiet about this, but you getting out of hand. Look at how you're acting. Sleeping with lesbians? I can't believe you." Shelby touched Kelly's skirt. "And your red fetish; red hair, eyebrows, cat hair, clothes. Damn skirt comes to the end of your butt cheeks and your top barely covers your nipples. Doesn't look like you've changed to me."

"Shelby, don't hate cause you don't have big tits like mine."

"Oh, this mouthful does the job. I'm just saying you need to assess your life. Look at where you are now versus where you come from. You have regressed. Where is that woman of God?"

Kelly didn't want to hear anything they had to say. She sat in the seat and struggled with herself internally. She wanted to be saved again, but then again she wanted revenge. She discreetly covered her mouth and nose with her hands like she was about to sneeze and popped seven more pills in her mouth. *There was nothing wrong with me. I was living life in the fast lane enjoying every minute of it and I didn't need anyone judging me. That's why I kept most of the shit I did on the down low. Hoes tend to fuck up a good nut. And that was their problem. They told too much of their damn bedroom business. One thing I did carry with me from the church is to never tell what you and your mate do in the bedroom. When you brag about what you have you make other people curious about your mate. And since they told me about their love affairs I felt there was nothing wrong with me sampling a taste or two.*

Blair nodded her head at Kelly and rolled her eyes. "You slept with my man and then Sapphire. I see you like coming behind me. All you had to do was ask if you wanted some of this sweet shit between my legs. You nasty, sick, deranged bitch."

"My red Jimmie Chimmie shoe or whatever Megan calls these, six-hundred-dollar shoes I'm wearing is about to connect with your head," Kelly screamed, struggling to pull her pumps off. "Bitch, you fucked up my arm and I didn't even fuck your husband that time," she yelled as she slammed the size 6½ shoe into Blair's skull several times. Blair blocked some of the hits with her arm as her hands tried to snatch the shoe away from Kelly. "I hate you, that's why I ate your bitch. You dirty whore, you had a good man until you ran him away." Kelly ranted like a wild woman, her breathing erratic and heavily labored. "I wanted to show you that I could have anything you had. Sapphire didn't give a damn about you. She slept with me with no persuasion. That is why the word says to run from sex sins. No other sin affects the body as this one does. When you sin this sin it is against your own body. Haven't you yet learned that your body is the home of the Holy Spirit God gave you, and that he lives within you? Your own body does not belong to you. For God has bought you with a great price. So use every part of your body to give glory back to God, because he owns it."

"Kelly, I'm sorry. Chill the fuck out. I'm not going to

fight you," Blair pleaded, attempting to take the shoe from her mangled hands, which were glued to the shoe.

Kelly didn't stop. Something was on her deep because she couldn't control her anger or actions as she tore into Blair, pulling at her long, red curly weave. "You know red is my color and yet you dyed your funky hair red," she spat, clawing deeper into her friend's scalp. "I'm mixed with the Holy Spirit and demons."

"Would somebody pull this crazy bitch up off of me?" Blair hollered with pain in her voice. No one moved. Everyone appeared stunned, frozen.

"I can't mess up my nails. And anyway I don't know what you two have. You won't give me HPV. Messing with lesbians and shit," Megan replied when no one else would speak.

"Walk humbly and do what is good; perhaps even yet the Lord will protect you from his rage in that day of doom," Kelly preached catatonically, then starting singing lyrics from Usher's song.

"What is she talking about?" Blair hollered, unable to break free from Kelly's strong grip.

"I'm talking about you. You dumb amazon bitch and yo stupid-ass friends," Kelly replied with a raspy voice and bloodshot eyes, pulling Blair's hair tighter, watching her eyes slant from the pressure. "Oh, Shelby not only did I fuck Megan's precious doctor boyfriend but your boo too. That's right, we had a threesome with Joel. You hear that, Shelby?" She chuckled profusely, feeling sick to the stomach. "Ain't that right, Fire?"

Sapphire grinned nervously. "Yeah, that's right. It was off the chain. But we can tell them about that later. We need to get you to a hospital. Come on Megan, Shelby, can't one of you do something. Kelly is turning colors and convulsing. Sweat is popping off of her forehead. It's oozing everywhere. Is she high or crazy?" Sapphire screamed, watching Kelly finally release Blair's hair.

Megan was going to help Kelly, but hesitated, wondering if she was telling the truth about her and Jackson. She reached down, looking for her cell phone. When she found it she sent Jackson a quick text message asking him if he slept with Kelly and if so did he use a condom.

Kelly has to be out of her mind. Jackson would never sleep with someone like her when he had me. How could he? I'm elegant, beautiful, and I have a perfect round ass that drives him crazy. Jackson loves me, he's my millionaire and I plan to marry him when I divorce Victor.

"It appears Kelly has overdosed on MDMA. The symptoms are an increase in blood pressure, high heart rate, muscle tension, involuntary teeth clenching, nausea, blurred vision, faintness, and chills or sweating," Shelby said, flipping through her prescription drug book, which she kept in her purse.

With blurred vision Kelly gasped for breath, barely able to sing more tunes by Usher. "*I mean I would never do the things I'ma 'bout to tell you I've done. Brace yourself, it ain't good or easy, but it would be even worse if you heard this from somebody else (oh no). These are my confessions . . .*"

"I've been sleeping with Dr. Jackson LeBlanc for a while and you were right, white men can lay that pipe and he loved the way these lips made him feel. Praise God, that man is blessed."

"What?" Megan questioned Kelly, wanting to choke her instead of feeling for her temperature. "Jackson would never sleep with someone like you. You have no class. You can't compete with me, Megan Cole Myru."

"Oh, I can and I did. You had a good man, a loving husband with money. You have a nursing degree, new baby, beautiful house, expensive car, good health, and you didn't have to work. But no, you were too greedy. Had to have you a millionaire? Well, I did too and he loved this Gucci-shaped pussy. See, I saved you because now you know Dr. LeBlanc would have never made a good husband. I did that for you." She made the sign of the cross. "Part of my work is to suffer for you; and I rejoice, for I am aiding to finish up the last of Christ's suffering for his body, the church."

"Come on, Megan. She's lying, just help her. She doesn't sound or look good," Shelby reasoned, staring at Kelly's dilated pupils and clenched teeth.

"Oops, I wouldn't be my friend if I were you, Shelby. I screwed your eighteen-year-old nephew and Dexter's brother, Damon too. Gave him the best blow job he ever had and I rode that dick like a rodeo star." Kelly lifted her red skirt and rubbed her naked vagina. "And you were right, Joel eats pussy very well. You should of tried that dick, though. Talkin' about delicious, it was long, thick, and very big. His crooked dick hit my G-spot every stroke, making a bitch scream." She stuck her thumb inside of her vagina. "Oh, I like it like that. How 'bout you? Didn't know you were a porn star. I liked the way you were taking it from the back in the rain. You and Dexter looked cute on the side of the house fucking." She licked her lips. "Yeah, Shelby, your husband is blessed. Blessed with some good dick. Dick that should've been mine."

Shelby froze, her hands inched off of Kelly's body. She pulled her hands into prayer motion. "In the name of Jesus, I rebuke this spirit from Kellyanna Swanson. Lord, I give her to you. For salvation comes from you alone."

The prayer relinquished all of the power Kelly had. Her pale, weak, frail body fought to stand up. Kelly's hands trembled as she staggered to the railing for support. The ex-nun begin to recited a verse from chapter one of Colossians, with the little bit of strength that remained in her body. "For God has rescued us out of darkness and the murk of Satan's kingdom and brought us into the kingdom of his dear son, who bought our freedom with his blood and forgave us all our sins."

"Next stop Vanburen and Jackson!" the conductor announced loudly over the intercom, not noticing the unruly behavior at the top of the train.

"Oh my God, it looks like her vitals are dropping," Megan cried.

"She's falling. Catch her before she falls over the rail," Shelby screamed to Blair, tears drowning her face.

"Give her CPR, Megan. Her pulse is low. It's faint," Blair shouted.

Kelly's body was limp, feeble, and lifeless. As she collapsed she reminisced on her escapades. All she wanted to do was marry Karl Hughes, the man sent to her by God himself. The numerous sexual sins she committed, the people she deliberately hurt, the abuse she executed on herself, was all done in vain. A crazed attempt to punish herself for being disobedient to the Lord for using lust and temptation to get what she wanted, not being humble or patient.

It was apparent this was the end, the end of Kelly's life of sin. God had saved her five years ago from this tempting vulture, but she had to go back for more. Now it was too late. Kelly's life was ending before her very eyes. The poison she poured into her body was finally erupting, killing the soul, killing her. "Tell Karl I love him and Megan, I'm sorry for sleeping with—"

Blair caught the stiff, possessed body and placed it on the floor of the moving locomotive. "Help! Stop the train! She's dying."

"Give her CPR now," Shelby screamed at the top of her lungs. "Someone call nine-one-one." Megan sprung to the floor of the train and pumped hard, pushing down on Kelly's delicate chest.

"Shelby, you do the chest compressions and I'll give mouth-to-mouth." Megan no longer cared about germs as she and Shelby worked on Kelly. Perspiration drenched their bodies as they attempted to save the women who betrayed them.

"She's not responding," Megan wailed.

"Don't stop!" Shelby shouted, beating on Kelly's unresponsive body. "We can't let her go."

"But she's not moving," Megan cried.

"Megan, don't say that," Blair blubbered, massaging Kelly's limp hair. "God, please help her. Don't let her die. She was only trying to help us."

Sapphire held on to Blair's daughter Bryanna and wept. She'd been weeping the entire time, kissing and holding Bryanna for dear life.

"Jesus, we need you," Shelby shouted as she continued to press hard on Kelly's lifeless chest, taking deep breaths and sobbing.

The girls were doing all they could. Not believing their childhood friend was vanishing before their eyes.

THIRTY-THREE

Kelly's mother, Estelle, walked to the light green doors and opened them. Her facial expression exhibited peace and relaxation. The tiny wrinkles under her eyes weren't as puffy as usual and her eyes weren't red. They were bubbly and blue. She extended her arms vibrantly, welcoming them into her home. Shelby, Megan, and Blair thought first before exchanging embraces with Estelle. They closed the door behind them and looked at one another in amazement of Kelly's mother's polite behavior. Any other day they would have been called all kinds of black bitches and whores, but today was a new day. Miss Estelle was a new person.

The girls looked about, surprised to see the Swanson home remodeled, clean, and thug-free. Shelby was really in awe because the last time she visited the place it looked like it had been targeted by Hurricane Katrina. Sorrow covered her face as she recalled the day before Kelly's wedding. She was so happy and in high spirits about her upcoming big day. Guilt overcame Shelby. Why wasn't she more understanding with Kelly? Why didn't she have more faith in her girl's dream? Maybe this awful tragedy would have never happened if she had been on her job and noticed the signs of Kelly's self-destructive behavior. As usual she was too caught up in her own identity crisis.

"Hello ladies." Miss Swanson smiled with sincerity, actually looking happy to see them. "Come right in. Have a seat." She patted down on the gold and cream sofa. "I'm so glad you girls came by. It's been very rough for me after Kelly's accident, but the Lord is good and I'm here. I've been drug-free six months today." They all smiled at Estelle in praise of her great accomplishment. "I have to say, you girls turned out to be three beautiful women. And I just want to apologize for being so evil and cruel to all of you throughout the years. It was the alcohol and drugs." She shook her head. "I just thank each and every one of you for being there for my sweet little angel," she said sympathetically with genuine tears forming in the corner of her blue eyes.

Shelby blushed. She knew Kelly would have been so proud to hear her mother say those words.

"It's okay, we *loveded* Kelly," Blair communicated with a sense of humor as she wiped Kelly's mother's eyes with a napkin.

Estelle rubbed Blair's belly and grinned. "How many months are you?"

"I'm four months."

"Well, praise God. I hope it's a little girl. Blairson needs another little sister to protect."

Blair had been through a lot, but she had finally made things right. She and Bryan attended anger management classes and biweekly couples therapy. Blair had found out all of her anger and frustration stemmed from the loss of her baby and her controlling nature. The controlling nature that pushed Bryan away and caused him to cheat. But everything was perfect now and they were happy as the day they first married.

"Well, Megan and Shelby, I know you two are fine." She winked at Shelby and giggled. "And I see you knocked off all of that extra weight. Now that's the sexy little Shelby I remember. You all need to remember to keep yourselves together, stay looking good, no matter what. I promise you that, and keeping them men hooked up with some good, wild, freaky sex will keep your man content, he'll never stray."

"They will stray no matter how much you fuck them," Megan mumbled for only Shelby and Blair to hear, but Miss Swanson heard too.

Estelle looked at the girls. "Yeah, you are right, that's why you always need to keep a spare tire." The girls giggled. "Don't laugh, don't you have one for your car? Well, you need one for you. These men will turn on you in a minute. Always have a spare and some money to go with it. 'Cause a man will leave you looking dumb and broke. I always kept me a spare even if it was just somebody to talk to." Miss Estelle rose up and led the girls toward the door. "Well, I guess we've chatted long enough. I just appreciate you ladies coming to see us." She looked down at the white, tan, and gray speckled cat that was rubbing her leg. "Isn't that right, Winnie?" She pointed to the basement stairs. "Kelly's room is still downstairs. You girls go on down there. Check it out. Her spirit is back. Satan couldn't get rid of my precious little girl."

An eerie feeling crept over Megan as they walked down the stairs toward Kelly's room in a trance. With each clack of her heels she thought about that incident on the Metra train. How Kelly betrayed her and slept with Jackson

LeBlanc. At first she was angry, but after time went on she realized Kelly did her a favor, a huge favor that saved her marriage. For that, Megan was grateful, but she often wondered what Kelly meant when she said, "I also slept with your . . ."

Shelby cried the minute her foot stepped in Kelly's room. She was always the most emotional out of all of them. However, Blair was strong. She sprinted to the white canopy bed and embraced Kelly, placing kisses on her forehead, rubbing her long nails through her friend's long black hair. "Look at you, pooky. You look like yourself again. You are so cute and your eyes are gray now. I love how they change colors."

Kelly lay in her white canopy bed watching the flower-shaped ceiling fan rotate on low. Not replying verbally or nonverbally to Blair. She just lay in the bed, reverting back to a child. Estelle had redecorated her room in pink and lavender with lilacs and butterflies. For once Kelly felt like a normal kid. She took pleasure in allowing her mother to make up for lost time. Estelle wasn't a good mother to Kelly, but now that she was sober things were changing drastically.

Megan positioned Kelly's hand in her hand. "You scared us. And you know I don't usually scare easy. . . . I'm glad to see you looking good. Glad you got rid of that dreadful red hair."

A smile lurked across Kelly's face and laughs poured out. "I want those diamond tennis bracelets and that pink diamond ring." She sat up in the bed. "And Shelby, stop crying. Look at you. You've lost so much weight. I'm not used to seeing you so skinny. It looks great on you, though."

"Anyway, let's talk about you. You scared us. Your ass stayed in that mental institution a long time."

"I wasn't in the mental institution. I was on a retreat and I am fine, reborn, like new. God has spared me again although I am not worthy. I can't believe how he continues to love me with all my mess." Kelly sighed softly. "Praise God! I'm glad he's forgiving."

Megan looked in her silver pocket mirror, with her initial inscribed on top. She glared at herself, wiping traces of tears from her eyes. Then she fixed her stare on the lavender comforter where her friend rested. She wanted badly to ask Kelly who else she slept with, but she couldn't. For months the thought haunted her. What if it was Victor? Megan didn't know how she'd react.

Kelly, what else did you have to confess to me before you passed out?

"Megan, are you okay?" asked Shelby, who was sitting on the end of Kelly's bed.

"Yeah, I'm cool."

Kelly clapped her hands. "Good, because I have an announcement, I will be preaching live on New Year's at midnight, the chapel on Seventy-third Street. In my sermon I will come clean about everything and explain why I did the things I did. I hope you girls can wait until then, because I really am sorry for everything I did to hurt you guys."

Fear graced their bodies. They resented her at first, but the Lord had dealt with them and they realized Kelly actually saved their marriages.

THIRTY-FOUR

The television crew was all set up at the small chapel on Seventy-third Street. There wasn't an empty mahogany pew in the church. Friends, family, and spectators cheerfully crowded the area to get their minute of fame on television. But Kelly's friends were not enthused about the upcoming sermon. They didn't know how many more confessions they could hear, especially Megan. And Shelby was also anxious and paranoid. She wondered if Kelly was going to tell her she slept with Dexter too. However, Blair was at peace. She was just excited about hearing her girl preach on live television.

The brass church bell rang twelve times from the attic of the church. Candles and poinsettias with pine fir branches decorated the altar as Kelly stood at the podium ready to give her sermon, looking like a true princess in her white wedding dress. Her coal black silky hair was drawn back smooth into a ponytail with lengthy loose curls surrounding her face with a pearl-beaded tiara on top of her head. The dress that adorned her body was graceful and ele-

gant. It was white with swirling beaded pearls on the satin
bodice with a triple-tiered chiffon skirt, empire waistline,
and a chapel train. Hints of makeup traced her face, natural earth tones.

"Last year I stood before this very altar awaiting a husband. God told me he was sending me a husband so I
waited and waited and no one ever showed up. And
church I became mad. Very angry, excuse my language,
but God pissed me off. He promised me a husband at this
place and at this time, twelve midnight to be exact and no
man showed up to marry me.

Open your Bibles to Proverbs sixteen:thirty-two, which
says better a patient man than a warrior, a man who con-
trols his temper than one who takes a city. Now turn to
Romans fifteen:five which reads patience and encouragement come from God."

Kelly slammed her hand down on the podium several
times. "I became impatient. I had been saved for five
years, dedicated my life to the Lord, remained celibate
and I deserved a husband. . . . When I didn't get that husband the day I wanted to, it hurt so bad, I'm talking about
excruciating pain topped with shame, embarrassment,
and an undesirable spirit. Weeks later, I became a warrior,
hunting out my husband. Taking measures into my own
hands, being impatient. I wasn't acting on faith. John
fifteen:seven—Jesus said if you abide in me, and my
words abide in you, you will ask what you desire, and it
shall be done for you. I didn't hold onto that faith. Because Hebrews eleven:one tells us faith is the assurance
of things hoped for, the conviction of things not seen.
Check it out, I didn't listen to the word, instead I played
God. I deliberately set out to make things happen for me,
using lust and temptation. Exploiting my body to get what
I wanted through the use of pills, cocaine, gin, and wild

sex. I wanted a taste of lust." Then she looked away from the congregation and turned back with a somber expression. "I want to apologize to all of you because on my pathway to destruction, I intentionally set out to hurt the people closest to me. God, my friends, and the man I wanted to marry. In my deranged mind I thought I was helping in a way. All of them had it going on, I mean had perfect lives in my Satan-distorted mind. I started to judge them and wanted to play God because I didn't think they were doing what they were supposed to be doing in their marriages. As sick as it seems I didn't want my friends to ruin their lives so I journeyed out to tempt and destroy. I wanted to show them that those men and women out there in the streets meant nothing to them." She hit her chest and locked eyes with Megan, Shelby, and Blair. "But I'm not God and I just want to say I'm sorry and please forgive me." Tears rolled down Kelly's eyes. "I love all of you and I'd die for you too, but Jesus already did. In Ephesians two:eight it says you have been saved by grace because you believe. You did not save yourselves. It was a gift from God." She bounced up and down and turned around in circles, repeating, "Blessed is the man who keeps on going when times are hard. Blessed is the man who keeps on going when times are hard. We must not become tired of doing good. We must not give up. Hallelujah! Hallelujah! Praise God! Blessed be your name. Blessed be your name." She chanted and her followers stood up and clapped. "Thank you Jesus for sending your only son so that we may not perish, but have everlasting life." Kelly danced around the pulpit. "I have been saved again. I thank you Jesus, 'cause I am not worthy, but you love me anyway. You love me with all my wicked ways." She shouted loud and the crowd yelled louder. "Thank you, Lord. Thank you, Lord. Blessed be your name. I am not worthy but you keep on blessing me." Kelly walked out into the crowded congregation. People became quiet, listening intently. Some were shedding a few tears. Shelby was one of them. Megan was still weary, waiting for the big testimony. She had pulled her silver vanity mirror out several times, reapplying makeup and dabbing tears. And Blair was at peace, sitting big and proud, rubbing her full belly.

"If anyone has a testimony, please follow me to the pulpit," Kelly ordered. "Bring it to God. Allow him to enter your life. Make a change today."

Sapphire stood up, blue contacts gleaming, as she followed Kelly. She was wearing a dress, black velvet at the top and blue satin at the bottom. Her platinum 'fro had been replaced with long black straight hair with bangs in the front.

"I too was like Kelly. I had to have every woman I saw." She giggled. "And some men." Sapphire paused and played with her blue diamond on her nose. "I let lust, jealousy, and envy rule my life. I set out to destroy marriages and friendships. But today I am giving it all up to live for the Lord. I have a daughter to raise and an example to set," she relayed to the church in a stressed voice.

She broke down and sobbed, shocking everyone. No one knew Sapphire had a daughter. The girls looked at each other in amazement, even Kelly appeared stunned as she rubbed on Sapphire's back.

"Bryanna, I am your mother," Sapphire mumbled out into the crowd, eyes focusing on Blair and her family. Bryan sunk into the pew. Blair grabbed Bryanna's hand and escorted her to the pulpit with her mother.

Sapphire screamed as she embraced her daughter and Blair with tight arms. "Lord, give me that new heart, put a new spirit in me."

Kelly moved to the microphone and raised her hands in the air. "Tell me the Lord isn't good and I'll have to tell you, you're a liar."

"Preach, sister," a man from the congregation yelled.

Kelly continued, "Jesus is in this church tonight and whoever calls on the name of the Lord shall be saved."

The church was fired up. Hands were clapping. People were standing, screaming, falling out to the floor, tap dancing, and waving their hands in the air. Kelly was really working the crowd, allowing the Holy Spirit to dominate her soul.

"I'm here to tell you. I haven't given up on the Lord. I can do all things through Christ who strengthen me. I shall have a husband, but this time I am going to do it right." She balled her fists up and raised them high over her head and shouted loudly, "And that means saying no to a taste of lust. No fornication, no liquor, no cursing, no lying, no stealing, no drugs, no jealousy, no evil thoughts, no to the worldly way of life."

She closed her eyes and wiped her face with a linen napkin. When her eyelids opened a man whom she knew very well was approaching the altar. A spine-chilling sensation vibrated through out her body. She couldn't interpret what her mind was thinking. She looked out into the crowd for her girls' support, but their chairs were empty. They had walked out on her again.

The tall, dark-skinned, well-built middle-aged man with mingled gray hair stood at the altar. Pastor Karl Hughes introduced himself to the church and immediately started to speak about love. Explaining that love is giving, selfless, kind, patient, rejoices in the truth, doesn't behave rudely, doesn't envy, but that love suffers long. "And church I have suffered long for love." His eyes fixed on

Kelly. He clutched her hand gently and walked her over to the pastor's chair, then motioned for her to pull her thigh-highs down. She followed his orders, still in awe. The minister of the church passed him a bowl. He slipped Kelly's foot in the water and commenced to washing her feet. "Husbands, love your wives just as Christ also loved the church and gave himself for her, that he might sanctify and cleanse her with the washing of the water by the word, that he might present her to himself a glorious church, not having spot or wrinkle or any such thing, but that she should be holy and without blemish."

Minutes later, Shelby appeared, carrying a lit candle. "Kellyanna Swanson, will you marry me?" Blair appeared. "Kelly, let's do it right this time." And then Megan appeared. "Kelly, will you marry my father?" It was at this point Megan realized this was the secret Kelly was trying to tell her. An essence of peace covered her consciousness as she stood with the girls, holding their lit candles, wearing their coral chiffon dresses.

Karl bent on one knee. "Kelly, I love you and I always have. God came to me too and that's why I'm here tonight. I don't care what you did in the past, I love you and I want you to be my wife. No one has ever made me feel the way that you have." The two shared a glance. "And yes, you can preach with me. Because God took Eve from Adam's rib, the two side by side, we are equally yoked." He kissed her hand and Shelby's son came forth with a pillow holding the biggest ring Kelly could have ever imagined.

"Kellyanna Swanson, will you marry me?"

Kelly's gray eyes lit up, becoming moist. She trembled. Her heart beat fast. "Yes, Karl Hughes, I will marry you," she said loud and clear, sparks of joy shooting her soul.

The two walked to the front of the pulpit, standing tall;

the girls followed holding Kelly's train. Kelly's minister stood tall at the podium proceeding with the wedding ceremony.

"For this reason a man shall leave his father and mother and be joined to his wife, and the two shall become one flesh."

Kelly forgot she was in church. She clutched Karl with firm hands, her arms swallowing his bulging muscles, their lips and tongues locked in maximum security. "Thank you, Jesus for sending me a husband!"

Excerpt from *Characters of Lust*

It was Friday night and I was bored again. I was sitting on the fluffy pink carpet in my bedroom, wearing only my bra and panties, looking at a box of letters. Again, I was thinking about him, Sebastian LaCroix. I was unsure if it was the lonely weekend feeling or the breeze of spring that made me think of him more than usual, but I was. I hadn't felt his touch in a year and my body was yearning for his loving. My panties became moist as I massaged the tender spot between my firm thighs and my mind consumed itself with thoughts of the man I gave my virginity to.

Sebastian traced my body with small intimate kisses. He licked my earlobes melodiously. The low suckling sounds made my vagina drip with sweet cum. As I stood facing him he lifted my skirt and pulled my panties down with his teeth. He sat on the park swing and I implanted myself on his deep tanned-colored baton. I bounced up and down his slippery penis, while I moaned his name, continuously. The faster the swing moved the more enmeshed our aroused bodies became. I clutched his back tightly as I slid to the bottom of his shaft and rose back up to the tip in a matter of seconds. Sebastian's lips locked my neck and he mumbled, "That's what I'm talking about. Baby, take all of this. Show me how much you love me." My muscles clinched his girth and I held him tight within my succulent walls. I love you Sebastian, I cried aloud as I buried my face in his chest. He pulled my head back and kissed away my tears. "Don't cry. I love you, Shelby Tate. You are my life. My everything . . . I will always love you."

The more I rubbed my hot pulsating flesh the madder I became. I rolled my eyes and shook my head.

How much longer can I do this saved thing? One year is too long to go without sex. I want to be fulfilled. Sebastian, you were supposed to be my husband. We should be married and making love right now. Why did you have to leave me? Why did I waste five years of my life with you?